T0285236

A CATERED QUILTING BEE

Books by Isis Crawford

A CATERED MURDER

A CATERED WEDDING

A CATERED CHRISTMAS

A CATERED VALENTINE'S DAY

A CATERED HALLOWEEN

A CATERED BIRTHDAY PARTY

A CATERED THANKSGIVING

A CATERED ST. PATRICK'S DAY

A CATERED CHRISTMAS COOKIE EXCHANGE

A CATERED FOURTH OF JULY

A CATERED MOTHER'S DAY

A CATERED TEA PARTY

A CATERED COSTUME PARTY

A CATERED CAT WEDDING

A CATERED NEW YEAR'S EVE

A CATERED BOOK CLUB MURDER

A CATERED DOGGIE WEDDING

A CATERED QUILTING BEE

Published by Kensington Publishing Corp.

A Mystery with Recipes

A CATERED QUILTING BEE

ISIS CRAWFORD

Kensington Publishing Corp.
www.kensingtonbooks.com

KENSINGTON BOOKS are published by

Kensington Publishing Corp.
119 West 40th Street
New York, NY 10018

All Kensington titles, imprints and distributed lines are available at special quantity discounts for bulk purchases for sales promotion, premiums, fund-raising, educational or institutional use.

Special book excerpts or customized printings can also be created to fit specific needs. For details, write or phone the office of the Kensington Special Sales Manager: Kensington Publishing Corp., 119 West 40th Street, New York, NY, 10018. Attn. Special Sales Department. Phone: 1-800-221-2647.

KENSINGTON and the KENSINGTON COZIES teapot logo Reg. U.S. Pat. & TM. Off.

Library of Congress Control Number: 203947327

ISBN: 978-1-4967-3497-6
First Kensington Hardcover Edition: March 2024

ISBN: 978-1-4967-3500-3 (ebook)

10 9 8 7 6 5 4 3 2 1

Printed in the United States of America

To my family. I couldn't have done it without you.

A CATERED QUILTING BEE

Chapter 1

Bernie noticed Cecilia Larson as soon as she and her sister walked into the Longely library for their meeting. She was leaning up against one of the shelves in the fiction section, arms folded against her chest, watching everyone who entered the premises. Later, when Bernie was giving a reporter from the *New York Times* a blow-by-blow of how she and her sister had solved the case, she realized that it was the way Cecilia held herself that had caught her attention. Like Cecilia had the answers to anything you might ask, even things you didn't know you needed the answers to. Or maybe it was because Bernie had expected someone who looked different. Someone frumpier.

She'd pictured a heavyset middle-aged lady wearing a cardigan sweater, a plaid skirt, and sneakers instead of a cool-looking, willowy blonde with perfect eyebrows, bright purple eye shadow, leggings, and a crop top that revealed toned abs decorated with a kaleidoscope of tattoos. In Bernie's mind, people who looked like Cecilia didn't teach kindergarten. Or quilt. Or hang out at libraries. They hung out around Rodeo Drive and lunched at the country club.

Cecilia brightened when she saw the sisters. "This way," she mouthed, beckoning for Bernie and Libby to follow her.

Libby nodded. She realized it had been a while since she'd been at the library. Built ten years ago, the large, one-story brick building had replaced the cozy ninety-year-old Queen Anne on Main Street. But what the new building lacked in charm it made up for with its floor-to-ceiling windows, cheerful interior, comfy chairs for reading, and plentiful parking. This early March afternoon, it was filled with an after-school crowd: mothers and toddlers paging through picture books in the children's section, elementary school kids doing class projects, gaggles of teenagers hunched over their computers, and adults checking out the latest bestseller or browsing through the library's collection of newspapers.

Bernie and Libby stopped to say hello to several of their customers from A Little Taste of Heaven while they wended their way through the reference section and past the children's corner to the back room where the library held classes and hosted art exhibitions of one kind or another. Which was why they were there now. Next month's show featured quilts made by the Longely Sip and Sew Quilting Society, and she and her sister had been hired to cater the event.

"I take it this is where the reception is going to be?" Bernie asked Cecilia as she glanced around the large room. She and Libby always liked to see where they'd be setting up before the actual event. That way they could catch any problems before they occurred.

Cecilia nodded. "This is the place," she said, gesturing to the pale yellow walls, then indicating the two long black folding tables in the middle of room. "What do you think? Do we need another table?"

Bernie shook her head. "I think two will be enough. One for the food and the other for the drinks and the plates and so on. Are we doing paper or the real stuff?"

"What's the difference?" Cecilia asked.

"Price," Libby answered.

"Then let's do paper," Cecilia said. "How about table-cloths?" Cecilia continued. "Will you supply them? Are they included in the price?"

"Yes, and absolutely," Libby replied, her eyes drawn to the other table. "Maybe something in a deeper shade of yellow to offset the patterns and provide a feeling of unity."

"Perfect," Cecilia said, following Libby's glance. The second table was piled high with square and rectangular quilts. Some were big, some were small, but together they formed a riot of colors and patterns. "I'm trying to figure out how I'm going to hang them," she informed Libby.

"Looks like a big job," Libby observed.

Cecilia rolled her eyes. "You can say that again. Had I only known." She shook her head. "Everyone is so touchy. So do or die. God forbid anyone should feel slighted about their place in the display. Really. You'd think we were talking about an exhibition at the Met."

Libby rubbed her chin with her knuckle. "My mom had quilts," she remarked.

"What happened to them?" Cecilia asked, noting the tense.

Bernie answered the question. "I'm not sure," she lied, not wanting to say her dad had donated them to Goodwill after her mom had died. Somehow, that seemed disrespectful. But in truth, her dad had never liked them, and neither had she. "The quilts on the table don't look like the ones my mother had," she said instead. Her mom's had been linear and subdued, all angles and dark-colored pieces of fabric. They had always reminded her of pioneer houses with smoke-blackened mantels, crying babies, and pots of stew cooking over the fire.

Cecilia laughed. "Well, the quilts on the table are modern. Or, I should say, modern designs. Free form. I bet your mom had log cabins and double stars." And she went on to explain about the history of quilting after seeing the blank looks on Bernie's and Libby's faces. "Historians think quilting might have started in ancient Egypt. Maybe even earlier. People have quilted throughout the ages, sometimes to make warm vests and blankets, sometimes to make art, sometimes to leave messages for one another, like the slaves did in the South. Did you know that the oldest example of a quilt is a remnant of a bedcovering from the thirteen hundreds? The thirteen hundreds! I ask you, how fantastic is that?"

Bernie wrinkled her forehead. "Oh yeah. That was stolen from the Met, right? The guard had a heart attack?" The story of the heist had been part of a documentary she'd seen recently on Netflix.

"Right," Cecilia said. She frowned. "I don't think the authorities ever recovered the fragment. Such a shame."

"I wonder what happened to it," Bernie mused.

"It's probably sitting in some rich collector's basement somewhere," Libby guessed.

"Probably," Bernie agreed. "That kind of stuff would be hard to sell on the open market." She shook her head. "Fabric from the thirteen hundreds. Wow. They sure don't make material like they did back then," she observed.

Cecilia laughed. "No, they sure don't," she said. "You're lucky these days if a T-shirt lasts a year. Nylon has been the death of fabric," she proclaimed. Then she laughed at herself. "Listen to me making pronouncements like an expert. It's all so fascinating, though. I mean, think about it. Who invented material? How did our ancestors go from wearing animal skins and palm leaves and coconut shells to wearing clothes made from cloth?"

"I never thought of it that way," Libby murmured.

"Most people don't," Cecilia replied. Her expression turned thoughtful. "In one sense, quilting saved my life," she said. "It gave me a community, a reason to be." Then she gave an embarrassed little grin and apologized. "Sorry about oversharing." She shook her head for the second time and waved her hand in front of her face, banishing the sentence she'd just uttered to the netherworld. "But that's a story for another time," she told the sisters, squaring her shoulders and setting her jaw. "Let's talk about the menu, shall we? I have some ideas."

Oh no, Bernie thought, remembering some of their other clients' brainstorms, but as it turned out, Cecilia's ideas weren't bad. Not inspired, but not awful, either. Her ideas centered around a fifties Americana retro menu featuring Jell-O molds, deviled eggs, pigs in a blanket, a variety of mini quiches and spanakopita, as well as a vegetable platter designed like a loom—although Bernie had no idea how they would accomplish that—and a cookie platter.

"And, of course, we'll want wine and hard cider, as well," Cecilia continued. "After all, we don't call ourselves the Longely Sip and Sew Quilting Society for nothing. Have to live up to our rep," she added brightly.

Bernie and Libby both smiled politely.

"And the cake," Libby prompted. "Have you decided what you want yet?"

"Ah, yes, the cake," Cecilia repeated. She was about to say she was thinking about something springlike—maybe an orange sheet cake with vanilla frosting decorated with flowers, either nasturtiums or Johnny-jump-ups—when Gail Gibson burst into the room.

Libby recognized her from their shop, A Little Taste of Heaven. She had come in once or twice a month for the past four years to get a dozen croissants, the featured fruit crostata of the day, and two portions of the shop's famous fried mustard chicken. A fireplug of a woman with short gray hair and an affinity for pink ruffled shirts and denim pencil skirts, she radiated a take-charge vibe. But today that vibe was gone. She looked panicked and on the verge of tears.

"Why don't you pick up your phone?" she demanded of Cecilia from the doorway. "I've been trying to call you."

Cecilia made a face. "Sorry. I guess I forgot to turn the ringer back on after work."

"Next time, don't forget."

"I said I was sorry, Gail," Cecilia snapped. "You know, you're not really one to talk."

Gail opened her mouth to retort in kind, thought better of it, and closed it. Instead, she said, "Thank God I remembered that you were supposed to be here."

Cecilia's expression changed from annoyance to concern. "Why? What's the matter?" Cecilia asked Gail. "You know, you don't look so hot," she commented after noting the tear in Gail's stocking and her smeared eye makeup.

"I don't feel so hot." Gail swallowed and bit her lip. "She's dead. I can't believe it. I just can't."

"Who's dead?" Cecilia asked as Libby got a folding chair from the corner and told Gail to sit down.

"Selene called and told me," Gail said, ignoring Libby's request.

"Selene White?" Cecilia asked.

Gail nodded and started to cry. "She's hysterical. I told her we'd be there. We have to go. I already called Judy. She said she'd get there as fast as she could."

"Who is dead? Where do we have to go?" Cecilia asked, looking alarmed. "What are you talking about?"

Gail hiccupped. She took a deep breath. "Ellen is dead."

"Our Ellen?" Cecilia asked incredulously.

"Yes, our Ellen," Gail replied.

Cecilia's eyes widened. "Ellen Fisher?"

Gail nodded.

"You're kidding me, right? I just got a text from her a little while ago," Cecilia said.

"I don't know what to tell you," Gail replied.

Cecilia put her hand to her mouth. "Oh my God. That's terrible. What happened? Was she in a car accident?" Ellen was a terrible driver. "Did she have a heart attack?"

Gail shook her head. "Ellen killed herself. Selene said she found her hanging from a plant hook in her sewing room. She used her binding."

Cecilia blinked. "I don't believe it. We talked this morning. She wanted to know if I had seen the latest edition of *Quilt Today*."

"It's true," Gail said, and she started to sob. Then her phone rang. She wiped her eyes with the back of her hand and reached in her bag to get it. "Oh my God," she exclaimed when she saw the caller ID. "I forgot. I'm supposed to be teaching Anthro 101 now. I have to call the departmental secretary and tell them to cancel the class."

"I'd go, but I have an appointment I have to show up for," Cecilia said. "I'm sorry."

Gail sniffed. "It's okay. I'll go after I make this call."

"Are you sure you can drive, Gail?" Cecilia said. "Your hands are shaking."

Gail looked down at them. "I guess they are. But someone has to. Selene needs us."

Bernie and Libby exchanged looks. Libby gave an imperceptible nod.

"It's okay. We'll go," Bernie told Cecilia and Gail. "Call Selene and tell her we're on our way."

Gail reached over and clasped Bernie's hand. "Thank you. Thank you so much. I don't think I could bear to see . . ."

She swallowed. "Well, you know." Then she collapsed into the chair Libby had pulled out for her.

As the sisters left, they could hear Cecilia saying, "I don't understand. I don't understand at all. When I talked to Ellen this morning, it sounded as if everything was fine. We were talking about restitching some of the binding. I can't believe she hanged herself with it."

Chapter 2

Two police cars, a small fire engine, and an ambulance were parked in front of Ellen Fisher's house when Bernie and Libby arrived. Three neighbors were standing on the sidewalk, talking in low tones, while a small group of first responders were standing off to the side, chatting with each other. Bernie parked the van across the street from the first responders' vehicles, and she and Libby walked over.

As they approached, a flock of sparrows rose from the bird feeder and landed on the lilac bush by the wooden fence, while a robin pecked at the birdseed scattered on the ground. A squirrel chittered at Bernie from the bottom of the white birch tree in the front yard.

Ellen Fisher's house didn't have much curb appeal, but then, Bernie reflected, neither did the other houses on the block. An undistinguished two-story gray colonial with black shutters, a matching black door, and scraggly arborvitae planted around its foundation, it was the kind of place you'd never give a second glance to when you drove by.

"Look, it's the Simmons sisters," a policeman yelled out

as Libby and Bernie started up the path to Ellen Fisher's house. "Come to save the day with chocolate cupcakes?"

"More like chocolate chip macadamia cookies," Bernie said, showing the officer the one she'd been saving to eat later.

The policeman laughed. "For me?" he asked.

Bernie pointed to the woman she assumed to be Selene. "No, for her, but stop by the shop and tell my countergirl, Amber, I said to give you a couple."

"I might do that," the policeman replied as Bernie and Libby approached Selene. She was half standing, half leaning against the large white birch next to Ellen Fisher's house.

If Gail Gibson was a fireplug, then Selene White was a stork—tall and thin, with a long nose. The pair of them reminded Bernie of Mutt and Jeff, her dad's favorite cartoon characters. She looked lost in her business suit and high heels, Bernie reflected. As if she'd shrunk.

"Gail sent us," Libby said to Selene when they got closer.

Bernie held out the cookie. "Here. Have it."

Selene shook her head. "Thanks, but I'm not hungry."

"Eat it," Bernie said. "It'll help you from going into shock."

Selene took the cookie.

"How are you doing?" Libby asked as she watched Selene take a nibble.

"Terrible," Selene said, straightening up and hugging herself. "Really awful."

"Of course you are," Libby murmured.

Selene swallowed. "I still can't believe it. I thought it was a really bad joke at first. I was going to tell Ellen off when she opened the door. Something along the lines of 'That's not funny, not funny at all.'" She stifled a sob.

"Talk about irony." Selene took a deep breath and let it out. "She . . ."

"You mean Ellen?" Libby asked.

Selene nodded. "Said she wanted my advice on the binding for the quilt she was finishing. She asked me to drop over." Selene bit her lip. "You think you know what's going to happen when you get up in the morning, but you don't. Not really."

Selene ran a finger down the trunk of the birch tree. Libby and Bernie waited for her to continue. A moment later, she did. "When I got here, I knocked on the door, because the bell is broken." She pointed to a sign taped on Ellen Fisher's front door that said KNOCK LOUDLY. The word *knock* was underlined three times. "It's been broken for a year now. Ellen kept saying she was going to get it fixed, but she never did, and now she never will." Selene sniffed. "When Ellen didn't answer, I knocked again. I figured maybe she was taking a shower or doing the laundry or something like that, you know?"

Both Libby and Bernie nodded to show that they understood.

Selene continued with her narrative. "Then I knocked a third time, and when she didn't answer, I went around to the back. I thought maybe she was gardening and she didn't hear me. She liked to listen to music when she did." Selene stopped talking for a moment and closed her eyes. A minute later, she opened them. "And then the cat meowed."

"The cat?" Libby asked.

"Miss M. She was sitting in the window. So, I turned. At first, I saw this bunch of orange flowers. And then I saw . . ." Selene stopped talking again.

"It's okay," Libby said. "You don't have to tell us."

Selene held up her hands. "No. No. I want to. I have to." She cleared her throat. "That's when I saw . . . Ellen . . . I thought it was a joke. I really did. Oh. I already said that! I'm sorry."

"It's fine. Don't worry about it," Bernie reassured her.

Selene thanked her. "There were orange flowers in a vase on the sewing table. Ellen really liked flowers. She always had a vaseful. For some reason, I remember thinking it was nice that they were the last thing Ellen had smelled. Funny how your mind works." Selene shook her head. "If the cat hadn't meowed, I wouldn't have turned, and I wouldn't have seen . . . her."

Selene stifled a sob and pulled on her bangs. "I thought everything was fine. Well, not exactly fine. I knew Ellen was having . . . issues. We talked, but I thought they were getting resolved." Selene blinked. "I should have seen it."

Libby reached over and patted Selene's shoulder. "You couldn't have known."

"Yes, I could have," Selene said, her voice turning fierce. "More to the point, I should have. I'm a psychologist, for heaven's sake. Maybe it's time for me to hang up my shingle and become a greeter at Walmart." Suddenly Selene stiffened. She swayed from side to side and closed her eyes. "Oh my God, what's happening to me? Everything is spinning."

"I think you're going into shock," Libby said as she took hold of Selene's arm, guided her to Ellen's front porch steps, and helped her sit down on the top one while Bernie went to get an EMT.

"I'm fine," Selene was saying to Libby when Bernie returned. She was still protesting to the EMT that she was okay when Bernie and Libby left her and went around to the back. Through the open door, they could see the morgue attendants cutting Ellen Fisher's body down. A moment later, their dad's friend Clyde came out the door. He was a senior detective on the Longely police force.

"What are you two doing here?" he asked when he spotted them.

Bernie replied, "Lending moral support to the woman who found the body."

"Selene White?" Clyde asked.

Bernie and Libby nodded.

"She's gonna need it," Clyde said.

Libby nodded. "She seems pretty shaken up."

"Wouldn't you be? That's not a nice sight to be greeted with," Clyde observed. He was a big guy at six feet, four inches and 260 pounds, but recently age—he was nearing sixty-five—had lent a slight stoop to his shoulders.

"No, definitely not," Bernie said. "It would be hard to unsee."

"For sure," Clyde replied. "Did you two know Ellen Fisher?"

Bernie and Libby both shook their heads.

"She never came into the shop," Libby told him. "Do you?"

"She taught one of my daughters," Clyde said. "How about Selene White?"

"She isn't one of our customers, either," Bernie told him.

Clyde nodded to show he was listening. Then he said, "According to the statement she made, she came by to give Ellen Fisher an opinion on the binding for her quilt."

"That's what she told us, too," Bernie confirmed.

"It's nice when things align," Clyde observed.

"Trust but verify," Bernie said, repeating what her dad, who had served as the Longely chief of police before he'd been forced out, always said.

Clyde grinned. "An oldie but a goody."

Clyde, Bernie, and Libby were quiet for a moment as

they watched the attendants load Ellen Fisher's body into the ambulance parked by the back door.

Clyde shook his head. "Such a waste. She was so good with my daughter," he reflected. "Miranda could hardly wait to get to school in the mornings. She used to cry when the weekends came because she couldn't go to class. And she was really nice to my wife. Helped her with a couple of quilts she was making." For a moment, he watched a pair of blue jays pecking at something on Ellen Fisher's lawn; then he continued with what he'd been saying. "You know," he said, "I can understand why you would kill yourself if you had something like ALS, but when you're healthy and relatively young . . ." He hitched his pants up. "I don't get it."

"You think she killed herself, then?" Bernie asked.

"That's what the evidence suggests," Clyde responded. "There were no signs of a struggle, no signs that Ellen Fisher had been involved in an altercation of any kind. According to the responding officer's account, Selene said she knocked, but when no one answered, she went around to the back, figuring maybe Ellen Fisher was in the backyard. She wasn't. Evidently, Selene was just leaving—she thought maybe she'd gotten the time wrong—when she heard Ellen's cat, at which point she turned and looked through the rear window. That's when she saw Ellen hanging from a hook in the sewing room ceiling and called nine-one-one."

"Did she try to get in after she called you guys?" Libby asked.

Clyde nodded. "According to the statement she gave to Officer Shaw, she tried the back door, but it was locked, at which point she looked for the key that Ellen usually kept underneath that ceramic turtle." Clyde pointed to the sculpture by Ellen Fisher's back door. "But the key wasn't there."

"So, someone took it?" Libby asked.

"Maybe," Clyde responded, "but Selene said Ellen Fisher was always forgetting her key, using her spare, and forgetting to put it back."

"Was anything taken from the house?" Bernie asked Clyde.

Clyde thought about what he'd seen on the first floor. There had been no signs of a struggle. Everything had looked in order. The living-room and dining-room furnishings were like the house—neat and unremarkable. The sofa and the chairs in the living room were gently worn, the coffee table was piled high with newspapers and magazines, and there was a cat tree near the fireplace and several random cat toys on the floor.

One half of the Queen Anne cherrywood table in the dining room was covered with neatly folded pieces of fabric of various sizes and patterns, while the other half of the table hosted packets of colored construction paper, boxes of crayons, and small white cardboard boxes.

"It doesn't look that way," he told Libby. "But considering we don't know what was in there to begin with, your guess is as good as mine."

"Fair enough," Libby said.

Bernie looked at her watch. It was time to get back to the shop. They had things to do. They left after they'd checked on Selene to make sure she was doing okay.

"So depressing," Libby said as she stared out the window at the dreary March landscape.

"The landscape or Ellen Fisher?" Bernie asked.

"Both," Libby replied.

The winter's snow had melted in the past two weeks, revealing season's detritus: streets dotted with rusted soda cans and discarded fast-food wrappers, front lawns carpeted with brown grass, and empty flower beds waiting for yellow daffodils to emerge.

"I can't wait for spring," Bernie remarked as she watched a squirrel running up the leafless branches of Mrs. Nevin's Japanese maple.

"Neither can I," Libby agreed, momentarily cheered by the thought of spring and summer's bounty. "We should do a special spring menu," Libby declared. "Something featuring fiddlehead ferns."

"And maybe a ragout of vegetables à la française," Bernie added as she turned onto Skyline Center Road.

"That too." Libby zipped up her jacket against the damp. "We could serve the ragout with a baguette or with smoked trout or sautéed shad roe. If we can get shad roe, that is." Recently, the spring delicacy had been in short supply.

"And then there's always roasted asparagus with duck eggs," Bernie suggested.

"Not to mention rhubarb and strawberry pie," Libby observed.

Bernie's mouth started to water at the thought of sweet strawberries and tart rhubarb enfolded in a buttery crust as she turned up the collar of her spring coat and buttoned the bottom button. It was definitely chillier out than she had thought it was going to be.

Chapter 3

Two weeks later . . .

Spring is definitely in the air, Bernie observed as she studied the forsythia bushes beginning to blossom across the street, along Old Lady Randall's white picket fence.

It was ten thirty in the morning, the rain that had been falling for the past two days had stopped, and the sun had come out and was streaming in through the windows of A Little Taste of Heaven, making patterns on the blue-and-white linoleum tile floor.

Bernie smiled and stretched, working out a kink in her back. This was her favorite time of the day; the morning rush had dissipated, and the lunch rush hadn't begun. She took a deep breath and inhaled the smells of freshly ground coffee, cinnamon, and butter while she listened to the chatter coming from the handful of women sitting at the four small round tables off to the side, enjoying their post–yoga class coffees and scones.

Bernie had just phoned in the shop order to the Pittsford Dairy and was sliding the tray of banana-ginger cupcakes with chocolate icing she'd made earlier that morning into the display case when the doorbell jingled and Cecilia walked in holding a bag. Today she was wearing a long-sleeved black boatneck sweater, a straight denim skirt that came down to just above her knees, nylons, and ballet flats.

Her makeup was subdued—a swipe of brown instead of purple eye shadow across the lids—and she'd put her hair up in a ponytail. Cecilia looked older and wearier than the last time Bernie had seen her. There were circles under Cecilia's eyes, which hadn't been there when she and Libby had met at the library in what seemed like forever ago. Bernie knew she hadn't been sleeping too well for the past two weeks. For some reason, she couldn't get the thought of Ellen Fisher out of her mind. She wondered if the same held true for Cecilia, as well.

"Can I talk to you?" Cecilia asked Bernie when she reached the counter. Then she corrected herself. "Both of you," she added, indicating Libby with a nod of her head. "I need to talk to both of you."

"Of course," Libby said. She gave the coffee machine she'd been wiping down a last swipe with her cleaning cloth before she turned around and gave Cecilia her full attention.

"Good." Cecilia absentmindedly tugged at her ponytail while she glanced at the women sitting at the tables. Three of them waved, and she waved back. "Perhaps we could talk somewhere . . . a little more private," she said to the sisters after exchanging pleasantries with the women about their children.

"We have an office in the back," Bernie volunteered, wondering as she did what Cecilia had on her mind. They hadn't spoken since the day Ellen had died and the exhibition had been postponed. "Will that work?"

"Perfect," Cecilia said as Libby offered her something to eat and drink.

"Now, what can I get you? Corn muffin? Bran muffin? Gluten-free blueberry muffin? Cheese Danish? Coffee? Tea? Espresso? Water?" Libby asked, laughing at herself as she reeled off some of the options.

Cecilia laughed, as well. "Cheese Danish and a coffee, please," she replied. She bit her lower lip. "After what happened with Ellen . . ." She sighed ruefully. "I'm back on carbs. No more keto diet for me. Life is too short to deny myself." Then she gave a half snort. "I mean, you never know, right?"

"Right," Libby echoed.

"All I want to do these days is eat chocolate and drink wine," Cecilia confided to Libby after Libby had handed Cecilia her coffee and Danish.

"Works for me," Bernie told her. She'd been doing a little of both of those herself. A little too much of both of those, if truth be told.

"How's Selene doing?" Bernie asked.

Cecilia sighed. "About as well as can be expected, considering. She's never seen a dead body before."

"Lucky her," Bernie observed.

"Well, that's not the way you want to start," Libby said. "Not that there's a good way," she added.

"No, there isn't," Cecilia agreed. "I should have known when I saw the crows," Cecilia reflected as she followed the sisters through the shop's swinging doors into the prep room, where their office was located.

Measuring ten by eight feet, the space felt closet-like, made even smaller feeling by the stacks of cookbooks, old newspapers, and cooking magazines piled up along the walls. Libby apologized for the mess, cleared a collection of files off the chair in front of the desk, and gestured for Cecilia to sit.

"Crows?" Libby asked, laying claim to the chair behind

the desk while Bernie carefully lowered herself onto the rickety chair off to the side.

"Yes, crows," Cecilia replied, taking her seat and putting her coffee on the scratched-up black desk. "They were there when I visited Ellen the day before she died. Six of them perched on the top of Ellen's house, cawing at me," Cecilia recalled, shuddering. "They were a sign. I was in too much of a hurry to stop and take notice. If I had, maybe I could have done something." She lifted her hand and dropped it in a gesture of hopelessness. "Perhaps I could have stopped Ellen from doing what she did."

"I'm sorry. I don't understand," Bernie told her. There were always flocks of crows around, roosting in the trees, raiding garbage cans, creating a racket, and making a general nuisance of themselves. They were like pigeons—only worse.

"Crows are a harbinger of death," Cecilia explained.

Libby sat back. "They are?" she asked, surprised.

"Yes, they are," Cecilia replied. "Everyone knows that."

"In Greek mythology, they carried messages to the gods," Bernie told her.

"Maybe they do both," Cecilia reflected after she took a bite of her Danish. "I still can't believe it. I can't believe Ellen is dead."

"It was a shock, that's for sure," Bernie replied.

Cecilia pointed to the Danish and changed the subject. "This is very good, by the way," she said after she'd swallowed. "Did you make it?"

Bernie nodded. "We make everything we sell."

"It's delicious," Cecilia said. "Very buttery." She looked at her watch. "I have an hour before I have to be back in school. Staff development day," she explained when she saw the blank looks on Bernie's and Libby's faces. "I snuck out. Didn't think I needed to hear another lecture on the need for structure in kindergarten." She shook her head. "If you ask me, what kids need is more playtime, not that anyone *is* asking me. After all, I've been teaching for only fifteen years, but God forbid they should ask someone with experience." Cecilia took a sip of coffee, then, seemingly lost in thought, pinched the rim of her take-out cup, realized what she was doing, and stopped.

"So, what can I help you with?" Bernie asked when Cecilia didn't say anything else.

Cecilia roused herself. "I've been told the two of you do detective work."

Libby nodded. "We've been known to on occasion."

"I also hear you guys are pretty good at it," Cecilia went on.

"We have our moments," Bernie allowed, going for a humble brag. Then she fell silent and waited for Cecilia to speak.

Cecilia took another sip of coffee, put the cup down on the black desk, took a deep breath, and let it out.

"Well?" Libby prodded.

Cecilia pointed at Libby and Bernie. "We—"

Bernie interrupted. "We?"

Cecilia clarified, saying, "The Longely Sip and Sew Quilting Society wants to hire both of you to find out who killed Ellen."

Bernie's eyes widened. "You're kidding."

"I wish I were," Cecilia remarked as Bernie shook her head. Talk about being surprised. This was not what she had been expecting when Cecilia walked into their place.

Chapter 4

Libby did a double take. "Seriously?" she said as the store phone rang. She ignored it. Amber or Googie would take a message.

"Seriously," Cecilia replied after she'd taken a sip of her coffee.

"I thought that matter was settled," Libby said. "I thought Ellen killed herself."

"I don't think she did, and neither do the rest of the crew," Cecilia declared.

Bernie leaned forward. "That's not what the ME ruled," she pointed out.

Two blotches of color appeared on Cecilia's cheeks. "I know what the medical examiner ruled, and he's wrong."

"Can I ask you why you guys have come to that particular conclusion?" Bernie inquired as she brushed a piece of lint off her black cotton shirt.

Cecilia pointed to her heart. "Because I know. In here. Because what the authorities are saying doesn't make sense."

"Have you talked to the police?" Bernie asked softly. "Told them what you think?"

Cecilia was indignant. "Of course I talked to the police. That was the first thing I did."

"I take it the results weren't satisfactory," Libby surmised.

Cecilia clenched her jaw at the memory. "That's one way of putting it."

"Who did you talk to?" Bernie asked.

"First, I talked to a detective, and then I talked to the chief of police."

"Lucas Broadbent?" Bernie asked to clarify.

Cecilia nodded. "Yeah. Neither one paid any attention to what I was saying. The chief patted me on the head—metaphorically speaking—told me I was in shock and needed to talk to a therapist, after which he told me to go home. Now he won't even take my calls."

"Have you considered that he might be right?" Bernie asked as she reflected that this could be one of the few times that Lucy, aka Lucas Broadbent, was correct.

"He's not," Cecilia declared.

"I see," Libby said.

"No, you don't," Cecilia retorted. "You don't see at all."

"And you told the chief why you thought Ellen didn't kill herself?" Bernie asked.

"Of course I did," Cecilia replied. "And like I just told you, he patted me on the head and told me to go home. And that's why I'm here." She took a deep breath. "Please," Cecilia begged. "You need to listen to me. You're my last hope. I don't know who else to turn to."

The sisters exchanged a glance.

"Of course we'll listen," Bernie replied.

Cecilia's face relaxed into a smile. "Thank you. Thank you so much."

"Don't thank us yet," Libby cautioned. "My sister just said we'd listen. That's all."

Cecilia leaned forward in her chair. "I know you'll help me when you hear what I have to say."

"We'll see," Libby said. Then she and Bernie folded their hands in front of them and waited.

"Aren't one of you going to take notes?" Cecilia asked, looking from one sister to the other and back again.

"I have a pretty good memory," Bernie assured her.

"Because in the movies the detective always takes notes," Cecilia told her.

"I will," Libby promised. "But right now, we'd prefer to concentrate on what you're saying."

Cecilia nodded. "Okay." She took another sip of her coffee and the last bite of her Danish as she gathered her thoughts. A minute later, she began. "I should start by saying I know Ellen was going through a rough time. I'm not blind."

"That correlates with something Selene said," Libby observed.

"No one said you were blind, Cecilia," Bernie added.

"Gail Gibson did," Cecilia responded.

"I take it that she doesn't agree with your assessment of the situation?" Libby asked.

Cecilia sniffed. "Gail thinks that because she's a college professor, she knows everything."

"So, she doesn't agree with you?" Libby repeated.

"No." Cecilia's eyes narrowed. "She doesn't."

"How many people in the group agree with Gail?" Libby asked out of curiosity.

Cecilia nibbled on a fingernail while she thought. "I'd say it's fifty-fifty. Maybe sixty-forty. Judy is on the fence. One moment she agrees with us, and the next moment she doesn't."

"Can you tell us why you don't think that Ellen hung herself?" Bernie inquired.

"I'm trying to," Cecilia said. She leaned forward and pointed a finger first at Libby, then at Bernie for emphasis. "See. Here's the thing. Ellen was really excited about her quilt. She was really excited about it being in the exhibition. She was really excited about it being chosen to be hung in the place of honor. And . . ." Cecilia paused for dramatic effect. "She had just found out her quilt was going to be photographed for a national magazine called *Quilts for All* and that it had been chosen to hang in a juried show in a museum when it was done. Those are very big deals."

"How big a deal?" Bernie inquired.

"Kind of like you having one of your recipes featured in *Bon Appétit*," Cecilia replied.

"So, a very big deal," Libby commented.

Cecilia nodded.

"But you said when the quilt was finished," Libby continued. "Isn't it unusual to have something like that chosen before it's done?"

"It was done. Ellen was just redoing the binding," Cecilia explained.

Libby moved a paper clip to the center of the desk. "How come?"

Cecilia shrugged. "Something about a couple of stitches being out of place. She wanted everything perfect."

"Maybe she felt she couldn't make it perfect. Maybe she felt that if she couldn't do that, it wasn't worth living," Bernie hypothesized.

"You're wrong. She wasn't depressed!" Cecilia stated. "Quite the opposite. I hadn't seen her so upbeat in quite a while. Ellen said it was the best thing that had happened to her in years! She was so happy she was crying. She was literally crying tears of joy."

"When did she find out?" Libby asked.

Cecilia wiped her hands on the napkin Libby had provided earlier before answering. "She found out about the magazine the day before we were scheduled to meet at the library, and about the museum the day before that. So, I ask you, why would she kill herself now, when she was succeeding? She wouldn't. And here's the other thing. She never, never would have used the binding of her quilt to hang herself. Never! That material was sacrosanct." Cecilia took a deep breath and let it out. "And then we come to point number three. Why would she send the text she did that day in the library if she was going to kill herself? It makes no sense. She knew Selene was coming over." Here Cecilia took another deep breath. "Why do . . . it then? Why not do it after Selene left? Or text Selene not to come?"

"I've read that suicide can be an act of anger," Bernie said. "Maybe she was trying to punish Selene for something she'd done."

"I can't imagine what that would be," Cecilia replied.

The three women were silent for a moment.

Then Libby spoke. "Maybe she didn't mean to kill herself. Maybe hanging herself was a cry for attention, and something went wrong," Libby suggested. "Maybe she thought she'd be found in time and cut down."

"That's ridiculous," Cecilia countered.

"I agree," Bernie remarked.

"Thanks," Libby told her sister.

Bernie nodded. "Sorry, but in this case, I think Cecilia is correct. What you're saying is that Ellen waited until Selene rang her doorbell to step off the table."

"I admit it's a bit of a stretch," Libby replied, "but sometimes people don't think clearly. Especially when they're upset."

Bernie shifted her position on the chair. It creaked ominously but stayed standing. "She would have really had to hate Selene to have done that."

Cecilia leaned forward. "What do you think?"

Bernie sighed. "You're probably not going to want to hear this, but even taking into account what you just told us, you must admit the case for Ellen killing herself seems pretty strong. For a start, the doors to her house were locked."

"Ellen could have let whoever did it in, and then they locked the doors on their way out," Cecilia hypothesized. "Or they could have taken the key under that ceramic thingy by the back door, or they could have had a key to begin with."

"Do you have a key?" Libby asked Cecilia.

Cecilia shook her head. "No, I don't. If I had one, I would have told you." She finished the last of her coffee. "But that doesn't mean Ellen didn't give out."

Libby leaned back in her chair. "Any idea who she would she have given a key to?"

"I don't know." Cecilia put her cup down. "Maybe a neighbor?"

"How about someone in your quilting group?" Libby suggested. "Would they have one?"

"They said they didn't," Cecilia replied as Bernie stood up, leaned against the wall, and stretched. "I already asked."

"I'm not sure it matters," Bernie said as Cecilia turned and faced her.

Cecilia wrinkled her nose. "What matters?"

"Who had the key," Bernie replied. "There were no signs of struggle evident on Ellen's body and no ligature marks on her wrists or ankles."

Cecilia readjusted the neckline of her black boatneck sweater. "Meaning?"

"It means that there's no indication that someone strung Ellen up against her will," Bernie explained. "Think about it."

Cecilia shuddered. "I don't want to."

Bernie apologized. "Sorry, but I think you're going to have to."

Libby took over the narrative. "I think what my sister is trying to say is that it would be very hard for someone to . . ." Here Libby hesitated for a moment, searching for more neutral phrasing before continuing. "To do what they did without your friend's cooperation. There would have been marks. In addition, Ellen's tox report came back clean." Clyde had called to give them the news.

"Of course it came back clean," Cecilia said. "She didn't do drugs."

"What Libby meant was that there was nothing in her system that would have rendered her unconscious," Bernie replied.

"Maybe the lab report didn't pick it up," Cecilia countered. "That happens on TV crime shows all the time. If you don't test for it, then you don't know. That happened on the last *CSI* I saw."

Bernie sighed. "We're not talking about *CSI* here, although it is true that a lot of those sorts of drugs clear the system pretty quickly." Bernie shook her head. "I'm sorry, but everything points to Ellen having done this to herself."

"Then how do you explain the timing?" Cecilia demanded. "How do you explain that?"

"It is off," Bernie admitted.

Cecilia smiled triumphantly. "Exactly." She turned to Libby. "And what about you? Do you have an explanation?"

"No, I don't," Libby admitted. "Any other reasons you think Ellen was murdered?"

Cecilia looked at Libby as if she was a moron. "Aren't the ones I just told you enough?"

"Okay, assuming you're right and someone killed her, who do *you* think did it?" Bernie asked Cecilia.

"I don't know. If I did, I wouldn't be here, would I? That's what I want to hire you to find out," Cecilia replied.

"Fair enough," Bernie answered.

"So, you'll do it?" Cecilia asked. "You'll look into Ellen's death?"

"And if we find out Ellen killed herself?" Bernie said.

"She didn't," Cecilia insisted.

"But if she did?" Libby inquired.

Cecilia hesitated for a moment. Then she said, "At least I'll know."

Bernie nodded. "Just so you understand."

Cecilia smiled for the first time since she'd walked in the store. "Does this mean you'll take the case?"

Bernie said yes before Libby could say no.

"I was hoping you'd say that," Cecilia said as she took a bank envelope out of her bag and slid it across the desk toward Libby. "There's four thousand dollars in there, and I can get more if you need it."

Libby nodded her thanks, took the envelope, and put it in the desk drawer off to the left.

"Aren't you going to count it?" Cecilia asked, rising to her feet.

Libby shook her head. "No need," she said. "We know where you live." Then she smiled to show she was kidding.

"We'll be in touch, Cecilia," Bernie said as she and her sister got up and started walking Cecilia out of the shop.

The sisters had reached the door when Cecilia stopped and turned to them. "One other thing," she said.

Bernie and Libby waited.

"The quilt that Ellen was working on," Cecilia continued. "It seems to have gotten lost in the shuffle. If you find it, could you bring it to me so I can finish it and take a picture of it for the magazine, then send it on to the museum for the exhibition? It seems like the least I can do, given the circumstances."

"Not a problem," Bernie reassured her. Then she gave Cecilia a hug and sent her on her way.

"So, what do you think?" Bernie asked Libby after the door had closed.

"I don't think that Cecilia is going to be happy with what we find out," Libby replied, flicking a spot of flour off her polo shirt.

"Neither do I," Bernie allowed. She readjusted the band of her pleated skirt. "On the other hand, Cecilia is right. There's something about this that doesn't make any sense."

"No, it doesn't, does it?" Libby agreed as she and Bernie walked over to the prep table and began assembling the ingredients necessary to make sourdough English muffins for the next morning.

Chapter 5

"**S**o, what did your dad say when you told him you'd agreed to help out Cecilia Larson?" Marvin asked Bernie.

"Why are you asking?" Bernie inquired.

Marvin shrugged. "No particular reason. Just curious what his opinion was."

It was a little after nine at night, and Bernie, Libby, and Libby's boyfriend, Marvin, were sitting at the bar at RJ's, having a drink. Marvin had just finished telling a long story about the dry cleaner ruining one of his suits, and they had gone on to discuss the day's events while Bernie's boyfriend, Brandon, hovered behind the bar, polishing glasses and keeping an eye on the customers as he listened to Bernie, Libby, and Marvin's conversation.

Except for a sprinkling of men, a group of five friends down at the end of the bar celebrating a promotion, and the dart players, RJ's was quiet, but then, Tuesday nights were always slow, Brandon reflected as he pushed a black bowl full of unshelled peanuts toward Marvin. These days, for some reason, Wednesdays, Thursdays, and Fridays were the busy nights of the week. No one went out on Saturday anymore.

"Have you ever thought about not telling him about the cases you take on?" Marvin asked, thinking about the difference in relationships between him and his dad and Libby and Bernie and their dad.

Libby laughed. "No. What would be the point? He would find out, anyway. He always does."

"This is true," Bernie replied, thinking back to when she was a teenager and used to sneak out of the house. No matter what she tried, her dad was always there to greet her upon her return home. Not only that, but he always heard if she got into trouble. She sighed. God, how she used to wish she wasn't the daughter of the chief of police.

"So, what does he think?" Brandon asked the sisters after he handed a customer an IPA. "Did Ellen Fisher kill herself, or was she murdered?"

Libby replied, "He agrees with the official verdict." She took a sip of her white wine. "But he said that if we wanted to muck around with it, more power to us. Miracles have been known to happen. That's a direct quote, by the way."

"That's not very encouraging," Marvin observed.

"No, it's not," Bernie agreed. "Actually, he called us the patron saints of lost causes, and then he said that he hoped that we were getting paid for our efforts."

"And are you getting paid?" Marvin asked, stifling a yawn. It had been a long day.

Bernie waved her hand in the air. "We're getting paid, but I think I'd take this on even if we weren't."

"How come?" Brandon wanted to know.

"For openers, I feel bad for Cecilia," Bernie told him after she'd taken another sip of her Scotch. "And secondly, there are a couple of things about the story that upon reflection don't make sense to me." Bernie thought about them as she held her glass up to the light and studied the golden color. Normally, she was a bourbon kinda gal, but recently she'd been branching out to single malts.

"Ellen Fisher's funeral is this coming Saturday," Marvin informed Bernie and Libby as he reached into the bowl. He took some peanuts, shelled them, and popped them into his mouth.

"So, I take it you're doing it," Libby asked him.

Marvin nodded as he swept the peanut husks onto the floor with the side of his hand, where they joined their brethren. "We are." He and his father owned one of the two remaining independent funeral homes in Longely. "The medical examiner is going to release the body to us tomorrow," Marvin noted. "Then she'll be cremated, and the ashes are going to be laid to rest in the cremation garden."

"It's taking them longer than usual to release the body, isn't it?" Brandon asked. He had to raise his voice to be heard over the sound of the television.

"Definitely. Between Covid and staffing problems, they're backlogged." Marvin made a face. "You didn't hear it from me, but bodies are piling up over there. They're talking about getting a couple of refrigerator trucks in the parking lot to help with the overflow."

Libby shuddered.

"Well, it's true," Marvin said. "I'm not making it up."

"I didn't say you were. The thought just gives me the creeps," Libby told him. Then she changed the subject. "Cecilia called and told us what was happening. I didn't see anything in the paper, though."

"That's because everything is online these days," Marvin informed Libby as he ate another peanut.

"Do you expect a big turnout?" Bernie asked Marvin.

Marvin shook his head. "Probably not. It's a graveside service. Pastor James is conducting it."

"Is the family coming?" Libby asked.

"There is no family," Marvin replied. "At least none that's come forward."

"No one?" Libby repeated. "Everyone has someone."

Marvin shelled another peanut and ate it. "Not in this case," he said. "Or if there is family out there," Marvin amended, "I haven't been able to locate them." He took another handful of peanuts from the bowl. "Of course," he added, "truth be told, I didn't look very hard, either."

Bernie half swiveled toward him. "Then who's paying?"

"For the funeral?" Marvin asked. "The Longely Sip and Sew Quilting Society. They took up a collection."

"They're helping with the investigation, too," Bernie commented as Brandon came over and topped off her glass with a little more Macallan. "At least two of them are."

"How can you drink that?" Marvin asked, indicating the glass Bernie was holding in her hand with a nod of his head.

"You mean the Scotch?" Bernie asked.

"I don't see anything else around," Marvin replied.

"Simple. I like it." And Bernie took another sip and let it roll around on her tongue.

"It tastes like diesel fuel to me," Marvin noted.

"Aren't you the person who likes Spam?" Bernie shot back.

"Be nice, Bernie," Brandon said.

"I'm simply stating a fact," she replied.

"What's wrong with Spam?" Marvin demanded. "I read there's a restaurant somewhere that's devoted to it. Anyway, the last I heard, you like Devil Dogs, so I don't think you're one to talk."

"Everyone has a guilty pleasure," Bernie responded.

"Exactly," Marvin said, at which point Brandon intervened and asked Bernie if she really thought Ellen Fisher had committed suicide.

"I think there's a small chance," Bernie allowed.

"A very small chance. Like infinitesimal," Libby said.

"I don't think I'd go that far," Bernie told her.

Libby rolled her eyes. "I would."

"Why wouldn't you?" Brandon asked Bernie.

"Because, like I said before, some things don't make sense. Like the timing. The timing is off," Bernie answered. She ran her finger around the rim of her glass. Then she took another sip of her drink before telling Brandon the same things Cecilia had told her and she'd told her father. "Ellen knew Selene was coming over—she'd asked her to—and she knew when she was expected, so why would Ellen pick that time to hang herself?"

"Maybe she was playing a practical joke on Selene, or rather thought she was," Brandon suggested.

Marvin snorted. "That's some joke. How do you come up with things like that, anyway?"

"I'll tell you how, Marvin," Brandon replied. "One of my friends did something like that in high school. Hung himself from the lamppost outside his house. Scared the crap out of us," Brandon revealed. "Of course, Mike was wearing a harness under his sweatshirt. And he was sixteen. You're an idiot when you're sixteen."

"True," Bernie said, thinking of the stuff she had pulled at that age.

"I wasn't," Libby said.

"No," Bernie said. "You were perfect."

Libby grinned. "I was, wasn't I?"

"I was being sarcastic, Libby," Bernie said.

"But I wasn't," Libby replied.

Chapter 6

"Sorry, but I was definitely the good daughter," Libby remarked after she took another sip of her wine. "While you, Bernie, were always getting into trouble."

Brandon laughed. "Now, there's a shocker."

"Yeah," Bernie countered, "but I had more fun."

"Well, Ellen didn't," Marvin observed. "That's a rotten way to died."

"Is there a good way?" Libby asked.

"Either in your sleep or getting hit by a bus," Marvin promptly replied. "So, I guess we're ruling out Ellen hanging herself as a joke gone bad," he continued.

"I think that's safe to say," Bernie replied. She began tapping her fingers on the bar. "Here's the thing. Ellen had just gotten two pieces of really good news about her quilt in the preceding days. At least according to Cecilia she had. Her quilt was going to be featured in a magazine, and it had been nominated to hang in a show in the Silverhead.

"That's a small museum in Auburn," Bernie explained when she saw the puzzled looks on Marvin's and Brandon's faces. "Evidently, they pick quilts from all over the world for their annual quilting exhibition, so this was a big deal." Bernie brushed a strand of hair off her forehead. "Anyway, that's why I think there may be a chance Ellen didn't kill herself. There are just too many details that don't fit together."

"What do you think the odds are?" Brandon asked.

Bernie thought for a moment, then said, "I'd say twenty percent."

"I'd put it at ten percent, if that," Libby said.

"Wanna bet?" Bernie asked Libby.

Libby grinned. "Sure. I can always use the extra cash."

"A dollar?" Bernie said.

Libby snorted. "Seriously?"

"Okay, two dollars."

"Ah, the last of the big spenders," Libby observed.

Bernie laughed. "So, are we on or not?"

"On," Libby told her sister as they shook hands. "Always happy to take your money," Libby continued. "Think about it, Bernie. Whoever killed Ellen would have had to have left just as Selene was arriving. And she didn't see anyone. Or if she did, she didn't tell the police."

"Whoever it was could have been lurking in the house and gone out the front door when Selene went around to the back," Bernie pointed out.

"Now what?" Brandon asked, interrupting Libby and Bernie's conversation. "How are you going to proceed?"

"The usual," Libby replied. "Talk to the neighbors. See if they noticed anyone coming in or going out of Ellen's house. Talk to the quilters and see what they have to say. If Ellen Fisher was murdered, it wasn't a random act. It took planning."

Bernie looked at Brandon. "And speaking of finding things out, I don't suppose you have any gossip to add to the mix?"

Brandon did outrage. "Gossip? Me?"

Bernie laughed. "Yes. You."

"Well, maybe I have a little something," Brandon conceded. "I'm not sure this is worth much, but if I were you, I might want to talk to Gail Gibson. She and Ellen were going at it the last time they were in here."

Bernie leaned forward. "What happened?"

"Nothing really. Ellen just stormed off. They usually come in at least once a month, sometimes two or three times," Brandon told her and Libby, raising his voice so he could be heard over the cheering of one of the dart teams.

"And?" Bernie prompted.

"And that's about it," Brandon said. "We're not talking lots of drama here. Members of their quilting group always sit in one of the booths in the back and have a couple of glasses of wine or a cocktail or two and then go home around ten. Maybe they'll stay to eleven if it's a late night. Sometimes, there are six or seven in the group, sometimes ten, and sometimes there are only three."

Libby finished her wine. Brandon went to pour her some more, but Libby put her hand over her glass to stop him. She'd had enough for one evening. "Has any of the group been in since Ellen's death?" she asked.

Brandon shook his head. "Not unless they've come in on one of my days off."

"When was the last time they did come in?" Bernie inquired.

"A couple of days before Ellen Fisher died," Brandon promptly replied. "There were three of them. Ellen Fisher, Gail Gibson, and . . ." He stopped speaking. "Jeez, my mind is going. I forgot her name."

"I've found that the key to remembering names is building a memory palace," Marvin said, trying to be helpful.

"Really?" Brandon told Marvin. "I've found the key is getting more than four hours' sleep a night." He snapped his fingers. "Cecilia. That's the name I was looking for."

"Cecilia Larson?" Libby asked.

Brandon nodded. "That's the Cecilia I'm talking about."

Libby frowned. Cecilia hadn't mentioned an argument between Gail and Ellen, but maybe she'd forgotten. Maybe she'd forgotten because it wasn't worth mentioning, but it would still be nice to know what the argument had been about.

"I don't suppose you happened to hear what they were fighting over?" Bernie asked Brandon.

He grinned. "Are you accusing me of eavesdropping?"

Bernie laughed. "You? Heaven forbid."

"Well, I did catch a snippet," Brandon allowed.

Bernie sat up straighter. "Well?" she said.

"Something about silk versus cotton thread, and whether Japanese thread is better."

Bernie snorted. "Seriously?"

Brandon nodded. "Told you."

Bernie tapped the bar with a fingernail. "Anything else?"

Brandon shook his head. "I couldn't hear. I was down at the other end of the bar by then. All I do know is that the discussion got pretty heated. I could tell from the expressions on their faces. Five minutes later, Ellen Fisher stormed off, and about ten minutes after that, the other two left, as well, and that, as they say, is all I got for you. But maybe Steve heard something. He took over for me while I was in the john." And Brandon motioned to the other bartender to come over.

"Yes?" Steve said a moment later. "What can I do you for?" he asked Brandon.

Brandon pointed at Bernie. "She wants to know what Ellen Fisher and Gail Gibson were fighting about."

Steve laughed. He ran his hand over his hair. "The usual. This time it was about something to do with thread. The last time it was about handsewn versus machine-sewn quilts. The time before that it was about how quilts should be displayed."

"They fought a lot?" Libby asked.

"All the time. Everyone in the group did. Sometimes, the arguments got really hot, although how you can care about what kind of backing a quilt should have is beyond me." Steve scratched his chin. "Can I ask what this is about?"

Bernie told him.

Steve frowned. He shook his head. "Ellen killing herself never made sense to me."

"You sound as if you know her," Libby observed.

"I do," Steve replied. "Sorry, did. Not well. We went out a couple of times. Nothing serious. Then she started seeing someone else, and that was that—not that we were going anyplace, anyway, relationship-wise."

"Do you know who it was?" Bernie asked.

Steve shook his head. "She didn't say, and I didn't ask, but I got the feeling it was getting pretty serious."

"Can you think of anything else we should know about?" Bernie asked.

Steve made a clicking noise with his tongue while he thought. Then he said, "She just seemed a little off the past month or so. Like something was bothering her. When I asked her what it was, she said it was just real estate stuff, that she was thinking about putting her house on the market in the future and trying to decide who to use as a Realtor, but I had a feeling something else was going on. Maybe with the new guy?" Steve stroked his goatee. "Of course, I could be wrong. Maybe Gail knows. Or Judy. Or Selene. You should ask them."

"Don't worry. We will. I take it you know them, too?" Libby inquired.

"As customers," Steve answered. "The sum of my knowledge about them is that I know that Gail drinks only red wine and Judy prefers rosé, while Selene prefers white, and they all like pretzels instead of peanuts." Then he pointed to a schleppy-looking man who had just walked in. "That's Dwayne Iodice, Gail's husband."

"Gail didn't change her name when she got married?" Libby asked.

"Not everyone does these days, Libby," Bernie observed.

"I'm aware, Bernie," Libby snapped back.

"I thought he was going on a business trip," Brandon said to Steve, interrupting the sisters' bickering.

Steve shrugged. "I guess it got canceled."

"He come in often?" Bernie asked.

"Probably two or three times a week," Brandon replied. "He usually has a couple of beers and leaves. Doesn't say much."

"What does he do for a living?" Libby inquired.

"I think he's a printer's rep, but I'm not sure," Steve replied. "I could be wrong."

"Can we meet him?" Libby asked.

"Sure thing," Steve said. "But he's not the friendliest guy in the bunch."

Dwayne grunted when Steve introduced him to the sisters. "I'm sorry," he said when he heard why they were talking to him, "but I don't have anything to say that would help you. It's been a long day, and I just want to drink my beer in peace and go home." Then he picked up his drink and walked off to the back.

"I did warn you," Steve said.

"Yes, you did," Libby agreed.

Marvin was fishing the last peanuts out of the bowl when Bernie and Libby sat back down next to him.

"So?" he asked.

Libby made a zero sign with her hand. "Nothing."

"Now what?" he asked.

"I was thinking it wouldn't hurt to take another look around Ellen Fisher's house," Bernie said.

"What do you expect to find?" Brandon asked.

"I don't know," Bernie told him.

Twenty minutes she and her sister had finished their drinks and were out the door.

Chapter 7

The fog the weatherman had been predicting greeted Bernie and Libby when they stepped out of RJ's. While they were inside, it had rolled in off the Hudson, bringing with it a penetrating dampness. Wisps of it clung to the parking lot lights and softened the darkness, shrouding everything in mist.

"It looks like San Francisco in the morning, before the fog burns off," Bernie remarked to her sister as she pulled out of the parking lot. She drove slowly, eyes glued to the road, alert for deer dashing across the road and cats out on the prowl. Ten minutes later she arrived at the street Ellen Fisher's house was on. The block was quiet. The houses were partly shrouded in the fog. TVs flickered in the windows, their jumbled sounds floating out onto the evening air.

"It looks as if everyone is in for the night," Libby observed.

"Indeed, it does," Bernie agreed as she studied Ellen Fisher's house. She noted that they hadn't taken the police tape off the house yet as she pulled into the driveway.

Libby frowned. "I'm surprised," she said to her sister.

"You'd think someone would have removed the tape by now. It's been a while."

"I'm guessing the real estate agent probably will remove it when the house goes on the market," Bernie hypothesized. "Unless one of the neighbors does it first. I know I wouldn't be happy passing that tape every day."

"Neither would I." Libby rubbed her arms. The damp was getting to her. She should have worn a heavier sweater instead of Bernie's embroidered black hoody. March was treacherous that way.

"I don't know about you, but I wouldn't want this house, not even if you gave it to me for free," Bernie noted as she studied the darkened building. The fog seemed to cling to it, wrapping it in its embrace.

"I'd slap a paint of coat on it and flip it," Libby opined. "Although," she allowed, "it wouldn't be an easy sell."

Bernie nodded. "No, it would not. People don't like to buy houses where a violent death has occurred."

"We don't know Ellen was murdered," Libby objected.

"No, we don't," Bernie agreed, "but suicide counts as a violent death, as well."

"I'm not so sure," Libby said doubtfully.

Bernie turned her gaze on her sister. "You're doing violence to yourself, Libby. How is that not a violent death?"

"I suppose," Libby allowed.

"There's no suppose about it," Bernie countered.

"How about if you take sleeping pills?" Libby asked. "That's not violent."

Bernie snorted. "Now you're being ridiculous."

"No. I'm being literal," Libby said as she watched a wisp of fog skitter across the street. A cold front was coming in, bringing thirty-mile-an-hour winds with it and thinning the fog out. She rubbed her arms again. "I gotta say I wouldn't tell people what happened here if I were the listing agent."

"I think you have to, Libby," Bernie told her. "I think it's the law. Full disclosure."

Libby reached in her pocket and took out two squares of chocolate, which she had just remembered she had. She handed one to Bernie, unwrapped the other one, and put it in her mouth. "I wonder if Ellen is going to haunt this place," she mused as the chocolate dissolved in her mouth. It was single origin from Venezuela and, God, was it good. Somehow, it made the night a little warmer.

"If I were going to haunt someplace, I'd like a place with a little more class—like a country estate . . ."

"Or a castle in Italy," Libby declared, finishing Bernie's sentence for her.

Bernie laughed. "Do you believe in ghosts, Libby?" Bernie asked as she savored the chocolate Libby had given her.

"I don't disbelieve, Bernie. What about you?"

Bernie considered her answer for a moment, then said, "Sometimes I do, and sometimes I don't."

"I guess you could say the same for me." Libby studied the street for a moment. "I wonder why that car is parked there," she said suddenly, indicating the Caddy Escalade on the other side of the road, two houses down.

Bernie shrugged. "Why shouldn't it be there?"

"No reason really," Libby responded. "It just stands out. Everybody else's vehicle is either in their driveway or their garage."

"It's probably a visitor's," Bernie suggested.

"You're probably right," Libby said.

Bernie turned to Libby again. "So, let's do this. Are you coming in or staying in the van?"

"Coming in," Libby replied.

Bernie nodded, turned off the van, exited, and started toward the backyard.

Libby followed her a moment later. The first thing she noticed was that someone had pulled all the window shades down, which made it impossible to see inside the house. The second thing she noticed as she hurried along was that the houses on either side of Ellen Fisher's were dark. Either the people who lived there had gone to bed or were still out for the evening. Libby was thinking that she and Bernie should talk to them, as well as to the rest of the neighbors, tomorrow or the next day when she and Bernie reached the backyard. It was pitch black because the floodlight mounted on the garage wasn't working.

"Better for us," Bernie noted as she walked toward Ellen Fisher's back door. When she got closer, she saw something white underneath one of the gold-needle pine bushes in the flower bed. She reached over and picked it up. A cigarette butt. Then she saw several more and wondered if someone had been standing by the door, smoking, and then had flicked them away when they were done.

"You don't see a lot of these anymore," Libby commented, holding one of the butts up.

"I wonder if Ellen smoked," Bernie asked as she put her hands on her thighs. She was just about to lever herself up when she heard a noise. "What was that?" she asked her sister.

Libby had heard it, as well. "It sounds like a door closing to me."

"It sounds like that to me, too," Bernie agreed. She listened carefully. "I think it's coming from the front of the house."

"Do you think someone was inside Ellen Fisher's house all this time?" Libby asked as they both ran to the front.

"I would say that's a yes," Bernie replied as she paused to watch the Escalade pull away from the curb, its taillights illuminating the fog. "And there they go. Whoever they are."

"I was right," Libby exclaimed triumphantly. "I told you we should have paid more attention to the Caddy."

"Yeah, yeah, yeah," Bernie replied as she opened the van door and hopped in. She fastened her seat belt and turned the key in the ignition. Mathilda coughed twice, then roared to life. Bernie pulled out of the driveway and sped down the street, but by the time she'd gotten to the end of the block, the Escalade had turned the corner. "Right or left?" Bernie asked Libby when they reached the same corner a moment later. "Pick one," she told Libby when she didn't answer immediately.

"Right," Libby replied, squinting into the fog. She'd read somewhere that 90 percent of people would turn right if given the choice, but that didn't prove to be the case this time.

Bernie turned onto Ashton and cursed under her breath as she looked down the empty street. The only thing moving in either direction was the tops of the cedars swaying in the wind, not that Bernie was expecting anything else, if she was being honest with herself. She spent the next ten minutes driving around the area. She and her sister saw two Toyotas and a Subaru on the road, and that was it. The Escalade had disappeared into the fog.

"I wonder where it went," Bernie mused.

"I wonder who was driving it," Libby said.

"Answer one question and we'll have the answer to the other one," Bernie observed. "It should be easy enough to figure out. All we need to do is find out who in the Longely Sip and Sew Quilting Society owns a Caddy Escalade."

"Assuming the person belongs to the group," Libby said.

"I would say that is the most likely possibility, wouldn't you?" Bernie responded as she slowed down for a racoon crossing the street. It was amazing how much wildlife was living in Longely these days, she reflected as she reached over and turned on the radio.

"Maybe Cecilia isn't so crazy, after all," Bernie reflected half a mile later. "Maybe she's right. Maybe Ellen Fisher didn't kill herself. Maybe she was murdered."

"And maybe someone read about what happened and decided to rob the house," Libby said.

"Also a possibility," Bernie allowed.

"We should call Cecilia and ask who in her group drives a Caddy Escalade," Libby suggested.

"Text her," Bernie said.

Libby did. A moment later she got a response. "Cecilia says she doesn't think any of the girls has an Escalade, but she'll try to find out if someone does."

Bernie yawned. It was getting time for bed. "We need to get into Ellen Fisher's house," she observed, yawning again. She definitely needed to get more sleep. "We have to find out what that person was looking for."

"If they were looking for anything," Libby amended.

"Well, I don't think whoever they were, were there to play Parcheesi," Bernie retorted as she turned onto Main Street and waved to Mr. Sullivan and his dachshund, Otto, both of whom were out for their last walk of the evening.

"And how are we going to get into Ellen Fisher's house?" Libby asked Bernie.

"The usual way," Bernie responded. "Through the back door."

A moment later, she pulled into A Taste of Heaven's parking lot. She and Libby got out of the van, went upstairs, and went straight to bed. Tomorrow was probably going to be a long day.

Chapter 8

Libby and Bernie left Brandon's house for Ellen Fisher's at ten the next morning, right after Bernie swapped out A Taste of Heaven's van for Brandon's six-month-old pickup truck.

"That way," Bernie had explained to her sister while she squatted down and ran her fingers inside the truck's rear fender, looking for the spare key Brandon kept taped there, "we won't be as conspicuous."

"So not only are you breaking into Ellen Fisher's house, but you're also stealing Brandon's pride and joy to do it," Libby had observed as she buttoned the top button of the pink plaid shirt she was wearing.

"I'm not stealing Brandon's truck. I'm borrowing it, and we are looking through Ellen Fisher's house," Bernie had retorted. "Emphasis on the 'we.' If Brandon reported his vehicle missing and the police picked us up, you would be charged, as well."

"Lovely, but semantics aside, he's going to be really upset," Libby predicted.

"He'll be fine. Anyway, he's not going to know," Bernie replied. "We'll have it back before he wakes up."

"You could have asked him last night, Bernie."

"And if it had occurred to me, then I would have. Aha." Bernie held the key up. "Found it," she announced before Libby could reply. "Coming?" she asked her sister as she straightened up.

Libby nodded.

Bernie unlocked the doors, and she and her sister climbed in. Then she backed out of Brandon's driveway and turned right at the end of the block. "It'll be fine," she reassured her sister as she adjusted Brandon's truck's side and rearview mirrors.

"All I know is that Marvin wouldn't be happy if I did that to him," Libby said as she studied the sky. It had been sunny at eight, but now clouds were massing overhead. It looked as if the weatherman was right. It was going to rain soon. Again. If this kept up, she was going to turn into a mushroom. Libby sighed and turned to Bernie. "So, what do you think we're going to find in Ellen Fisher's house?" she asked her sister.

Bernie shook her head. She didn't know. "Hopefully, something that will either help or allay Cecilia's suspicions," she replied as she stopped to let a class of little kids accompanied by their teacher and two aides cross the street to the park.

Libby started to say something and stopped.

"What are you thinking?" Bernie asked her.

"Nothing really. It's just that you don't expect a kindergarten teacher, let alone a quilter, to get murdered. If she was murdered. At least in the manner she was. It would be different if Ellen Fisher had been killed in something random, like a drive-by shooting or a carjacking, but she wasn't. If Cecilia Larson is correct. This is a whole different ball game. Ellen Fisher's death wasn't the product of a random act. It was personal. Very personal. And it took a fair amount of strength to achieve it. And planning. It wasn't impulsive. In addition, the act was intended to mislead." Libby tucked a strand of hair that had come loose from her top-knot behind her ear.

"Meaning?" Bernie asked.

"Meaning that our killer is smart and disciplined. Ellen probably knew the person," Libby added. "She probably let him or her in."

"It wouldn't surprise me if Ellen had," Bernie agreed.

"What was Ellen involved in that got her killed?" Libby mused.

"So, we're ruling out the boyfriend?"

"I didn't say that, but this sure wasn't a crime of passion," Libby observed.

"No, it wasn't," Bernie agreed.

Libby took a sip of the coffee she'd brought with her, leaned back in her seat, and began eating one of the chocolate croissants she'd taken from the shop. She nodded toward the second one. "Want it?" she asked her sister.

Bernie shook her head. She'd tried on her bathing suit this morning, and it hadn't been a pretty sight. On the other hand, it was early March. Lots of time before swim season. "Oh, what the hell," she said, holding out her hand. "I could use the chocolate." She sighed with pleasure as she took the first bite. She could feel her nerves quiet. Chocolate and butter. Two of the better things the world had to offer.

The sisters arrived at their destination ten minutes later. Bernie parked the truck by the curb in front of Ellen Fisher's house. Then, as she got out, she patted her denim skirt's right front pocket just to make sure her lockpicks were still in there.

"Ready?" she asked Libby.

"Ready," Libby said, gulping down the last bit of her coffee.

"Then let's do this," Bernie said. First, they were going

to talk to the neighbors, and then they were going to go through Ellen Fisher's house. At least that was the plan.

Libby nodded while Bernie stopped to take a pebble out of her loafer. When she straightened up, she held out her hand. She felt a drop. It was starting to sprinkle. Again. She sighed and picked up the pace. God, she wished it would stop. They had had one northeaster after the other blowing through. According to the weatherman on the local news, this March was in the running for being the rainiest one ever. She just hoped that the storm drains on Main could handle the overflow.

According to the town engineers, there was a good chance they wouldn't if the rain came down too fast. Who knew the pipes in the town were almost one hundred years old? And to make matters worse, evidently, A Little Taste of Heaven was in a flood zone, a fact neither she, Libby, nor her father had been aware of until they'd gotten a letter from their insurance company last month informing them of that fact. Maybe they should get some inflatable sandbags. Just in case.

Bernie thought about that as she looked around. The block Ellen Fisher lived on was quiet at this time of the day. An empty school bus drove by. Libby waved, and the driver waved back. A postal worker was delivering the mail. Bernie watched a woman being pulled down the street by a large goldendoodle and another woman chasing after a toddler. She watched a DHL van stop in front of a pale green colonial and drop off a package while a ginger tabby sunned itself on the front steps. Next door a woman dragged a garbage can to the curb.

Then Libby counted ten robins looking for worms in Ellen Fisher's front yard. "I've never seen them in a group before," she noted. "Usually, there are just one or two."

"That's because they're highly territorial," Bernie said.

"Maybe the way they're acting has something to do with climate change."

"Could be," Libby agreed.

"I think they're called a round of robins."

"Like a mob of crows."

"Exactly, Libby," Bernie said.

A couple of minutes later, the sisters stopped in front of the neighbor on the right side of Ellen Fisher's house.

"There's no car in the driveway," Libby noted as Bernie rang the bell. No one answered. She waited a minute and tried again. The result was the same. No one came to the door. "They must be at work," Libby observed.

"It would seem so," Bernie agreed. "On to the next house?"

Libby nodded.

A moment later, the sisters were standing in front of the small white colonial on Ellen Fisher's left. There were a couple of bikes lying in the grass, a basketball hoop near the garage, and chalk stick figures on the driveway.

"Kids," Bernie observed while Libby rang the bell.

A minute later a heavyset elderly lady answered the door. "Yes?" she said. "Can I help you?"

Bernie smiled at her and introduced herself. The lady in front of them did likewise.

"I like your hair," Bernie said. "Blue suits you."

Mrs. Elison smiled back. She touched one of her curls. "Thank you. I like it, too. My daughter not so much. She says I looks silly. My mother would have said I look like mutton masquerading as sheep, but I don't care. At my age, you have to have fun where you can find it."

"Well, I think you look great," Bernie told her. "Very colorful."

Mrs. Elison looked down at her clothes. She was a vision in lilac sweatpants, a purple sweatshirt, and orange sneakers. "I am, aren't I?" She leaned on her walker. "My granddaughter did my hair," she confided. "My daughter wasn't happy, but I thought she was about to die when she came home and took a look at this." She lifted her arm and displayed the tattoo of a rose on her wrist. "My grandson and I got matching ones." She chuckled at the memory. "What do they say about karma being a bitch? But enough about me. Now, how can I help you ladies?"

She shook her head when Bernie explained about Ellen Fisher. "That was so terrible. Just horrible." She shook her head again. "Poor lady. I don't know which is worse, feeling so awful that you kill yourself or having someone hate you so much that they would do that to you." Mrs. Elison blinked several times. Her eyes misted. "Why would anyone do something like that to her?"

"That's what we're hoping to find out," Libby told her gently. "Did you know her very well?"

Mrs. Elison shook her head again. "Not really. I knew her to say hello to, but that was about it. She'd come home and go straight into her house. Poor dear." Mrs. Elison shook her head for the fourth time. "She never had any visitors."

"Not even a boyfriend?" Bernie asked.

"Not that I saw," Mrs. Elison answered. "She must have been terribly lonely to do what she did. My daughter and I tried to make friends with her, but she never accepted our invitations. She never came to the block party or any of the potlucks we do once a month or invited anyone into her house. At least not from the neighborhood." Mrs. Elison was quiet for a moment. Then she said, "I should have tried harder."

Libby assured her that what had happened to Ellen Fisher wasn't her fault.

"Thank you for saying that, dear," Mrs. Elison said. "I

know that's true, but somehow it doesn't help much." She was turning to close the door when Libby asked her how long she and Ellen Fisher had been neighbors.

"Ten years," Mrs. Elison promptly said, turning back to face Libby. "I remember because she and I both moved in at the same time, but even back then she kept to herself. My daughter went over to welcome her, and Ellen practically shut the door in my daughter's face." Mrs. Elison sighed. "It seems like just a moment ago. Why is it that the older you get, the faster times goes?"

"I think there's a scientific explanation for that," Bernie said.

"Probably," Mrs. Elison replied. "There seems to be a scientific explanation for everything these days, but the explanations never answer the question, do they? Not really."

"What's the question?" Libby asked.

"The meaning of life, of course."

"Of course," Libby echoed as Mrs. Elison shut the door.

"You know, she's got a point," Bernie commented while she and her sister walked away.

They spent the next half an hour going up and down the block, knocking on doors, and talking to the people who were home. The general impression was that Ellen Fisher was a person who kept to herself. No one had anything bad to say about her, but no one had anything good to say about her, either.

Chapter 9

L ibby put up the collar of her windbreaker and studied the rear of Ellen Fisher's house. The place looked even more abandoned in the light of the day. For some reason, the phrase *detritus of despair* popped into her head as she began scouring the ground around the back door for something they might have missed last night.

"You see anything?" Bernie asked Libby.

"No. Yes. Possibly."

"Which is it?" Bernie demanded.

Libby bent over and picked up a crumpled empty pack of Camels that was hidden under a pile of leaves. "What do you think, Bernie?"

"I think it goes with the cigarette butts laying on the ground."

"It could be from our killer," Libby said.

"Or a first responder."

"What do you think? Bag or leave?"

"Leave," Bernie said as she took note of the trampled grass, the ruts made by the stretcher when the EMTs had wheeled Ellen Fisher's body out of her house three weeks ago, and the footprints overlaying them. Nothing looked like it had been made recently.

Libby sneezed. She put out her hand. Another drop. It was starting to sprinkle. She was just about to say something about it when Bernie started talking.

"So, it seems as if our latest visitor to Ellen Fisher's house went in through the front door, because I don't see any fresh footprints here from yesterday."

"It definitely looks that way," Libby agreed.

"Which means she . . ."

"Or he . . ."

"More probably she . . . We're talking quilting here."

"Men can quilt . . . ," Libby told her sister.

"They can, but most don't," Bernie replied.

"Meaning we're ruling out the guys?"

"I didn't say that," Bernie replied. "I just said it was unlikely."

"And the neighbors?" Libby asked.

"It sounds as if no one on her block had much to do with her."

Libby rubbed her chin as she watched her sister try the door handle. No go. The door was locked. No big surprise there. In fact, she would have been surprised if it hadn't been. "So?" Libby said as Bernie took her lockpicks out of her pocket.

"Sew buttons," Bernie answered, setting to work on the lock.

Libby smiled. She, her sister, and her mom had been saying that to each other ever since she could remember. "I wonder if Nana said that to Mom, Bernie."

Bernie grunted. "Probably."

"What does it even mean?"

Bernie stopped what she was doing and thought. "You know, I don't know." Then she went back to focusing her attention on the lock, while Libby kept an eye out for anyone coming by.

"What's taking so long?" Libby asked after a minute.

Bernie exhaled, told herself to be nice, and turned toward her sister. "Do you want to do this, Libby?"

"No."

"Then be quiet and let me concentrate."

"A little grumpy today, aren't we?"

"Yes, I am, Libby."

"Do you want to talk about it?"

"No. I want to work on the lock," Bernie replied.

"Fine. I just hope the cops don't come back when we're here."

Bernie gritted her teeth. "Libby, can you please be quiet!" she snapped.

Libby lifted her hands up in a gesture of surrender. "Sorry!"

Bernie didn't answer. She kept working. "Got it," she said, straightening up after another couple of minutes had gone by.

"Feel better?" Libby asked.

"Yes, as a matter of fact, I do." As Bernie said it, she realized it was true.

"I thought you were losing your touch there for a minute," Libby commented.

"So did I," Bernie admitted.

Then she opened the door, bowed, and stepped inside Ellen Fisher's house. Libby followed. For a moment neither sister said anything. Libby was the first to speak.

"Wow," she said, surveying Ellen Fisher's studio.

"What a mess," Bernie commented.

"That's one word for it," Libby opined. "Well, now we know that the person we spotted was definitely looking for something."

Bernie clicked her tongue against her teeth. "I wonder if they found it."

"I wonder what it was," Libby mused.

"Heaven only knows," Bernie replied.

"And it's not telling us," Libby said.

What had been a happily disorganized place of activity was now a shambles. The piles of fabric that had been neatly stacked on a long table had been thrown on the floor. Boxes of needles, thread, and edging materials had been emptied out, as had boxes of patterns. Bernie picked up a few of the books that had been thrown on the top of the fabric and quickly leafed through them as she read the titles out loud. "*History of Quilting. Quilting for Idiots. Who Needs to Quilt? Quilting Patterns.*" Bernie looked up. "Nothing in here."

She put the books down, stepped over an empty glass, and moved on to Ellen Fisher's portable sewing machine. Someone had taken it apart and left the pieces scattered on the floor. Bernie nudged one of the bobbins with her foot. Then she picked it up, tossed it in the air a couple of times, and caught it while she watched her sister open the drawers to the table the sewing machine had been on. They were filled with what she would have expected to see: needles, a pincushion full of pins, several different types of scissors, a couple of tape measures, and spools of thread.

"What could they possibly want that would be in the sewing machine?" Libby wondered out loud as she closed the drawers. Then she and Bernie moved on to the other side of the room, taking care to walk around the spot where Ellen Fisher had died.

"I don't know, but whatever they were looking for must not have been very big," Bernie reflected as she examined the quilt that was splayed out on Ellen Fisher's worktable. It was on the large size—Bernie estimated six by eight feet—and had been slashed with a knife in multiple places.

"I wonder if this is the quilt that was supposed to have been hanging in the library," Libby said. "The one Cecilia called Ellen's pièce de résistance."

"Let's see," Bernie said, and she texted Cecilia a picture of it. A minute later she got her answer back.

"That was fast," Libby noted. "What did she say?"

"It's not," and Bernie showed her sister Cecilia's text.

Libby said, "I wonder where it is."

"Good question," Bernie replied. Then she picked up the quilt she had texted Cecilia about and ran her hands over it, checking to see if there was something in there that the person searching had missed. "I wonder if whatever the person was looking for is what got Ellen killed," Bernie mused.

"*If* she was killed," Libby said.

"It's sure beginning to look that way," Bernie replied.

"I suppose it is," Libby reluctantly agreed. She chewed on the inside of her cheek while she thought. "So, what the hell were they looking for?"

"Something larger than a toaster but smaller than a bread box?"

"Ha ha."

"I don't know, Libby. A thumb drive? A piece of paper? Diamonds? Money? The secret to world peace?" Bernie guessed. "You could hide a fair number of one-hundred-dollar bills in the quilt."

"Yes, you could," Libby agreed. "But would you do that and then hang the quilt in a public place?"

"You know the expression 'hidden in plain sight'?" Bernie asked Libby.

Libby frowned. She thought for a minute. Then she said, "On a different note, if that were the case, if I thought there was money in here"—Libby gestured toward the quilt—"I wouldn't be slashing this thing. I'd be taking it apart very, very carefully."

Bernie nodded. "This is true. It's not as if you can glue the money back together again. Well, actually, you can if you've got most of the bill there . . . but still, why take the chance? So why this, if that's the case?" Bernie asked, lifting the quilt for emphasis.

"Why indeed?" Libby clicked her tongue against her teeth. "Anger? Frustration at not being able to find what they were looking for? I wonder what the rest of the house looks like."

"Let's find out, shall we?" Bernie said, putting the quilt back down.

"That's what we're here for," Libby replied.

The sisters went through the rest of Ellen Fisher's house quickly. The dining room and living room had been ransacked, as well. Colored sheets of construction paper, crayons, Magic Markers littered the dining-room floor, as did some of the dishes from the china cabinet.

"Rosenthal china," Libby noted as she stopped to pick up the plates lying on top of an expensive Oriental rug. It would be a shame if they broke.

"She had good taste," Bernie commented, taking a detour around Libby and walking into the living room. It hadn't fared much better than the dining room had. The sofa and club chair pillows had been slashed, and the sofa had been turned upside down. Someone had ripped off the muslin covering the bottom side, exposing the sofa's wood and springs.

"Talk about a blast from the past," Libby said as she bent over to look through the DVDs stacked on the shelves of the TV console. They were all the kind of documentaries you'd see on PBS. No zombie movies here. When she was done, she straightened up, and she and her sister walked into the kitchen.

"The kitchen isn't as bad as I thought it would be," Bernie commented, heading for the kitchen table to check out the two travel guides for Mexico sitting on it. She picked up the first one and thumbed through it. It was heavily annotated. So was the second.

"It looks as if Ellen was going on a trip," Libby remarked as Bernie put the guides down.

"That's what Steve said. Too bad she didn't get to go," Bernie remarked as she surveyed the open bags of flour and the cereal that had spilled out of boxes on the counters.

"Yes, it is," Libby remarked. "So why would you be planning a trip if you were thinking of committing suicide?" she asked.

"You wouldn't. Cecilia was right," Bernie said, checking the cabinets, while Libby went through the refrigerator.

They spent another ten minutes checking under the kitchen chairs and table and removing the range hood filter, and when they didn't find anything, they moved on to the office. The file cabinet was open, and various folders had been thrown on the desk. Libby quickly went through them. They contained the usual household stuff: tax records, utilities, medical bills, gardening expenses, appliance warranties, and instructions.

"Nothing out of the ordinary here so far," Libby told Bernie as her sister studied the desk.

"There's something missing," Bernie noted as Libby picked up another folder.

Libby cocked her head. "Like what?"

"Like a computer," Bernie said. "There's a docking station for a laptop, but the laptop isn't here."

"Maybe it's upstairs in her bedroom," Libby suggested. "That's where mine is."

"Or maybe whoever was going through her stuff took it."

"That is also a possibility. I guess we'll find out when we get up there," Libby said to Bernie as she put the folder she'd been looking at back on Ellen Fisher's desk. She sighed. If there was anything here that would shed light on Ellen Fisher's death, she wasn't seeing it. "You know what else we're not finding?" she said to Bernie as she headed out of the office.

"What?" Bernie asked.

"We're not finding a carton of cigarettes. Or a pack. Or ashtrays."

"Further confirmation that whoever was smoking outside the door wasn't Ellen. It was either a friend or . . ."

"A workman or one of the first responders," Libby said.

"Or her killer," Bernie said. "Too bad we can't send those cigarette butts to the lab and find out."

"We could if we were in a TV crime series," Libby said.

"Yeah, and then we'd get our results back in twenty-four hours."

"Instead of six months," Libby said as she started up the stairs to the second floor.

"If we were lucky," Bernie noted, remembering a story she'd recently heard from Clyde.

Chapter 10

The stairs up to the second floor were carpeted with a thick blue runner, which absorbed the sound of Libby's and Bernie's feet.

"You wouldn't hear anyone coming," Libby noted as she ran her hand along the oak banister. It was polished and smooth under her fingers. "And speaking of missing," she said to Bernie as they climbed the stairs to the second floor, "there is something else I didn't see downstairs."

"And what is that?" Bernie asked.

"Any photographs. I didn't see any pictures of friends and family."

"Because she doesn't have any. That's what Marvin said."

"I know what he said, but everyone has someone," Libby protested.

Bernie shrugged. "Maybe she has pictures of them on her phone."

"Which we also can't find," Libby pointed out.

"Well, there is that." Bernie brushed a strand of hair out of her eyes. "The police probably have Ellen's cell," she hypothesized. "We should ask Dad to find out."

"Definitely," Libby agreed, and she did.

Sean called back a few minutes later. According to her dad's best friend, the police didn't have Ellen's phone or her computer.

"But they probably didn't look for them, either," Bernie guessed as she studied the upstairs hallway. The walls were painted a pale yellow and hung with posters of quilt exhibitions, while the floor was covered with the same blue runner the stairs were. They stopped in front of the bathroom.

"How very mid-century modern," Bernie proclaimed, taking in the mint-green bathroom fixtures, walls, and floor. She pointed to the lid of Ellen Fisher's wicker clothes hamper and the door to the linen closet. Both were open, and their contents were strewn over the floor. "I'm going to assume that Ellen didn't do this," Bernie said.

"I would say that's a good probability," Libby observed, stepping inside the bathroom. She squatted down and looked through the towels and the dirty clothes. One of the towels had a small bloodstain on it. She showed it to Bernie. "What do you think?"

"I think she probably nicked herself shaving her legs," Bernie replied as she opened the medicine cabinet door. "I guess Ellen didn't use makeup," Bernie observed as she looked through the shelves.

"Or too much in the way of hair products, either," Libby added, looking in the shower stall.

"But she did use sleeping pills, though," Bernie said, holding up a bottle of Ambien.

"I could have used one of those last night," Libby said.

"Ditto," Bernie told her sister. For a moment, Bernie thought about taking a couple with her for emergencies, but then she decided it was a bad idea. "You know," she continued, "whoever killed Ellen went to a great deal of trouble to make it look like a suicide. Why?"

"That is the question, isn't it?" Libby acknowledged. "There had to be something gained. But what?"

Bernie nodded. "And how did they manage? She wasn't tied up. Apparently, she didn't resist."

"Maybe she was doped up. Maybe someone put something in her tea," Libby suggested, thinking back to the rinsed-out teapot and the mugs they'd seen in the kitchen sink.

"Or in a glass of juice," Bernie said, thinking of the empty glass on the floor of the sewing room. "But like what?" she challenged.

"Something that cleared her system quickly."

"Far-fetched, but possible, I suppose," Bernie conceded. "Which takes us back to the fact that whoever did this knew her."

"Maybe not so far-fetched," Libby pointed out. "It would certainly explain what happened. It would be relatively easy to hang someone if they were all doped up. Otherwise, I imagine it would take more than one person. Ellen Fisher wasn't that light."

"I guess that's one advantage to being a little overweight. More to love and harder to hang," Bernie said. "Not funny?" she asked, catching the expression on her sister's face.

"Not even a little bit." Libby checked her watch. "We need to get a move on."

Bernie nodded and put the bottle of Ambien back where she'd found it. Libby was right, Bernie thought as she returned to the hallway. They needed to get going.

"Just like the living and the dining room," Libby noted as she surveyed the first guest bedroom.

The bed had been stripped, and its sheets and the pillows tossed on the floor, while the mattress was leaning against the bed frame, its guts leaking out onto the rug. In addition, the drawers of the oak dresser had been pulled out, and their contents had joined the mess on the floor. The closet door had been left open, as well, revealing a row of empty hangers and a mint-green comforter that had been pulled out of its zippered plastic bag. The second guest bedroom mirrored the first one. Ellen Fisher's bedroom, on the other hand, hadn't been touched.

Bernie paused on the threshold and surveyed the scene. "Whoever was searching the place must have stopped when she . . ."

"Or he . . ."

Bernie waved her hand in dismissal. "Who cares? Heard us."

"And saw us," Libby said. She pointed to the two bedroom windows. They looked out on the backyard. "I bet he or she was just starting on Ellen's room when we arrived . . ."

"And they were afraid we'd get in the house," Bernie said, taking up the narrative, "so he or she decided to get out of Dodge—metaphorically speaking."

"What is Dodge, anyway?" Libby asked.

Bernie blinked. "Seriously?"

"Yes, seriously."

"It was a town out West. I can't believe you don't know that."

Libby sniffed. "Maybe we should concentrate on the matter at hand." And she pointed to the suitcase on the bed. "Wanna bet that suitcase has everything for Ellen's Mexico trip in it?"

"I do not," Bernie said as she opened it. She took out a bathing suit, T-shirts, shorts, two sundresses, sandals, and a tube of sunscreen. "I always pack for a trip and then kill myself, don't you?"

"Maybe Ellen was one of those 'pack three weeks in advance' kind of people," Libby suggested.

"Maybe," Bernie said, "but I doubt it."

"Me too," Libby agreed.

"Still have doubts?" Bernie asked her sister.

Libby shook her head. "Not anymore. The suitcase sealed the deal as far as I'm concerned." At which point, she and her sister began to search the room.

Libby took the dressers and the closet, while Bernie took the nightstands and the bed.

"Nothing here," Libby announced when she was finished with the dresser. "Just clothes. Lots of cheap T-shirts, sweaters, and blouses. Pajamas. Cotton underwear. Socks. Tights. No leggings. Judging from what's in here, I don't think Ellen cared about what she wore."

"Ah, Libby, a kindred spirit," Bernie couldn't help remarking.

"Why do you always have to be so snotty?" Libby asked.

"I wasn't being snotty, Libby. I was being factual."

"So you say, Bernie."

Bernie didn't answer. All her effort was going into pushing and pulling the mattress off its box spring and onto the floor. She leaned over and picked up a pair of underpants and a bra that had been lying under the mattress. "I wonder how these got here," she mused, putting them back where they'd been. She rubbed the small of her back to ease the ache that was developing. "Nothing of interest here," she said as she moved to the right-hand side of the bed and began investigating the nightstand while Libby moved on to the closet.

It was stuffed full of shirtdresses, slacks, tunics, a ballgown, and a stack of boxes. Libby opened them. The first one contained fabric swatches, the second one contained scraps, and the third one held larger pieces of fabric. Libby opened the fourth box. There was a quilt in it. She was just about to tell Bernie she thought she might have found the quilt Cecilia had asked them to find when Bernie said, "Now, this is a little more interesting."

Libby turned to look. "What's more interesting?"

"This," Bernie said, and she held up the gun she'd found in the nightstand drawer. "And, by the way, it's loaded."

Chapter 11

Sean laid the gun Bernie had handed him back on the coffee table and sat down in his chair. "Interesting," he commented, using the same word Bernie had used when she'd found it. Then he started eating the lunch Bernie and Libby had brought upstairs for him. "Very interesting, indeed." He took a couple of bites of his sandwich, grilled salmon on a brioche roll with bacon, fennel coleslaw, and basil mayonnaise.

"What do think of the sandwich, Dad?" Libby asked, changing the subject, as Sean broke off a small piece of the fish and fed it to his cat, Cindy. Libby was asking because she and Bernie had been arguing about the sandwich's composition since Bernie had first suggested it.

Sean took a third bite, chewed slowly. After a moment's thought, he said, "You know I love bacon, but in this case, I think it overwhelms the salmon. Maybe just using one strip would be a better balance?"

"Or using none at all," Libby said. She turned to Bernie. "See? You're outvoted. That's two to one."

Bernie threw up her hands. "Fine. You win. No more bacon. What about the fennel slaw, Dad? What do you think about that? Is that too much, too?"

"Absolutely not," Sean replied. "That should stay. It's excellent. So is the brioche, by the way." He fed Cindy another piece of salmon, then gestured toward the gun. "I noticed the serial numbers have been filed off the Glock."

Bernie took a sip of her coffee and followed it up with the last bit of her peanut butter and radish sandwich on walnut-raisin bread. "We did, too."

"That's why we called Clyde," Libby said. Sean's best friend was coming by in about twenty minutes or so to take possession of the weapon. "Well, one of the reasons," Libby said in response to Sean's lifted eyebrow.

"We're hoping he can tell us something about its history," Bernie added.

"That would be nice," Sean said, "although I understand forensics is pretty backed up these days, what with everything that's going on." He gave a wry smile. "I'll tell you one thing, though. That gun isn't something I would have expected you to come across in Ellen Fisher's bedroom."

Bernie crumpled her napkin up and tossed it in the trash basket. "Frankly, neither would I," she said. "I wonder where Ellen acquired it."

"That is the question, isn't it?" Libby commented as she finished her leftover bagel and salmon from her morning's breakfast. "Somehow, I don't see her going down to the hood to get it."

Sean nodded. "Well, she didn't buy that thing in a gun shop, Libby. That I can promise you."

"Maybe she got it on the dark web," Bernie suggested.

"A definite possibility," Sean said as he stood up and walked over to the coffee table. He picked up the gun again, weighed it in his hand, and put it back down. "A Glock forty-three. Nine mil. Six-plus-one capacity. Enough to get the job done. Also, one of the most popular guns for women."

"I didn't know that," Libby said.

Sean nodded. "It's true. This model is lighter than some of the others. Makes it more popular with the ladies. Same with the Galaxy."

"And let's not forget the magazines," Bernie pointed out. "There were three of them. What about those?"

Libby clicked her tongue against her teeth. "She was prepared for whatever came her way. At least she thought she was."

"Yes, she did," Bernie said. "But what was coming her way?"

"Or maybe she just liked to shoot," Libby suggested.

"Like target practice at the local gun club?" Bernie asked.

Libby nodded.

"I can call Roland and check." Roland was president of the Longely Gun Club. "Although I will be surprised if she was a member," Bernie said.

"Me too. Usually, those guys are pretty good about locking their guns up in their gun safes. They don't leave a loaded weapon in their nightstand. Too many possibilities for disaster," Sean noted as he sat back down. Cindy jumped up on his lap. "I have to say, I never would have pictured Ellen Fisher with a nine-millimeter. Maybe a twenty-two." He shook his head. "No. Not even that. She didn't like guns."

Bernie and Libby looked at each other.

Bernie leaned forward. "How do you know that?"

Sean drew himself up. "Because I remember her saying something to that effect."

Bernie opened her eyes a little wider. "You never told us you know . . . knew Ellen Fisher."

Sean turned his attention back to his sandwich. "I don't . . . didn't, really," he mumbled through a bite.

"What does that mean?" Bernie asked.

Sean readjusted the collar of his polo shirt. "The brioche is perfect. How'd you get that crust?"

"We used a pan of steaming water on the bottom of the oven," Bernie replied. "Now talk."

"I am."

"Cute. About Ellen Fisher."

"There isn't much to tell, Bernie," Sean replied.

"Well, tell us what there is to tell," Libby told him.

Sean fastened his gaze on the window and watched a titmouse and three sparrows fighting over a crumb on the sidewalk outside of A Little Taste of Heaven. "I never used to find birds interesting," he remarked.

"You're not answering the question," Bernie noted.

"Now you know how I used to feel when you were a teenager," Sean told her.

Bernie laughed. "Well played."

"You went out with her, didn't you?" Libby guessed.

Sean snorted. "For coffee."

"And?" Bernie asked.

"I met her a few times," Sean told Bernie. "That's all."

"Why didn't you mention it?" Libby asked.

Sean shrugged. "It didn't seem relevant."

Now it was Bernie's turn to snort. "When you were working a case, didn't you always tell us that there was no such thing as a detail too small to consider?"

Sean smiled. "When it was germane to the case. This isn't."

"Tell us, anyway," Bernie instructed.

Sean raised his hands. "If you want to waste your time, that's fine with me."

"We do," Libby said.

Sean frowned. He took a deep breath and let it out. Both girls leaned forward in anticipation as Sean began.

"You know, after your mom died . . ." He looked at his daughters. Both girls nodded. "I wasn't in the best shape."

The girls nodded again.

"Neither were we," Libby said, remembering a time she preferred to forget.

Sean rubbed his hands together. "I was looking for something to do. Something with these." He lifted his hands up and wiggled his fingers. "To get my mind off things, you know?"

Bernie and Libby nodded for the third time.

"I wanted to start woodworking again, but there's no room here for a shop." Sean paused. Libby and Bernie waited. "Anyway, evidently, Clyde was discussing my problem with his wife, and she had a suggestion." Sean cleared his throat. "She introduced me to this bunch of women who . . ."

"Pole danced?" Bernie asked.

Sean chuckled. "That would have been a lot more fun. No. Who quilted."

"And Ellen Fisher was one of those women?" Libby asked, surmising that she was.

Sean finished off his coffee. "As a matter of fact, she was."

Bernie and Libby couldn't help it. They burst out laughing.

Sean sniffed. "See, this is why I didn't tell you," he said.

"Tell them what?" Clyde asked as he walked into the room.

Chapter 12

Bernie and Libby jumped. They'd been so focused on their dad's story that they hadn't heard Clyde come up the stairs.

"You're awful quiet for a big guy," Sean commented while he rubbed the spot on his thigh Cindy had dug her claws into.

Clyde grinned. "It's a talent acquired through years of midnight refrigerator raids." He turned to the girls. "Now, what was your dad telling you about?"

"Nothing," Sean said at the same time Libby said, "Quilting."

Clyde chuckled. "Yeah, that was quite the quilt your dad made."

"You made a quilt, Dad?" Bernie cried. "Wow. Can we see it?"

"No, you may not," Sean replied. "I threw it out."

"Why?" Libby asked him.

Sean crossed his arms over his chest. "Because."

"I don't understand why you don't want to talk about it," Bernie said.

Clyde answered for Sean. "He's embarrassed."

"Why?" Libby repeated.

Clyde grinned. "Because real men don't quilt."

Bernie snorted. "How unPC."

Sean glowered at his friend. "That's not the reason."

"Then what is?" Bernie asked her dad.

"It was bad."

"Well, it was your first attempt," Libby told him.

"Okay. It reminded me of your mom," Sean said, his voice gruff with emotion. "Now, can we keep to the topic at hand?"

"Sure," Clyde said. He pointed at the Glock. "Is this what we're talking about?"

All three of the Simmonses nodded.

Clyde rubbed his chin. "Interesting," he remarked as he plopped himself down on the couch next to Bernie.

"That's the word that keeps popping up in connection with this case," Sean told him.

Clyde grunted as he reached over and picked up the Glock. "I wouldn't have expected to find this in Ellen Fisher's house."

"That's what Dad said," Bernie observed. "For that matter, so did I," she added.

"Me too," Libby said.

"When was the last time you saw Ellen Fisher?" Bernie inquired of Clyde.

Clyde shook his head. "A long time. It's been years since my daughter went to elementary school, and it's not as if we exactly move in the same circles."

"And is that true for Mrs. Clyde, as well?" Libby asked, Mrs. Clyde being the woman they called Martha.

"I don't think my wife has, either. She stopped quilting a long time ago. Now she's on to journaling."

"Can you text her?" Bernie asked.

Clyde nodded. The answer that came back was no. She

hadn't. "As for Ellen's phone," Clyde continued, "I checked again. It was never logged in, meaning it wasn't on her person when she was delivered to the morgue."

"And your guys didn't look for it, right?" Libby asked. "At least that was my impression."

"No, they wouldn't have," Clyde replied.

Bernie jumped into the conversation. "They wouldn't have had any reason to, Libby," Bernie said. "The responding officers would have assumed that Ellen Fisher was a suicide, just like we did."

Libby nodded. What her sister had said was true. "I wonder where it went."

Clyde shrugged. "Heaven only knows. It'll probably show up in the most unlikely place. They usually do," Clyde said, thinking of his own, which he'd finally located in the pocket of his windbreaker after a two-day search.

"Of course, the killer could have taken it," Bernie suggested.

"If there is a killer," Clyde said.

"We think there is," Libby said, and she told Clyde about the guidebooks and the suitcase they'd found in Ellen Fisher's house. "That clinches it for me."

"There could be other explanations," Clyde pointed out, although both Bernie and Libby noticed he didn't seem as sure of himself, as his gaze wandered to the food Bernie and Libby had brought upstairs earlier for him to eat. He smiled in anticipation of tasting the cup of corn chowder, the salmon sandwich, and the two chocolate cupcakes. "Looks good," he said, rubbing his hands together in anticipation.

"It is good," Sean told him as Clyde spooned some of the corn chowder into his mouth.

"Tasty," he remarked. "Very tasty." Then he changed the topic. "But I do find Ellen's choice of weapon unusual.

Most women own twenty-twos," he observed after he'd swallowed. "They're easier to handle. Maybe it wasn't even hers."

Sean corrected him. "That was then. According to an article I recently read," Sean said, "a lot of females are carrying nine mils these days. The manufacturers are sizing them down, so they fit in women's hands. At least that's what the *Times* business section said."

"Terrific," Clyde commented after eating more soup. "Just what we need. More people armed. Makes the world a scary place."

"Yes, it does," Sean agreed. "For everyone," he added.

"Tell me about it. We've had two homicides this year so far," Clyde said as Libby flicked a bagel crumb off her denim skirt.

"Ellen was obviously expecting trouble," she noted.

"And she was right," Sean commented.

"Or she liked to shoot," Clyde suggested.

"Nope." And Bernie showed him the text she'd gotten from the president of the Longely Gun Club. "Or if she did, she wasn't doing it here."

"Another possibility," Clyde went on. "Maybe she was paranoid? Have you thought of that? Maybe she just thought someone was coming after her. Maybe that's why she'd armed herself."

"Right. And that's why she committed suicide, instead of lounging on the beach in Mexico?" Libby said, sounding skeptical.

"People have done crazier things," Clyde replied.

"You mean Ellen figured she'd kill herself before they"—Sean marked the word *they* with finger quotes—"did it for her? That she'd be nice and save them the trouble? Is that what you're saying?"

"And if that was the case, she had a gun. Why not shoot

herself?" Bernie added before Clyde could answer. "It certainly would be an easier exit. I mean hanging?" She made a face. "Not a good way to end things, from what I understand."

Clyde looked sheepish. "I was just spitballing ideas," he said, defending himself. "But I guess my last one does sound pretty silly."

"Well, none of them are sticking to the wall," Sean informed him.

Clyde pushed the empty soup cup away. "I take it you're beginning to think Ellen Fisher didn't commit suicide, after all?" he asked Sean.

"I have to admit I am leaning in that direction," Sean replied. "I didn't think so before, but given everything— the gun, the trip, the timing, the fact that she was expecting company—I'm beginning to change my mind."

"What kind of trouble was she expecting, anyway?" Libby wondered aloud as Clyde started in on his sandwich. "A malfunctioning sewing machine? Getting sprayed with water by a six-year-old? I mean, she doesn't seem like the kind of person things happen to." Libby turned to her dad. "What do you think?"

"I have to agree." Sean rubbed the tips of Cindy's ears. Her purring filled the room.

"Well, she must have had something going on," Bernie told her dad. "This wasn't a random crime."

"No, it was not," Sean agreed.

Clyde rubbed his chin. "I must admit, I'm wondering if things are a little more complicated than they appeared at first glance. It's the lack of a serial number on the Glock, not the possession of it, that's swaying me," he declared. "A Glock is a serious weapon, but then, lots of people have them these days. Much as it pains me to say it, it's not a red flag. On the other hand, having a gun without a serial number is a whole different matter. It raises a whole slew of new questions." He reached for his sandwich and took a bite.

"This is excellent," Clyde said. He beamed. "Love the bacon," he told Bernie and Libby after he'd swallowed. "In fact, I love the whole deal. The sandwich is perfect. My compliments to the chef."

"See, Libby?" Bernie said triumphantly. "I told you."

"That's one for and one against," Libby said.

"I can count, Libby," Bernie said as she turned to Clyde. "As you were saying?"

"I was saying I think we may have misjudged Ellen Fisher. I think there might have been a lot going on under that mousy exterior of hers."

Bernie smiled. "Do you think the gun might persuade Lucy to change his mind about Ellen Fisher killing herself?" she asked.

Clyde laughed. "You're kidding me, right?"

"Sorry. I forgot who I was dealing with." Bernie sighed. It was a well-known fact in the department that once Lucy got something in his head, that was where it stayed.

"Let me see if I can persuade Roy to spend a little time matching the Glock up with any recent crimes," Clyde said. "It's a long shot, but you never know."

"It would be nice," Libby said, and it would be, although she wasn't counting on it happening.

Clyde finished the sandwich and started on the first chocolate cupcake. "What's in the icing?" he asked after he'd taken his first bite.

"Cinnamon and a tiny amount of red pepper," Libby answered. "Why? Don't you like it?"

"I love it," Clyde said as he licked a dab of icing off his finger. "So now what?" he asked Libby.

"Cecilia is hosting a gathering at her house after Ellen's funeral tomorrow," Libby replied.

"Are you guys going?" Clyde asked.

"We're supplying food for the gathering, so that would be a yes," Bernie told him.

Libby leaned forward. "It'll give us a chance to talk to everyone at once."

"We're hoping that someone will drive their Caddy Escalade there, as well," Bernie added.

Sean laughed. "Good luck with that. I don't think the person you're after is that stupid."

Clyde chuckled. "Sean, you always were a negative son of a bitch."

Sean corrected him. "I think the phrase you want is 'realistic son of a bitch.'"

Chapter 13

The air smelled like rain when Bernie and Libby arrived at Cecilia Larson's home the next afternoon.

"Nice place," Libby remarked as Bernie parked the van in the driveway.

Located in the middle of Ash Street, which was on the outskirts of Longely, the brick and stucco house had been built in the 1930s as part of a development by ICD Inc. for its middle managers.

"It should be a nice place, given its price point," Bernie commented. "You used to be able to buy one of these houses for between three and four hundred thousand dollars. Now you'd be doing well to get it for a million cash, as is, with no inspection or negotiation."

"Amazing, isn't it?" Libby said as she studied the house. "I wonder what the ceiling is going to be. Lucky for Cecilia, she bought it before the insanity started. I mean it's nice, but . . ."

"We're not talking about Windsor Palace here," Bernie said, finishing Libby's thought for her.

"Exactly," Libby told her sister as Bernie turned Mathilda off. Bernie got out, walked over to the garage, and peeked in the window. The garage was empty.

"No Escalade," she informed Libby, not that either woman had expected to find it here, but it was always good to check.

"Are you surprised?" Libby asked as she exited the van.

"No. I would be surprised if it was here, but you know what Dad always says . . ."

"Trust but verify," Libby replied.

"Exactly," Bernie said as she and her sister started off-loading the supplies they'd brought with them. Bernie grabbed the carton filled with pies, while Libby took the coffee urn, and they both started up the redbrick path to the back door.

"Look, Bernie. Snowdrops," Libby cried, nodding at the small white flowers peeking out of the laurel bed that flanked the house's foundation. Snowdrops were the first flowers to appear after winter, sometimes poking their heads through after a late-season snowstorm, and Libby was glad to see them. "And there are buds on the forsythia bushes."

Bernie grunted as she put down the carton she was carrying and picked up the small ceramic turtle Cecilia had said she had hidden the house key under.

"I bet Ellen and Cecilia got them at the same place," Libby said, referring to the turtle.

"I bet you're right," Bernie said, lifting the key out. Then she opened the door, picked up the carton, stepped inside, and carefully placed the carton down on the counter nearest to the doorway, while Libby did the same with the coffee urn she was carrying.

They both took a minute to study the kitchen. It was small but adequate for their needs. The cabinets were an off-white, as were the fridge, the stove, and the dishwasher, while the counters were a gray-and-white-patterned Formica and matched the oval kitchen table, which was set off to the side. The table was surrounded by a white leather banquette and two black chairs. The only bit of color in the room was the large square red sink and the matching red bread box.

"A bit monochromatic for my tastes," Bernie noted as she checked the time on her cell. They were still on target.

Bernie figured she and Libby had a little over an hour and a half to get ready, which, barring unforeseen incidents, should be more than enough time to accomplish what they had in mind. They'd come on the early side so they could take a quick look around the house before everyone came back from Ellen Fisher's graveside service.

"Let's do this," Bernie said to Libby after she and her sister had finished unloading the van. She didn't really expect to find anything of interest in Cecilia Larson's house vis-à-vis Ellen's death, but over the years she'd learned the hard way that it was a mistake to take things for granted.

Libby nodded. "Let's do this quickly."

Cecilia Larson's house turned out to be your standard three-bedroom, two-bathroom affair. It was a "place for everything, and everything in its place" kinda deal. Libby noted that Cecilia had followed the kitchen color scheme throughout her home. She'd painted the walls white and selected furniture that was either black or gray, which had the effect of highlighting the multiple quilts hanging on the walls, draped over the sofa, and covering the beds and living-room walls upstairs.

The only thing that stood out to Bernie and Libby once they'd gone through the house was Cecilia's sewing room. It, like Ellen Fisher's, was stuffed to the gills with materials and sewing projects in various stages of completion, books on quilting, two sewing machines, and a sketchbook filled with design ideas.

"So how do you want to play this?" Bernie asked Libby

when they were back in the kitchen twenty minutes later. "What are you thinking?"

Libby pointed to the white dishes that Cecilia had left out for them to use. "I'm thinking that we could use some color on the table."

Bernie snorted. "True, but I was talking about the Escalade. About chatting up people. About this case."

"Such as it is," Libby said.

"Which is why we have to get our act together," Bernie reminded her. "We don't have much at the moment."

"We have the gun in Ellen's nightstand," Libby pointed out.

"Unfortunately, lots of people have those," Bernie told her.

"Not guns with the serial number filed off," Libby said.

"True," Bernie replied, "but the gun doesn't point to whether Ellen killed herself or was killed. It's certainly not enough to get Lucy to launch a homicide investigation. What we have now is a lot of conjecture but nothing substantive."

Libby sighed. What her sister had said was true. "Hopefully, we'll hear something here that will help," Libby said as she arranged the white roses and peonies Cecilia had left for them in a tear-shaped glass vase. She stood back and studied the results. "What is it with Cecilia Larson and white?"

"White is the color of death in a lot of Asia," Bernie remarked.

"Meaning?"

"Meaning nothing, Libby. I was just making an observation."

Libby checked her watch. People would be arriving soon. "So, what's the plan, Stan?"

Bernie smiled. "Glad you asked, man. Serve pie, hand out cupcakes, listen to what people are saying."

For the next half an hour, she and Libby made the coffee; set out the drinks, pies, and cupcakes; and arranged the cups, glasses, silverware, dessert plates, and handmade quilted napkins on Cecilia Larson's white linen tablecloth.

"I hope we have enough food," Libby commented as she cut a small sliver out of each pie. Over the years, she'd found that, in general, people were reluctant to be the first to cut into something. Taking a sliver out was a surefire way to get people to serve themselves.

"We definitely do," Bernie replied. "I estimated on the generous side."

When she and Libby had asked Cecilia about the number of guests to expect, Cecilia hadn't been sure how many people would show up for the funeral or come back to her house. She had put the number at somewhere between ten and fifteen but then had said it could be more or less depending on how many teachers from Ellen Fisher's school showed up.

"Or it could just be the quilting ladies," Cecilia had told Bernie and Libby. "Ellen really didn't have many friends. She was on the quiet side, you know, one of those people who are more comfortable at home than at a party." She tilted her head. "Although," she had been quick to point out, "that's not to say people didn't like her. They did."

"Not everyone did," Bernie had pointed out.

"Obviously," Cecilia had replied.

"And speaking of not getting along, what was the thing with Gail Gibson and Ellen Fisher?" Libby had asked, curious to see what Cecilia's answer was going to be.

Cecilia cocked her head and looked puzzled. "What do you mean?"

"I heard they had an argument at RJ's," Libby said.

Cecilia laughed. It was not the reaction Bernie was expecting.

"They did indeed. It was about whether hand stitching was better than using a machine and whether Gail should use a certain brand of thread."

"Really?" Libby said.

"Really," Cecilia repeated. "I know it's hard to believe, but Ellen was quite passionate about the subject. Actually, we all are."

Chapter 14

Libby was remembering her conversation with Cecilia when the front door opened and Cecilia came in. She was followed by a group of people. Ten to be exact. She smiled as she surveyed the room.

"Looks good," Cecilia said to Bernie and Libby after she'd helped everyone store their umbrellas in the umbrella stand by the front door.

Bernie and Libby nodded their thanks while Cecilia introduced Bernie and Libby to the people they didn't already know.

"Your cinnamon rolls are the best," Judy Fine gushed after the introductions had been completed. Today her hair looked even more like a bird's nest than it usually did, Bernie reflected.

"Thank you," Bernie replied. Then she added, "Nice style choice," referring to the sweater set and the box pleated skirt Judy was wearing.

Judy beamed. "Ellen gave the outfit to me. She said it didn't fit her anymore. I wore it today to honor her."

Bernie was about to tell Judy Fine what a nice thought that was, but Selene White spoke first.

"How could that have been Ellen's?" she asked. "You're so much . . ." She stopped.

"Thinner than she was," Judy Fine said. "I know. Ellen told me she'd been holding on to it, hoping she'd lose weight. Evidently, she used to be quite thin. I remember her telling me she liked the way she looked better when she was young."

"I don't know why we women are so hard on ourselves," Selene White observed.

"Well, losing weight is hard," Judy said. "Especially when you get older, what with your metabolism slowing down and all."

"I say screw the patriarchy," Selene commented.

"Oh please," Gail said. "Spare me the rhetoric."

"I don't understand why you find that comment so offensive," Judy Fine said.

"I don't find it offensive. I find it hypocritical coming from her." Gail pointed to Selene's shoes.

"And why is that?" Selene asked.

"Look at your shoes."

Selene looked down. "I'm wearing heels. What's wrong with heels?"

"They're bad for your feet, not to mention being a symbol of male enslavement," Gail commented. "If you read the book I suggested, you would understand."

"I think it's a matter of developing good eating habits when you're young," Cecilia observed, hastily steering the conversation back to the original topic before things got more heated. "Otherwise, it's almost impossible to do it when you're older."

"That's ridiculous, Cecilia," Gail protested. "You're saying people can't change, and they certainly can. According to you, I shouldn't have been able to stop smoking ten years ago, and yet I did."

"That's great for you," Selene told her. "I'm glad you did, but I've observed in my practice that most people find it difficult to change their eating habits, exercise habits, whatever. If it wasn't so hard, all of us would be perfect."

"You mean I'm not?" Gail asked.

Everyone laughed.

Gail patted her stomach. "Of course, I did substitute sugar for cigarettes."

"What kind of cigarettes did you smoke?" Bernie asked, thinking of the crumpled pack of Camels she'd found next to Ellen Fisher's door.

"Cools. Why?"

Bernie shrugged. "No reason. Just making conversation," she replied.

"And speaking of sugar," Selene White said as she turned to Bernie. "I don't suppose you brought some of your amazing cinnamon rolls with you?"

Bernie smiled. "We certainly did."

"What makes them so good, anyway?" Gail wanted to know.

"It's the cinnamon from Vietnam we use in them," Bernie replied.

"Does it matter where the cinnamon comes from?" Cecilia asked.

Libby nodded. "It certainly does. The cinnamon from China, Ceylon, and Vietnam all have different flavor profiles. Like the tomatoes you eat in Italy taste different from the ones raised in New York State. Different growing conditions lead to different outcomes."

"Makes sense," Selene replied as she went into the dining room. The other women followed.

For the next three-quarters of an hour, Bernie and Libby served coffee and tea, listened to Ellen Fisher stories, handed out cupcakes, slices of pie, and cleared away the dirty plates and cups.

"I'm sorry for your loss," Libby said to Gail Gibson as she took her plate from her. "This must be hard. I understand you were besties," Libby continued.

Gail motioned to the women standing next to her. "Along with Selene, Judy, and Cecilia."

"Yes, we were," Cecilia said as she cut herself another small slice of apple pie.

"We are all passionate about quilting," Gail explained. "That's the bond that united Ellen and us."

Cecilia amplified this by saying, "We have met every week for the past four years."

"Four years and three months," corrected Selene. "There were more of us originally, but they dropped out over the years for one reason or another, while we stayed." And she made a circle with her hand, indicating herself, Judy, Gail, and Cecilia.

"Yeah," Judy said. "We're hard core."

Gail sniggered. "Hard-core quilters. Now, there's a picture for you." She sighed. "I still can't believe Ellen is gone."

"Neither can I," Selene said as she readjusted the jacket of her pink pants suit.

She was about to say something else when a heavy-set woman named Joyce came bustling up to the group. "Excuse me," she said.

Everyone stopped talking and turned toward her.

"Sorry to interrupt," Joyce continued. She held up a phone. "But I just found this. Does anyone know who it belongs to? I'm sure they'd like it back."

Cecilia's eyes widened. "Oh, my God," she cried. "I've been looking all over for that."

"That's Ellen's," Gail replied. "I recognize the case."

"Where did you find it?" Cecilia asked.

"In the cabinet under the bathroom sink," Joyce answered. "It was under a bunch of cleaning supplies." She looked sheepish. "I didn't know if someone had lost it or not. I thought I'd better ask instead of leaving it there."

Bernie thanked her. "I'm glad you did."

Joyce continued with her explanation. "I was looking for toilet paper. There was none on the roll."

Cecilia apologized. "Sorry about that," she said. "I've been a little . . . overwhelmed these days."

Judy Fine patted Cecilia on the shoulder. "We all have," she said.

Cecilia thanked her. Then she crossed her arms over her chest and hugged herself. "This is so weird," she said. "It's like a message from the beyond."

"Can you imagine if Ellen called us on it?" Gail said.

Judy shuddered. "I'd faint if that happened."

Libby pointed to the phone. "Are you sure this is Ellen Fisher's?" she asked everyone.

Selene answered, "Absolutely." She pointed to the two tiny flowers and the heart stuck on the outside of the pale lilac case. "Ellen told me a little girl in her class gave those stickers to her, and she put them on her phone. She was going to take them off later that day, but I guess she forgot."

Joyce sniffed. "Ellen was always good with the little ones that way. Always had the kids' best interests at heart. I'm going to miss her."

"We all will," Selene said as Bernie took the phone out of Joyce's hand and tried it. Dead. Not that she expected anything more.

"I guess I'll plug it in and see what we get," Bernie said.

"You're probably not going to get much," Cecilia told her. "Ellen told me she was going to wipe it. Of course, I don't know if she did. Ellen wasn't very good with technology. I was supposed to sell it for her on eBay," Cecilia explained. She grimaced and slapped her forehead with the palm of her hand. "I feel terrible. I don't know how I could have forgotten. All the stress, I guess."

"So, this is her old phone?" Libby asked, just to make sure.

Cecilia nodded. "She'd just gotten a new one a couple of days before . . . before . . . she did you-know-what."

Bernie looked down at the Samsung Galaxy in her hand. "I wonder how this one ended up under the bathroom sink."

Cecilia brightened. "Now, *that* I can answer," she said. "One word. Trini."

"Who is Trini?" Bernie inquired.

"My cleaning lady. She does a great job. The only downside is that I never know where anything is when she's done. Either Ellen or I must have left it out somewhere, and Trini put it away." Cecilia smiled ruefully. "Ellen was always forgetting things."

"She was here?" Bernie asked Cecilia.

Cecilia nodded. "The day after our last meeting." Cecilia's eyes misted. "We made Manhattans and talked about her quilt. By the way, thank you for bringing it over."

Bernie and Libby both nodded.

Cecilia turned to the other women standing there. "I thought we could finish the binding together."

"That would be a good thing," Judy said.

"I thought so," Cecilia agreed.

"I still can't believe she killed herself," Judy said.

"I can," Gail said. "I mean, you never know how other people are feeling, do you?"

"I don't think that's true," Selene said.

"You would say that," Gail replied.

"Meaning what?" Selene asked.

"After all, it's your business, isn't it?" Gail responded.

"You sound as if you think that therapy is a bad thing," Selene replied.

"I guess that depends on the therapy, doesn't it?" Gail retorted.

Selene was about to ask Gail what she meant by that comment, but before she could, Bernie broke into the conversation. "So how many of you think that Ellen didn't kill herself? That someone did it for her?"

"She didn't kill herself?" Joyce asked, looking shocked. "What do you mean?"

Bernie filled her in on what she and her sister were working on.

Joyce shook her head. "Murdered? I really can't believe that. I don't understand. Ellen didn't have an enemy in the world," she declared. She dabbed at her eyes with a crumpled napkin. "She was so nice. Always eager to help. I mean, she loved her kids and her quilting. They were her world. The two things that meant the most to her. She wouldn't harm a hair on anyone's head. She even took the spiders that she found in her house outside. Who would want to kill her?"

"That's what we're trying to find out," Bernie told her. She held up Ellen Fisher's phone. "Maybe after we charge it and figure out the password, there'll be something in here that will steer us in the right direction. Even if she did wipe it. Sometimes, that doesn't work too well."

"I can try if you'd like," Cecilia said, holding out her hand for Ellen Fisher's cell. "I'm pretty good with technology."

"No need," Bernie said. "I think we can manage, but thanks for the offer."

Cecilia shook her head. "I can't believe I forgot about it. Well, actually, I can. If it's not out, if I can't see it—"

"I'm the same way," Libby interrupted.

"Me too," Bernie said. "Once it's filed, it's as if it never existed."

"Maybe we'll get lucky and get something off the phone," Libby said later, as they were loading everything back in the van.

"Hopefully," Bernie agreed. "What do you think about Cecilia's story about Ellen's phone?"

"It's plausible," Libby said.

"But do you believe it?" Bernie insisted.

Libby thought for a moment. Then she said, "Yes, I do. Sounds like the time our workmen's comp papers ended up in the freezer. Only that wasn't the maid's fault." And she gave her sister a meaningful look.

"Give me a break. That was five years ago, and I already said I was sorry about a hundred times," Bernie replied. "It's not my fault the papers were under the frozen corn, and I was in a hurry."

Chapter 15

Later that evening, after Bernie and Libby had closed A Little Taste of Heaven, had had dinner, and had gone over the afternoon events with their father, the sisters drove over to RJ's. The neon beer signs in the window blinked on and off, welcoming them.

"It looks busy," Libby noted while Bernie scouted for an empty spot in the crowded parking lot.

"I'd say," Bernie replied as she gave up and parked in the back, next to Marvin's vehicle. Usually, Saturday nights weren't as busy as Tuesday nights, but not tonight. Tonight the bar was bustling. A wave of noise hit the sisters when they opened the door and walked inside. It took them a minute to spot Marvin.

"There he is," Libby said, pointing. He was sitting off to the right at the bend in the bar, sipping a beer and watching the game on the television.

She and Bernie headed straight for him.

"You're late," he said when Libby tapped him on the shoulder and kissed his forehead.

"Amber had to leave early," Libby explained, "so I ended up mopping the floors and taking out the trash." She looked around. "This is zoo city," she observed.

"Ya think?" Brandon said, popping up in front of them.

"Busy night," Bernie observed, reflecting as she did that Brandon looked tired.

"Tell me about it," he said. "And to make matters better, our bar back didn't show up." He wiped his hands on the kitchen towel slung over his shoulder and looked over the bar. Thank God it wasn't Saint Paddy's Day deep, but it was crowded enough. "Definitely a lot of celebrating going on. Must be spring is in the air." He leaned in toward them. "So, tell me what I can do for you, ladies?" he asked, raising his voice to be heard over the laughter of the dart team ensconced nearby. "You were very mysterious on the phone."

Bernie ordered a Scotch for herself and a white wine for Libby. Then she slid Ellen Fisher's phone across the bar. "I need help," she told Brandon.

Brandon grinned. His eyes crinkled. "I've been saying that for years. I'm glad you finally got the courage to admit it."

Bernie snorted. "Ha. Ha. Ha. I meant with Ellen Fisher's phone." After she'd charged it, Bernie had spent two hours on and off trying to unlock it. She had failed miserably.

"And you tried the obvious passwords like—"

"One, two, three, four, five, six and zero, zero, zero, zero, zero, zero," Bernie said. "They didn't work."

Brandon pushed the phone back to Bernie. "Well, I'm afraid that exhausts my area of expertise."

"May I take a look?" Marvin asked.

"Be my guest," Libby said, passing the phone to Marvin.

Marvin studied the cell for a moment. Then he asked Libby for Ellen Fisher's birthday.

"No idea," Libby answered.

"And you googled her?"

"Bernie did," Libby replied, "and got a big fat nothing."

"Odd," Brandon remarked.

"I guess some people like their privacy," Libby observed.

Marvin was silent for a moment. Then he said, "Does she have a cat or a dog?"

Bernie and Libby shook their heads in unison.

"Not that I know of," Bernie told him.

"Hmm." Marvin took a sip of his IPA and sat back on his stool. "Too bad we cremated Ellen Fisher," he reflected.

Libby looked puzzled. "Why are you saying that?" she asked. "What do you mean?"

"It's simple. If we hadn't cremated her yet, we could have tried facial recognition, seen if that worked, or tried a finger scan."

"But she's dead," Libby exclaimed.

Marvin patted her on the shoulder. "Yes, I know that, and you know that, but the phone doesn't know that."

Bernie shuddered. "That's gross."

"No," Marvin said, "that's practical."

"No, Marvin . . . that's weird, bro," Brandon said as he reached across the counter and grabbed Ellen Fisher's cell.

"What are you doing?" Bernie demanded.

"Wait and see," Brandon replied.

Then, as Marvin, Libby, and Bernie watched, he brought the cell over to a slightly built, balding middle-aged man sitting two seats down. "Here," he told him, setting the phone down on the bar.

The man looked up from the beer he was nursing. "What's this?" he asked him.

"They need some help," Brandon said, nodding in Marvin, Bernie, and Libby's direction. Then he explained the situation. "I thought you might like to give it a try."

The man smiled. "Let's see what I can do." And he picked up Ellen Fisher's phone and his beer and walked down to where everyone was sitting. "Mike Gregor, at your service," he said, putting his beer down and introducing himself.

"Do you think you can unlock it?" Libby asked.

"Does a cat like milk?" Mike said, sitting down next to her.

"Mike does tech support for—" Mike held up his hand, and Brandon stopped talking.

"If he told you, I'd have to kill you," Mike said.

Bernie laughed. "Unpleasantly, I presume."

"Very unpleasantly," Mike told her. "Seriously, this is just a side gig of mine." He wiggled his fingers, cracked his knuckles, and rubbed his hands together. "Let's see what we can see, shall we?"

"It might be wiped," Bernie told him.

"Doesn't matter," Mike said.

As they all watched, Mike studied the phone. Then he pressed two buttons. Nothing happened.

"Damn," he muttered. "That's usually enough."

"What's enough?" Bernie asked.

Instead of answering her, Mike said, "Let's see what happens when I try this instead."

"What's this?" Marvin asked.

Mike laughed. "And give away my trade secrets?" he said. "No. I don't think so."

But whatever *this* was didn't work, either, because a moment later, Mike straightened up and massaged the back of his neck. "This is going to be a little more complicated than I had anticipated," he informed everyone.

"Do you think you'll be able to do it?" Libby asked.

"Of course I'll be able to do it," Mike replied. He rubbed the back of his neck again, then stretched his arms over his head and brought them back down. "I gotta say, though, this phone has some serious voodoo on it. I'm impressed. This lady knew what she was doing." Mike took a sip of his beer. "I can unlock it for you, but it's going to take me a little while." He continued studying the phone, turning it over in his hands as he did. "So how did this chick make bank?" he asked without looking up.

Libby answered, "She was a kindergarten teacher, but evidently, her real love was quilting."

Mike raised an eyebrow. "Quilting?"

"Yes, quilting," Bernie responded.

"Not what I would have expected," Mike commented. "I'll tell you one thing, though. She knows her technology really, really well."

"That's not what her friend said," Libby replied. In addition, there'd been nothing she'd noticed in Ellen Fisher's house that had screamed techie. In fact, it had been just the opposite.

Mike put the phone down and began drumming his fingers on the bar. His foot started jiggling. "I mean, I wouldn't have expected this level of protection on this phone. Most people don't bother."

"Like you, Libby," Bernie couldn't resist saying.

"I don't care," Libby told her. "I don't have anything on it, anyway."

Mike extended his hand. "As I was just saying . . ."

Libby frowned. "I don't see why it's such a big deal, anyway."

"Because someone can use your phone to hack into your or other people's accounts," Mike explained as he picked up Ellen Fisher's phone again. "I have another idea," he said.

"And if that doesn't work?" Libby asked. "If you can't unlock it?"

"Oh, I will," Mike assured her. "I'll figure it out. Don't you worry." And he pocketed the phone. "I need to make a call," he explained as he stood up and walked away.

"Are we taking bets?" Brandon asked.

"Yeah," Marvin said. "Sure. Why not?" He put a dollar on the bar. "I say he won't be able to unlock it."

"I stand with Marvin," Libby said, tossing four quarters on top of the bill on the bar.

Brandon added his dollar. "And I say Mike will."

"Ditto," Bernie said, forking over a dollar.

"It's even odds, folks," Brandon noted.

"I wonder how long Mike is going to take," Marvin said.

"We can bet on that, too, if you'd like," Brandon suggested.

Marvin laughed. "I don't think I can stand that much suspense in one day."

Chapter 16

Mike rejoined the group fifteen minutes later. Bernie was finishing her Scotch when she saw Mike threading his way through the scrum of people around the pool table. He had a broad smile on his face and a lilt to his walk. "No cell can resist the efforts of Mike Gregor for long," he crowed as he slid the phone across the bar.

Bernie caught it and thanked him as Brandon handed her his money.

"Stick with me, baby, and I'll make you rich."

Bernie laughed and turned to Mike. "Can I pay you?" she asked him.

Mike shook his head. "Not necessary. I like the challenge, but I won't say no to a drink."

"Fair enough." Bernie smiled. "Whatever he wants," she told Brandon.

Mike pointed to the bottle of fifteen-year-old Macallan sitting on the top shelf. "I'll take a shot of that, if you please. I think I've earned it."

"I think you have, too," Bernie agreed.

Mike smiled. "Always glad to help out if I can." He

watched while Brandon poured him a drink. "Any great revelations?" he asked Bernie after he savored his first sip.

"I think she did wipe it," Bernie said after having given Ellen's phone a cursory inspection. "For openers, she doesn't have any photos. No selfies. No shots with friends. No 'This is what I ate' shots. No 'This is where I spent the weekend, and it was fantastic' shots. And no quilt shots, as in 'This is the quilt I'm working on' or 'I saw this quilt, and I love it' or 'I saw this quilt, and I hate it.' "

"You're right," Marvin said after he looked. "There aren't any," he noted as he handed the phone back to Bernie.

Bernie continued her examination. "I wonder if she had any social media accounts."

"The world would be a better place without social media," Marvin observed. He rubbed his chin. "I wouldn't be on any of them if I didn't have to use them for business."

Bernie continued, "She doesn't have a lot of apps, either. Just the ones that came with the phone."

"How about games?" Marvin asked. "Does she have any of those?"

Bernie showed him Ellen's screen. "Not a one. No *Candy Crush*. No *Wordle*. Also, no Amazon Prime. No Uber or Lyft. No Apple Pay. No Instagram or Facebook. We are talking bare bones here."

"Fascinating. Given the way she's using it, it might as well be a burner phone," Mike opined after he'd taken another sip of Scotch. "You'd think that given the level of protection she put on this device, she'd have some serious stuff on it."

"Too bad we can't find her other phone," Libby said.

"Isn't it, though?" Bernie said.

"I wonder where it went," Marvin mused.

Brandon shrugged. "It probably got stolen by someone when they were taking Ellen's body out."

Libby sighed. "I keep on thinking we're getting somewhere, but we always end up back where we started."

"The story of my life," Brandon noted as he poured a Guinness from the tap into a glass.

"What happened to the quilt?" Marvin asked, changing the subject.

"Cecilia has it," Libby replied.

Marvin frowned. "I thought you said whoever was going through Ellen's house ripped it up."

"That was a different quilt," Libby replied. "The one slated for the exhibition was in a box in Ellen's bedroom—the only room in the house besides the attic whoever was searching the house hadn't gotten to. Talk about a lucky break."

"That's weird," Marvin observed. "I wonder why it was there, instead of in her sewing room."

"Maybe she was going to use that box to send it, and she brought the quilt upstairs to see if it fit," Libby suggested.

"It makes more sense to take the box downstairs than to bring the quilt upstairs," Marvin pointed out.

"She could have been hiding it," Brandon suggested as he surveyed the head on the Guinness he'd finished pouring.

"Why would she do that?" Bernie challenged.

Brandon shrugged. "Damned if I know." Then he went and served the beer to a man sitting four seats down from Bernie and came back.

"Maybe she was killed because of the quilt," Marvin said after a minute. "Maybe someone wanted to stop Ellen from showing it."

"Why?" Libby asked him.

Marvin shook his head and pointed to Brandon. "I'm going with what he just said. I have no idea."

Bernie laughed. Then she held up the phone. "Then we come to this."

"You don't believe Cecilia's explanation?" Brandon asked.

Bernie replayed her conversation with Cecilia in her mind. "No, I do."

"Who is this Joyce character, anyway?" Marvin asked.

"She worked with Ellen," Libby replied. "She's an elementary school teacher."

"Maybe she pretended to find the phone. Maybe she had it all along and was lying about finding it in the bathroom," Marvin suggested.

"Why would she do that?" Libby asked.

"To frame Cecilia," Marvin suggested.

"And the reason for that would be?" Bernie inquired.

"To divert suspicion from herself obviously," Marvin responded.

"So, you're saying Joyce is our killer?" Bernie asked.

Marvin nodded.

Bernie thought about that for a minute. She couldn't imagine anyone less likely.

"Not a possibility?" Brandon wanted to know, correctly reading the expression on Bernie's face.

"I don't think so," Bernie replied. "First of all, she wasn't part of the quilting group. I don't think she was friends with Cecilia, either. I got the impression she'd never been in her house before."

"That would make things more difficult," Marvin allowed.

"She would make the perfect assassin, though," Libby observed.

"This is true," agreed Bernie.

"How so?" Brandon asked.

"Think about it," Bernie said. "Joyce is just . . . average. Average height. Average weight. Mousy brown hair. Brown eyes. No identifying marks. Blah clothes. No one would notice her until it was too late. Then blammo." And she mimed getting shot.

"I take it you guys are no further along in solving this thing?" Marvin asked.

Bernie took a sip of her Scotch. "No, we are not." Then she put her glass down and ran her finger around its rim.

"Why not just shoot or stab her?" Marvin asked.

"Because then her death wouldn't look like a suicide," Libby answered.

"Which sounds to me like the object of the exercise," Brandon said as he wiped his hands on the towel he had slung over his shoulder.

"Agreed. But why?" Bernie asked. "What's the motive? What was Ellen's killer trying to accomplish?"

"Getting away with murder," Brandon told her. "I'll be back in a sec." And he nodded at the woman with the short blond hair down the way, who was holding up her wineglass.

"Why indeed?" Marvin repeated. He tapped his finger against his beer stein, then took a couple of pretzels out of the bowl next to him and ate them. "Obviously, whoever did this had a reason." He drummed his fingers on the bar. "I mean, people don't do things without a reason, even if it's a crazy one."

"Ellen Fisher had to have had something that someone wanted," Bernie said, remembering the person they'd seen exiting Ellen Fisher's house and the condition they'd found the house in. "And, obviously, they didn't have time to find it after they killed her. Otherwise, they wouldn't have come back."

"We could be talking about two different people,"

Libby suggested. "One person killed her, and another ran-sacked her house." She looked over at Bernie. "Although, admittedly, that's a stretch," she said in response to her sis-ter's raised eyebrow. "But it is possible."

For a moment everyone was quiet while they listened to the cheering that had erupted at the other end of the bar. Judging from the yelling, someone had won five hundred dollars on their New York State lottery ticket.

"But you know what I find really strange," Marvin con-tinued once the noise had died down. "Well, maybe *strange* is too strong a word. Maybe a little odd. Some-thing that stands out to me."

"What's that?" Libby asked.

"Actually, two things." Marvin reached over, drew the bowl of pretzels to him, and began to finish them off. "One is that Ellen has no family—at least none that we could find. I know that's not that unusual, but most peo-ple have someone. An aunt. An uncle. A second cousin twice removed. Someone. Anyone."

"And two?" Libby prompted.

"And two," Marvin continued, "is that once I started talking to her friends about her, no one seemed to know things, basic things, like where she was born or what high school she went to. Things like that. Not that that matters if everything else is normal . . ."

"But it's not," Brandon said.

"No, it certainly isn't," Bernie agreed. She sighed. "Let's talk about something else for a while. This is just depressing."

"Works for me," Libby said.

Libby, Bernie, and Marvin left an hour later. The front parking lot had emptied out, and the wind had picked up, rustling the tree branches and carrying the mournful sound of a tugboat's cry.

Marvin pointed at the clouds scudding across the sky. "Looks like a cold front is coming in," he said as he and the sisters walked to the back lot. It was dark there because the lights were out, so they were halfway to Mathilda when they saw it.

"Crap," Bernie said.

Libby groaned. Then she said, "Great. Just what we need."

Chapter 17

Sean and Cindy were watching the evening news when Bernie and Libby walked through the door.

"How are Brandon and Marvin?" Sean asked as Cindy got up, readjusted her position, and sat back down.

"They're fine," Libby said. Then she and Bernie both started talking at once, filling him in on what had happened to Mathilda, their voices rising and falling, braided together in a cacophony of sound.

Sean raised a hand. "Hey, slow down," he ordered. "One at a time. I can't understand a thing either of you guys is saying."

"Someone went through Mathilda," Bernie said.

"When we were at RJ's," Libby added.

Then the sisters both started talking over one another again.

"So, nothing is missing out of the van," Sean clarified when Bernie and Libby had stopped speaking.

His daughters shook their heads.

"You checked?" their dad asked.

"Twice," Libby said.

"But it is obvious someone went through it," Bernie

added, thinking of the dumped-out cartons of paper plates, towels, condiments, and cleaning supplies, which they should have, but hadn't, unloaded yet.

"And they were looking for?" Sean asked as he muted the television and gave his full attention to his daughters.

"We don't know," Libby answered.

"We think it has something to do with Ellen Fisher," Bernie added.

Sean looked at Libby for confirmation. She nodded, and Bernie explained. "We think whoever went through the van did so because they were under the impression that we took something from Ellen Fisher's house."

"Yeah," Libby added.

Sean raised an eyebrow. "That seems like a stretch to me. How do you get that?"

"Easy," Bernie said. "Of course, we could be wrong, but this seems like too much of a coincidence, and you always say . . ."

Sean laughed. "I know what I always say. Go on."

Bernie did, ticking the reasons off on her fingers as she went. "Number one. We were parked in back of RJ's, so we weren't visible from the road, which means whoever went through the van knew where we were."

Sean shifted his position. "Or being in the back could have been the reason they picked the van in the first place," Sean said. "No witnesses. Just sayin' . . ."

"True," Libby replied. "It could have been, but then we get to reason number two. None of the other vehicles in the lot were broken into. Usually, they would be in situations like this."

Sean nodded. What Libby had said was true. "Okay. Agreed. That appears to diminish the odds of the van break-in being a random robbery. Doesn't nullify them, but it does reduce them."

Bernie continued. "And our third, and most important

reason, is this." She held up an AirTag. "Ta-da! We found this stuffed in the crack in the seat in the van."

"What's this?" Sean said, reaching for the small round object.

"It's a tracking device, something that allows you to find your things," Libby answered.

"Or follow someone," Bernie added.

"I know what a tracking device is, thank you very much," Sean said, annoyed.

Bernie grinned. "So you say."

Sean grinned back. "Yes, I do." Sean turned the small tag over in his hand. "It's amazing what's around these days, and I don't mean that in a good way."

Bernie went on laying out the scenario. "We're betting that whoever put this in the van did it when we were in front of Ellen Fisher's house."

"Although they could have done it anytime after we left Ellen Fisher's house, as well," Libby reflected. She glared at her sister. "Especially with the car alarm disabled."

"I thought we had this discussion, Libby," Bernie said. "I thought we all agreed having it on wasn't worth upsetting the neighbors. Or losing sleep."

Libby sighed. It was true. The last time the alarm had gone off, it was three in the morning, and a racoon had jumped on the hood of the van.

Sean handed the AirTag back to Bernie. "If what you say is true—and I have no doubt that it is true—I'm not liking the way that sounds."

"Me either," Libby said as she and her sister sat down on the sofa.

"What did the police say?" Sean asked.

Bernie shook her head. "I don't know. We didn't call them. We figured we'd take a look at the security camera footage first and see if it picked up anything."

"And did it?" Sean prompted.

"No. The camera wasn't working," Libby said as Cindy the cat jumped off her dad's lap and onto hers. She began rubbing the tips of Cindy's ears. "Neither were the cameras in the front, for that matter," she added.

"Nothing like the appearance of security instead of its reality, I always say," Sean observed. He chewed on the inside of his cheek. "And you have no idea what this person was looking for in the van?"

"None," Bernie answered. "The only thing this proves to me is that they—whoever they are—didn't find what they were looking for at Ellen Fisher's house. Whatever that is." She stifled a yawn. The day had hit her suddenly, and she realized how tired she was. "And"—Bernie yawned again—"I might add, we still are no closer to finding out anything about Ellen Fisher than we were when we started. We don't have a motive or a suspect in her death."

Sean leaned back in his chair and steepled his fingers together. "What do you have?"

"Like I just said," Bernie answered, "we have absolutely nothing."

"That's not quite true," Sean told her. "Sometimes what's not there is more valuable than what is there."

"I'm not sure I understand," Libby said as she and Bernie leaned forward in anticipation of what her dad was going to say.

"It's simple," Sean replied. "For openers, you have a reasonable possibility that Ellen Fisher isn't who she said she was," Sean told her as Cindy meowed, jumped back on his lap, circled four times, kneaded his leg with her claws, and settled down.

Bernie wrinkled her brow. "How do you get that?"

"I'm getting that from everything you've been telling me." Sean rubbed his leg where Cindy had scratched him. "It sounds to me as if Ellen didn't want to be recognized."

"You're saying she was in witness protection?" Libby asked.

"That's one possibility," Sean said.

"And another?" Bernie inquired.

"She could have changed her identity on her own. Maybe she had warrants out on her, maybe someone was after her for something she'd done, or maybe she was escaping an abusive relationship."

"That's a whole lot of maybes," Libby noted.

"Yes, it is," Sean agreed equably.

Bernie put her hands on the small of her back and stretched. "But if that's the case, why would she do something that would attract attention to herself?" Then Bernie proceeded to remind her dad about the accolades Ellen's quilt was about to receive.

"That's simple," Sean said as he scratched at a mosquito bite on his nose. "People do the same things, even when they're on the run. People who like hamburgers will continue to eat hamburgers. Someone who golfed will usually continue to golf if he or she can, no matter where they are. You can change your address and even your appearance, but most people can't or won't change their interests and their habits. You'd be surprised at how often fugitives are caught because of that." He stifled a yawn. "And by the way," Sean added, "you might want to talk to Clyde tomorrow morning. It's too late now."

"Why do I need to talk to Clyde?" Bernie asked. "Has he discovered anything interesting?"

"You might say that. There's a chance he might have found the Caddy you guys are looking for," her dad told her.

"Seriously?" Libby said.

"What do you think?" her dad replied as Cindy repositioned herself on Sean's lap for the hundredth time that evening.

Bernie glanced at her phone. It was a little after eleven. Her dad was right. It was too late to call Clyde. He went to bed by nine. She sighed.

"And by the way," Sean added. "He wants his favorite cupcakes as payment."

"Fair enough," Libby said, standing up and stretching. "This has been quite the day," she observed.

"Yes, it has been," Bernie agreed. Even her eyes were tired.

"I don't know about you," Libby said, "but I need some ice cream."

"I don't know about needing it," Sean replied, "but wanting it—now, that's a different story."

"Works for me," Bernie said.

"Baileys over the vanilla ice cream we made yesterday?" Libby suggested.

"Perfect," Bernie replied. Like her sister had just said, it had been that kind of day. Besides, maybe some Baileys over vanilla would help with the bad feeling she was developing in the pit of her stomach.

Chapter 18

It was a little after ten o'clock in the morning by the time Libby and Bernie made it over to the Longely Police impound lot. They'd wanted to get there earlier, but Clyde hadn't been able to get to the lot before ten, and even if he had been able to, it had turned out that they couldn't have. First of all, Libby and Bernie had woken up late, because they'd both slept through their alarms, so they'd been behind to begin with. Then the credit card machine had malfunctioned during the morning rush, they'd had a run on their cardamom-ginger muffins, and Amber had accidentally knocked a pound of flour off the top of one of the prep tables onto the kitchen floor.

After they'd cleaned that up, Libby and Bernie had had to finish baking and icing the ten-layer cake that Mrs. Stein was picking up for her book club luncheon at one thirty, the chocolate cake with the volcano on top that Lucy Chen was bringing to her son's third grade class for his birthday celebration, and the chocolate chip banana cupcakes with chocolate frosting they were baking for Clyde as payment for his help.

"I thought it was supposed to be sunny today," Libby

commented as she and Bernie turned onto the road that led to the impound lot.

"It was," Bernie said, looking at the overcast sky. The clouds were darkening in the west, and it looked as if rain was coming later in the day.

The impound lot was located five miles from the Longely police station, between a used car lot that specialized in wrecks and a shop that sold plumbing supplies. The drive took ten minutes longer than Bernie had expected because of a crash on Oakland and Sheffield, so they and Clyde ended up arriving at the same time.

"Oh, my God, is that a new car?" Libby asked Clyde as she watched him unfolded himself and wiggle out of a light blue Prius. "Can you even get out of that thing?"

"It's like you're getting out of a clown car," Bernie added helpfully. "What happened to your Jeep?" she inquired.

Clyde scowled. "I don't want to talk about it."

Bernie persisted. "Did you sell it?"

Clyde's scowl deepened. "I said I don't want to talk about it."

"It died, didn't it?" Bernie guessed. After all, the Jeep did have almost two hundred thousand miles on it. "I bet your wife is happy." Clyde's wife had been after him for over a year to swap out his vehicle for something that was a little less Rambo and a little more ecologically correct.

Clyde's scowl became a full-on glower. "Hey, I'm doing you a favor here. If you're going to make fun of me, I can go back to the station. I have plenty of work to do there."

"I'm not making fun of you," Bernie replied. "It's just that you look . . ." And she couldn't help it. She burst out laughing.

"Ridiculous?" Clyde asked.

"No, no. Not at all," Bernie lied before going off into

another gale of laughter. "I'm sorry," she apologized as she wiped the tears from her eyes. "I really am."

"I can see that," Clyde snapped.

"I'm not laughing at you," Bernie told him.

"Then who are you laughing at?" Clyde demanded. "Because you certainly aren't laughing with me."

"I'm not laughing at anyone. I was just thinking of something one of our customers said earlier," Bernie said, lying for the third time.

Clyde raised an eyebrow. "Would you care to elaborate?"

Bernie's mind drew a blank. "Not really."

"Figured," Clyde said.

"Hey, I was just trying to be funny," Bernie told him.

"And not succeeding," Clyde told her. "Now, do you want to look at the Caddy or not?"

"Look at it," both Libby and Bernie chorused.

"Okay then," Clyde responded.

"What's the story with the car?" Libby asked.

Clyde rubbed the back of his neck. It was sore from the ride over, not that he'd ever admit that. "An officer found the vehicle abandoned in a ditch when he was on a call investigating a loud noise complaint late yesterday afternoon," Clyde informed the sisters. "I had to come back to the station last night because I forgot something, and I saw the report, remembered what your dad had told me, and gave him a heads-up. It probably has nothing to do with what you're working on, but I figured you'd want to check it out."

"For which we thank you," Bernie said.

"Any idea how long the vehicle was in the ditch?" Libby asked Clyde.

Clyde shook his head. "Nope. It could have been a week. It could have been a day or two. There's really no way to tell. The one thing I do know is that it wasn't reported missing. I checked the database."

"Interesting," Libby remarked.

"Who owns it?" Bernie asked.

"Don't know that, either," Clyde replied. "There are no license plates on the vehicle or documents in the glove compartment. The responding officer checked."

"No VIN number, either?" Bernie asked.

Clyde shook his head. "Filed off."

"Of course it was," Libby said. They couldn't seem to catch a break. "Where was the vehicle found?"

Clyde stifled a yawn. "Near James and Perl, over by the old Eastman strip mall."

Bernie looked at Libby. "That's near where Judy Fine lives, isn't it?"

Libby nodded. "Indeed, it is."

Clyde scratched behind his ear. "Judy Fine. Why does that name sound familiar?"

"Maybe because she gave a talk at the Y a couple of weeks ago on the history of quilting," Libby replied.

Clyde snapped his fingers. "Oh yeah, my wife went to that," he said as he watched two crows squabbling over a chicken wing someone had left on the ground.

"So can we see the Caddy?" Bernie asked as Libby went and got the cupcakes out of the van.

"That's what we're here for," Clyde replied.

"This is really overkill security-wise," Bernie said, commenting on the impound lot, while they waited for Libby to return.

Five years ago, the lot had been unfenced, but after a rash of car thefts from the lot, the town council had decided to install a six-foot chain-link fence topped with double strands of barbed wire, surveillance cameras, and a hefty chain secured by a padlock on the gate.

"Agreed. But I wasn't consulted," Clyde replied as Libby came back a moment later with the cupcakes. He opened the box, selected a cupcake, and took a bite. "Ah, the smell of butter in the morning," he said, paraphrasing a line from *Apocalypse Now*.

"How are they?" Libby asked.

"Delicious," Clyde said and finished off his cupcake.

"Are you going to give any to Mrs. Clyde?" Bernie asked.

"The person that loves tofu and hates all things tasty? No. I don't think so." Then Clyde put the box with the rest of the cupcakes in his car and returned as another crow swooped down and joined the chicken wing fray.

"Here we go," Clyde said as he took a key out of his pants pocket, inserted it in the padlock, and turned it. There was a click, and the lock opened. Clyde carefully unwound the chain, then opened the gate. "After you," he said, bowing and extending his arm in invitation.

"I'm glad I didn't wear heels," Bernie observed a few minutes later, as the grass squished beneath her feet. Even with the flats she was wearing, she could feel herself sinking into the clayey soil.

"It's definitely been a wet year," Clyde observed as he stepped around a puddle of standing water. "At least the frogs like it."

"Well, I don't," Libby pronounced as she almost stepped in another puddle.

Five minutes later, they reached the Escalade. "This is it," Clyde said. "What do you think?"

"Well, it's black, just like the car we saw," Libby commented.

"As are most other Escalades," Bernie said as she opened the passenger side door and peeked inside.

Her first impression was that the vehicle had just been

detailed. The inside was spotless. No candy wrappers or soda bottles or coffee cups. Which was odd. In Bernie's experience, most people had stuff lying around. Who kept a car like this? Bernie wondered. Certainly, no one she knew. That was for sure. Obviously, whoever had driven the Caddy had taken pains to take their trash with them, which ruled out joyriding teenagers, a group not known for their fastidiousness, in Bernie's experience.

Or maybe the Escalade's owner was OCD, Bernie decided as she checked out the glove compartment, the side pockets in the front and rear doors, and the compartment in the middle. They were empty, which pointed to the second and most likely possibility: that the person who had driven the car didn't want its owner found.

"We should go," Clyde said, looking at his watch. "I gotta get back to work. This is a waste of time. Like I told your dad, the Escalade is clean."

"Give me another sec," Bernie replied, and she squatted down and ran her hands under the passenger-side front seat. "Found something," she sang out a moment later, as she straightened up. "See?" she said, waving two small squares of light green cotton cloth in the air. "There was something in there, after all."

Clyde looked. "So?" he said. "They're fabric scraps."

Libby corrected him. "They're squares, not scraps."

Clyde sighed the sigh of the long-suffering. "Pardon me for misstating. And your point is?"

Libby responded, "My point is that these scraps, as you are calling them, were found in a vehicle that might belong to the woman whom we think was searching Ellen Fisher's house."

"That's a lot of 'thinks' and 'maybes,'" Clyde commented.

"Possibly," Bernie conceded, taking over the conversation. "But this vehicle was found near where Judy Fine lives, and she's a quilter, which suggests there might be a connection of some sort."

Clyde put his hand over his heart. "My God, you solved the case," he cried. "I'll have her picked up immediately and transported to the county jail for booking."

"No need for sarcasm," Bernie told him.

"How about a need for reality?" Clyde responded. "You do know that the description you just came out with could cover a multitude of people, up to and including my wife, don't you? Talk about a stretch. Ask a judge to sign a warrant for something like that and they'd throw you out of their office."

Bernie turned to her sister. "But we're not asking a judge to do anything like that, right, Libby?"

"Right," Libby replied. "Not that we could do that, anyway."

"Maybe this is a stretch," Bernie conceded, "but it's the only lead we have right now. I think it's worth pursuing."

Clyde shrugged. "Hey, if you want to go on a wild-goose chase, be my guest. If you want to believe that Ellen Fisher was murdered, that she didn't kill herself, despite all the evidence to the contrary, go right ahead. Have at it."

"There is one other thing," Bernie replied, at which point she told him about the AirTag they'd found stuffed down in Mathilda's seat. "Why would someone do that if we hadn't hit a nerve? If there isn't something to Cecilia Larson's story? Tell me that."

Clyde humphed. "Are you sure?"

"Of course my sister is sure," Libby responded. "You think she'd make something like that up?"

"No." Clyde tapped his fingers against his thighs while he considered what Bernie had just told him. "You might have a point. Perhaps there's something going on, after all," he conceded.

"That's what my dad thinks," Bernie said as she felt

raindrops on her nose. She looked up. The sky had darkened. Gusts of wind were whipping the tree branches around. There was a crash of thunder. A bolt of lightning cut through the sky, leaving the smell of ozone lingering in the air.

"I think it's time to go," Libby observed.

"Agreed," Clyde said, and he, Libby, and Bernie started hurrying toward the gate. They reached their respective vehicles just as the sky opened up.

"I wonder what Judy Fine is going to say for herself," Libby mused as she watched sheets of water coming down and listened to them pummeling the top of their van.

"Hopefully, something that will move this case along," Bernie answered, raising her voice so she could be heard over the claps of thunder.

Chapter 19

The storm stopped as quickly as it had begun. By the time Libby and Bernie arrived at Judy Fine's house half an hour later, the wind had blown the clouds away, the sky was a bright blue, and the air smelled of spring. The only reminders of the downpour were the puddles on the ground and the water dripping off the trees and bushes.

The area Judy Fine lived in was one of Longely's earliest suburbs. Located a mile away from the Hudson, the residences in it had been built in the twenties and the thirties. Time had been kind to the houses. Most of them looked as if they were in immaculate condition. As Bernie drove through Hillsdale's winding streets lined with elms, silver maples, and birches, she noted that half of the brick and stucco homes had large screened-in front porches attached to their facades reminding her of the neighborhood she'd lived in during her brief stint in Oakland.

"Cute house," Libby commented, referring to Judy Fine's residence, as they pulled up in front of it. The sharply sloping roof, the curved bright orange door, and the diamond-shaped leaded windows made it look like something out of a fairy tale.

"Cottage," Bernie corrected. "It's a cottage."

"Cottages are small houses in the country or at the beach," Libby replied. "This house is in the suburbs."

"At least we can both agree the house is small," Bernie said. She estimated that it was twelve hundred square feet at most.

Libby frowned. "And that no one is home," she said, noting the empty driveway.

"Unless Judy's car is in the garage," Bernie replied while she parked in the street.

She and her sister sat there for the next five minutes, studying the house and finishing the coffee and the brioches they'd brought from their shop.

"The garage is almost as large as the house," Libby reflected as she flicked a crumb off her tan quilted jacket. "It's even got a second floor."

"I think that's what they used to call a carriage house," Bernie said. She screwed the cover of her thermos back on and rested it on the floor.

The sisters got out and walked up the redbrick path lined with fairy lights to the house, both of them carefully avoiding stepping on the earthworms that had been flushed out by the downpour.

"Maybe Cecilia was wrong about Judy being home," Bernie said. On the drive over, she'd called to ask Cecilia where she could find Judy.

Libby stopped to pick up an earthworm and put it on the grass. "We should have called Judy first," Libby said.

"Then we would have lost the element of surprise," Bernie replied as she rang Judy Fine's doorbell.

"True, but then we wouldn't have to make two trips," Libby observed while Bernie rang the bell again.

There was no response.

"Oh well," Bernie said. "I guess this isn't our day."

"Back to the shop?" Libby asked.

"We should," Bernie said, thinking of everything they had to do. But instead of walking back to the van, she followed the path to the garage and peeked in. "Now, this is interesting." She said, motioning for Libby to come and have a look.

"I don't see anything," Libby complained as she glanced through the window in the garage door. It was dark, and the glass was streaked with dirt, making it difficult to see the garage's interior.

"Over there," Bernie said, pointing to the garage's far corner.

Libby concentrated. She still didn't see anything. "What?"

"That green thing in the corner."

Libby squinted. "I think that's a bolt of cloth."

Bernie patted her coat pocket. "Exactly. It looks as if it matches the cloth we found in the Caddy."

"I don't know. It's hard to tell without any light."

"Let's find out, shall we?" Bernie said.

"Was that a question or a statement?" Libby asked.

"A statement," Bernie said.

"Figured as much," Libby told her.

Bernie studied the lock on the garage door. "This is an old lock. Getting in shouldn't be a problem. In fact, I think I can probably pop the latch with a credit card."

"Oh, goody. Dad will be so proud."

Bernie grinned. "Hey, he should be. He's the one who taught me how to do it," Bernie responded as she searched around in her bag for her wallet.

"That's because you and your roommates kept on forgetting your key to your apartment, and he got tired of having to drive over and let you in. Boy, was Mom not pleased," Libby said, reminiscing, remembering the scene when Rose had walked in on her father and sister.

"No. She wasn't, was she?" Bernie said, recalling the scene, as well. "I thought she was going to kill Dad. Metaphorically."

"And speaking of killing," Libby said, thinking back to the case they were working on, "we're assuming that Ellen let her killer in."

"That's what I'm assuming, anyway," Bernie said as she took her wallet out of her bag, opened it, and chose her AAA card. "The lock at her house wasn't tampered with. Besides, given the scenario we're postulating, whoever killed Ellen Fisher had to have been invited over."

"Or dropped by," Libby said.

"Same thing," Bernie said as she began working her AAA card between the door plate and the lock.

"Which means," Libby continued, "that whoever did it intended to."

"Well, you don't hang someone by accident," Bernie said. Then she stopped talking, turned back to the lock, and concentrated on opening it.

Libby folded her arms, leaned against the garage, and watched her sister work. It took Bernie less than a minute to open the door.

"Told you it would be fast," Bernie said to her.

"I didn't say you couldn't do it. I was just questioning whether you should do it," Libby replied as Bernie stepped inside. Libby followed. "There's a difference."

"I know," Bernie told her as both sisters looked around. "There's a lot of stuff in here," Bernie remarked.

"Indeed, there is," Libby said. "Any more stuff and there won't be room for the Caddy. As it is, it can't be fun maneuvering it in here with all this," she noted, waving her hand around to indicate the two sewing machines, the piles of cartons, the gardening supplies, the folding chairs and tables, and the old furniture, as she and her sister carefully threaded their way through to the corner where the bolt of material Bernie had seen was sitting.

"See, Libby?" Bernie said as she pulled the pieces of material she'd found under the Caddy's seat out of her pocket. "It's a match."

"What's a match?" Judy Fine asked.

Libby and Bernie whirled around. Judy Fine was standing in the garage's doorway with a gun in her hand, and it was pointed at them.

"Jeez," Libby said, putting her hand over her chest. "You almost gave me a heart attack."

"No hello?" Bernie asked Judy Fine. "No how are you doing?"

Judy Fine's eyes narrowed. "I repeat. What the hell are you doing in my garage?"

"What the hell are you doing with that gun?" Bernie replied as she and her sister exchanged glances.

"What does it look like I'm doing?" Judy Fine asked.

"I don't know," Bernie replied. "That's why I'm asking."

Chapter 20

Libby moved a step closer to Bernie. "Judy, why don't you put that down," Libby said, referring to the weapon Judy was holding. "It's not as if you don't know who we are. Unless, of course, you're the killer."

"Ha. Ha. How do I know that you're not?" Judy replied.

"You got us," Bernie said.

"You still haven't told me what you're doing here," Judy answered.

"And we will once you put the gun down," Libby said.

"That's a pretty big gun for you," Bernie noted, referring to the Smith & Wesson Judy Fine was pointing at them. "You can hardly get your hands around the grip." Which was true. "Maybe you should try something smaller next time."

"And lighter," Libby said. "A twenty-two would probably work."

"I'm fine with this," Judy Fine replied.

"We're just trying to help," Bernie added.

"You could shoot yourself in the head," Libby told her. "Well, maybe not the head, but definitely the foot. That

Smith & Wesson has quite the recoil, if I remember correctly."

"And it doesn't even go with your outfit," Bernie pointed out. Judy Fine was wearing another pleated skirt, a white blouse with a Peter Pan collar, a tan cardigan, and tasseled loafers. "That gun is more of a nineties gangsta movie thing, and you're dressed for a fifties rom-com. I think it's always good to coordinate one's accessories with one's weapons, don't you?"

"Seriously, Judy," Libby said, picking up where her sister had left off. "Your hand is shaking. And, by the way, did you know the safety is still on?"

Judy looked down. It was.

"You're just lucky we're nice. Some people would take that gun away from you and shoot you with it," Bernie said.

Libby chimed in with, "Or pistol-whip you."

"Do you have a license for that thing?" Bernie asked.

"As a matter of fact, I do," Judy replied, lowering the weapon and placing it on top of the large carton from IKEA she was standing next to. This wasn't working out the way she had pictured it would, she decided.

"Did Ellen?" Libby asked.

Judy wrinkled her forehead. "Did Ellen what?"

"Have a license for her gun?" Libby inquired.

Judy's eyes widened. "I didn't know she had one."

"Well, she did," Bernie told her. Then she changed the subject. "That's a serious piece of firepower you've got there, Judy," Bernie noted. "Sometimes smaller is better."

"I got it after I was carjacked last year," Judy explained. "I keep it in my glove compartment now. Just in case," she continued. "So I repeat. Do you want to tell me what the hell you're doing here?"

"Oh, that's simple," Bernie said. "The police found

your Caddy in a ditch, and we just came by to tell you. You know, save them the trouble, their being short staffed and all."

Now it was Judy's turn to startle. She swallowed. "What Caddy? What are you talking about?"

"I'm talking about the Caddy you were driving the day you decided to break into Ellen Fisher's house and search it," Bernie said. "Tell me, did you find what you were looking for? Inquiring minds want to know."

"Maybe inquiring minds do, but like I just said, I don't know what you're talking about," Judy told Bernie.

"Judy," Libby continued, "you're really a very bad liar. And the whole 'leaving the safety on' thing?" Libby shook her head, a more sorrowful than angry gesture. "If you're going to do this kind of thing, you need to practice more if you want people to take you seriously."

"Very funny," Judy snapped.

"We thought you'd be happy finding out about the car," Bernie said, taking over the conversational reins from her sister. "Obviously, we were wrong."

Judy frowned. "Obviously, you were, since I don't own a Caddy, but even if I did, that still doesn't explain why you're in my garage," Judy pointed out.

"That's easy," Bernie replied. "We rang the doorbell, and no one answered."

"That's because I was out doing an errand," Judy explained.

Bernie turned to Libby. "See, I told you she wasn't home."

"And you were right, Bernie."

"I usually am."

"Not always."

"But most of the time," Bernie replied. As she watched Judy Fine shift her weight from one foot to the other, Bernie reflected that she looked as if she'd lost weight since Ellen Fisher had died. A lot of weight. Judy Fine had been thin to begin with, but now she was downright skinny, as if she was being sanded down to nothingness by the events of the past weeks.

"We were going to leave a note," Libby said, "but then we saw the door to the garage was open, and we decided to check in here before we did."

Judy shook her head. "You're lying. The garage door was locked. It always is."

"Maybe you forgot to lock it," Libby suggested.

"There's no need to be embarrassed. Stuff like that happens all the time to me," Bernie told Judy. "Once I left the teakettle on. I thought I'd turned the burner off, but I hadn't. I nearly burned down the house."

Judy sniffed. "Good for you. Stuff like that doesn't happen to me," Judy told her. "Why are you really here?"

"I just told you," Bernie said. "The police found your Caddy, and we came around to break the news."

"The Caddy isn't mine," Judy repeated. "I already told you that."

"Yeah, and we don't believe you," Libby told her.

"Are you calling me a liar?" Judy spluttered.

Bernie laughed. "We already have."

"Yeah," Libby said. "You want a piece of advice? Save the moral outrage for the cops."

Bernie pointed to the bolt of green cloth in the back of the garage. "We found two squares of fabric underneath the Escalade's seat that match that material, so don't even bother trying to deny that the Caddy is yours."

Judy laughed. "That's what you're basing this whole thing on?"

"It's enough," Libby said.

"Really? Because it's pretty slim, if you ask me," Judy retorted.

"Maybe it is," Bernie allowed, "but it's enough to point the police in your direction."

"Be my guest," Judy told her. "Point away. If you want to play that way, I can call the Longely PD and have you arrested for trespassing."

"We weren't trespassing. Like I said, the door was open," Libby repeated.

"That's called an attractive nuisance in legal parlance," Bernie added helpfully.

Judy snorted. "Talk about being bad liars," Judy said. "At least come up with a better story."

Bernie looked at Libby. "I thought this one was working, Libby."

"I did, too, Bernie."

Bernie turned back to Judy. "Have it your own way. We were just trying to help." She drew the two squares of fabric out of her pocket and showed them to Judy Fine. "The police don't know about these yet."

"What about them?" Judy asked.

"This is what I found beneath the seat in the Caddy," Bernie replied.

"So?" Judy said, pretending indifference and doing a bad job of it.

"So," Bernie continued, pointing to the back, "the pieces of fabric match the bolt of fabric in the corner of your garage. And by their cut, it looks as if they're intended to be part of a quilt."

"That's quite an assumption you're making," Judy replied. "Two assumptions, actually. If you were my student and this was a paper, I'd give you an F on logic."

Bernie put the squares back in her pocket. "All right then. If that's the way you want to play it." She motioned to her sister. "Come on. Let's get back to the shop. We can make the call to the police from there."

"Works for me," Libby said.

Chapter 21

Bernie and Libby had just exited the garage when Bernie turned around and spoke to Judy Fine. She'd decided to give it one last try. "Judy, don't you care about what happened to Ellen Fisher?" she asked.

"Of course I care," Judy Fine replied.

"Don't you want her murderer caught?" Bernie asked.

Judy frowned. "I'm still having trouble believing that. I know I told Cecilia I agreed with her, but that was to make her feel better. She's always seeing things that aren't there. Making things up."

"Maybe she is, and maybe she isn't," Libby replied, "but Cecilia is correct about one thing. Something about Ellen Fisher's death doesn't add up. Don't you want to know what it is?"

Judy Fine took a deep breath and bit her lip.

"I can see that you do," Libby said gently. "Please help us figure this thing out."

Judy Fine touched her collar. She coughed. Libby and Bernie waited.

"Please," Bernie repeated after a minute had gone by and Judy hadn't said anything.

"Pretty please with a cherry on top," Libby added.

Judy couldn't help it. She laughed. "Okay. You win."
She paused for another moment, and then she began to talk.
"Hypothetically speaking, let's suppose that the Caddy is
mine," she said.

"Go on. We're listening," Bernie said, indicating herself
and Libby with a wave of her hand.

"Only I don't drive it," Judy continued.

"I see," Bernie said, wondering where this was leading.

"Then who does?" Libby asked.

"My ex. Hypothetically speaking."

Libby nodded, while Bernie crossed her arms and leaned
against the doorframe. "Go on," she urged.

"That's it," Judy said.

Bernie and Libby exchanged another look.

"Is that why you didn't report the vehicle missing, hypothetically speaking?" Libby asked, adding the hypothet-
ical when Judy didn't answer.

Judy Fine smiled and nodded. "I didn't know it was
missing."

"Did your ex borrow it?" Libby said.

"That's one way of putting it."

Bernie raised an eyebrow. "He stole it?"

"You said it. I didn't," Judy replied.

"And you didn't report him?" Libby asked.

Judy looked down at the floor. "I didn't want to get him
in trouble," she murmured.

"I see," Libby said, even though she strongly suspected
Judy was lying and there was something else involved.

"Most people don't harbor tender feelings toward their
exes," Bernie observed. "I know I certainly don't. If one of
my exes took my car, I'd be calling the cops immediately."

Judy looked up. "He's having problems . . . lots of problems."

"What's your ex's name?" Bernie asked. "I can find out easily enough," she added when Judy Fine didn't answer. "All I have to do is ask around."

Judy swallowed. "It's Richard, Richard Dunne."

"How can we get in contact with him?" Libby inquired.

"Are you going to speak to him?" Judy asked Libby after she'd told her where to find him.

"That's the plan," Libby replied.

Judy rubbed her chin with her free hand. "Okay, but he can be scary when he gets upset."

"Define *scary*," Bernie demanded.

"Are we talking violent here?" Libby asked.

Judy put her hand to her mouth. "You didn't hear it from me." Her eyes widened as a new thought occurred to her. "Oh my God, you don't think he . . . was the one who did . . . that thing . . . to Ellen, do you?"

"I don't know. What do you think?" Bernie asked Judy.

"I . . . can't believe he would do something like that," Judy replied, but Bernie reflected that her voice lacked conviction.

"You don't sound so sure," Bernie told her.

"Oh, I am," Judy said, sounding the opposite.

"Do you have any idea who would?" Libby inquired.

"None," Judy answered quickly. "Ellen was always so . . . quiet. I can't imagine her doing anything that would cause anyone . . . to do that. All she cared about was quilting and teaching, really."

"That's what everyone says," Libby observed.

Judy bit her lip. "I mean, Ellen's idea of a wild night was going out with the girls and having a couple of glasses of wine."

Judy's comment made Bernie remember something Brandon had said to her the other evening. "You guys used to meet at RJ's, right?" Bernie asked Judy.

Judy Fine nodded. "At least one Thursday a month, after one of our quilting sessions. But usually it was more."

Bernie continued. "I heard that Gail and Ellen got into a fight before Ellen died, and Ellen stormed out of there."

Judy Fine corrected her. "Actually, it was Gail who stormed out."

"What was the fight about?" Libby asked, curious to hear what Judy had to say.

Judy shrugged. "The usual nonsense."

"Which was?" Libby asked, prodding.

"It started with Gail being angry about something that Ellen had said about one of Gail's relatives and ended with a full-on argument over the merits of hand versus machine stitching."

"You're kidding," Libby said. "I mean, really, who cares?"

"They did . . . do," Judy Fine replied. "Some quilters take their quilting very seriously." She paused for a moment, then said, "And I think there was something else going on, as well."

"Like what?" Libby asked.

Judy shook her head. "I don't know. It's a feeling I had. And now, if you two don't mind, I have to get ready to teach." And she turned and started toward her house.

"Hey, what do you teach?" Libby called after her.

Judy Fine turned back around and smiled at her. "I teach a course called Feminism, the History of Fabric, Female Aesthetics, and the Crafting of Quilts." She raised her hand to stop any comments. "And yes, I know, the course title is unwieldy, but the material in it is fascinating, if I do say so myself. Did you know that the earliest quilting example we have is from nine hundred AD—"

Bernie interrupted. "I thought it was the thirteen hundreds."

"That's the more well-known fragment," Judy said. "The

fragment I'm referring to was recently found in a bog in Scotland."

"The one from the thirteen hundreds was stolen and held for ransom, wasn't it?" Bernie said, remembering what she'd read.

Judy nodded.

"How much money were they demanding?" Bernie asked. "I forget."

"They weren't asking for money. They were asking for recognition of a feminist aesthetic," Judy informed her.

"I think I'd ask for money," Libby said. "More fun."

Judy laughed. "I guess that depends on your point of view. The truth is that if men quilted or embroidered, those activities would be lauded as art forms." Judy's voice rose as her emotions took over. "Women's contributions to society are frequently ignored. And it goes further. Think about fabric. Before industrialization, women were the weavers. Without weavers, where would we be?"

"Naked?" Bernie joked.

This time Judy chuckled. "Pretty much. But think about it—fabric encapsulates the history of civilization. How did people, and by people, I mean women, go from using animal pelts for clothing to weaving fabric and fashioning it into clothes? What people wear, who wears what and when, says a great deal about who we are."

"I never thought of that," Bernie admitted as she buttoned up the middle button of her jean jacket. The damp was getting to her.

"Yup," Judy said. "Feminism and fabric. The two are inextricably linked." She glanced at her watch and groaned. "I'm going to be late. Sorry to go on a rant. It's just something I feel passionate about." And then she disappeared into her house.

Chapter 22

The sun had come out from behind the clouds by the time Libby and Bernie walked back to their van. Bernie unbuttoned her denim jacket. Suddenly, she was hot. That was the trouble with this time of year, she reflected. First, she was cold; then she was hot; then she was cold again. She never knew what to put on in the morning. She was thinking about that and the folly of spring clothes—after all, in this part of the country, you got to wear them a couple of weeks at most—while she watched the five robins on Judy Fine's lawn. Three were pecking in the dirt near a birch tree, while the other two were hopping around, carrying twigs in their beaks. Yes, spring was in the air. Bernie just wished it would hurry up and get here.

"What do you think?" Libby asked her sister once they were back in the van.

"I think I'd like to take Judy Fine's course, if I could find the time," Bernie replied as she started Mathilda up. "It sounds interesting. I wonder if there's a course on the history of food that I could take, as well. I read somewhere that snails were the first farmed animal back in Neolithic times. Do you think that's true?"

Libby snorted. "I have no idea. I'm talking about Judy Fine. Do you think she's telling the truth?"

"I don't know," Bernie replied after a moment of thought. "I'm not sure. What do you think?"

"Same as you. She could be," Libby said. "On the other hand . . ."

"She could be a really good liar," Bernie said.

"Exactly," Libby answered.

Bernie sighed. "It's not as if we haven't met some of those before."

"For sure," Libby replied. "Remember Marty? Remember him telling us he couldn't pay us the ten thousand dollars we lent him, because he had cancer?"

"Oh, I remember," Bernie said as she put her seat belt on. "He was sitting in the prep room with tears in his eyes, telling us he was dying, and I knew he was lying, but a part of me believed him, anyway. It was so weird."

Libby nodded. "Wasn't it, though?" She stopped talking for a moment to watch two squirrels chasing each other around the trunk of the silver maple in the middle of Judy Fine's front lawn. Then she turned back to her sister. "I wish we'd seen the person who came out of Ellen Fisher's house."

"And I wish we could discover the secrets of the universe, Libby, but that's not happening."

"At least not yet." Libby tore at a hangnail with her front teeth, realized what she was doing, and stopped. Then she said, "You know, the Smith & Wesson surprised me. I didn't peg Judy Fine as the kind of person who'd be waving one of those around. Her and weapons don't compute in my mind."

"No, they don't," Bernie agreed. "But then, this whole thing doesn't compute. Maybe Clyde is right. Maybe we are crazy. On the other hand, someone did put a tracker in the van. We're not making that up."

"No, we are not," Libby replied. "And to me, that indicates we've hit a nerve."

"It would be nice to know whose nerve," Bernie pointed out.

"Indeed, it would," Libby said as her sister hung a left onto Piermont Place and swerved to avoid hitting an Amazon Prime truck double-parked on the side of the road.

"Your guess is as good as mine," Bernie told her.

Libby rolled the window back up. She was getting chilly again. This weather was making her nuts. "What did Ellen Fisher have that was so valuable that it was worth killing for?"

Bernie readjusted the rearview mirror. "Maybe it wasn't a thing. Maybe it was something that she knew. Something she was going to tell someone."

"Like what? State secrets?" Libby demanded. "Ellen was a kindergarten teacher, not a nuclear scientist."

"She could have been blackmailing someone," Bernie hypothesized. "And don't say she doesn't look like the type who would do something like that. Remember Roberta?"

"Of course I do," Libby replied. The story had been splashed over the local paper for a week and had even made the national news. Roberta Twitchell had been a mousy-looking pastor's wife who'd gone missing and been found stuffed in a duffel in back of the Eastgate Mall a week later. Turned out she'd been blackmailing another pastor with a sex tape, and he'd gotten tired of paying. "But who would Ellen Fisher be blackmailing?" Libby asked.

"The obvious answer would be her boyfriend," Bernie answered.

"True," Libby agreed.

Bernie continued. "Or one of the quilters. Or maybe she was slipping down to the city for some fun and games. I guess we can add that to our ever-growing list of things we need to find out." Bernie drummed her fingers on the steering wheel. "And then there's this," she said a moment later, turning to Libby and changing the subject. "What would you do if your ex stole your car?"

"I'd report him to the police, of course," Libby answered.

"So would I," Bernie said.

"At the very least, I'd call the police and report the vehicle missing," Libby added. "That way if it was involved in an accident, I wouldn't be held responsible."

"Exactly," Bernie said. "As would any right-thinking person. So why didn't Judy Fine do that?"

"Because she still loves him?" Libby guessed.

"My thoughts exactly. I wonder what her ex would say," Bernie answered. "Let's find out, shall we?" she added as she slowed down at the Concord and Bayridge intersection before hanging a right onto Pine Street.

Libby leaned back in her seat. "Wendell's Hardware, here we come."

"And we can stop on the way and get some coffee at the Cup," Bernie added.

She suspected it was going to be another long day and she was going to need all the coffee she could get. A couple of shots of bourbon in it wouldn't hurt, either. Plus, she had a few questions to ask the shop's owner.

Chapter 23

The Cup was a hole-in-the-wall shop that served the best coffee in Longely, at least it did in Bernie's and Libby's estimation. On the way there, Libby looked up Richard Dunne on Google. There wasn't much information on him there, or if there was, she couldn't find it. Ten minutes later, they arrived at their destination. They were one of three vehicles in the lot.

"I guess we won't have to wait in line," Libby observed as she and her sister walked into the shop.

"As opposed to Starbucks," Bernie replied before greeting the owner and giving her order. Five minutes later they had their coffees in hand.

Libby sighed with pleasure as she took a sip of her cappuccino. "Perfect," she told Dominic, the owner of the place.

He smiled and nodded. "Haven't seen you guys for a while," he said.

Bernie shrugged. "You know how things are."

"Busy?" Dominic asked.

"We're holding our own," Libby replied. "And you?"

"Hanging on," Dominic said. He pointed to the holes in

the parking lot macadam, the overflowing trash cans on the strip mall's sidewalk, and the two empty shops sandwiched between the cleaners, the nail salon, and the medical lab. "This doesn't help."

"Have you talked to Oscar?" Libby asked. Oscar was the rental agent for CB Properties.

Dominic frowned. "He keeps on saying they're going to fix this place up, and I keep on asking when. At least the rent is cheap."

"Would you think of moving?" Bernie asked.

Dominic gave a dry laugh. "I'm okay for now. Now anyone who wants me knows where to find me. If I move . . ." His voice trailed off.

Bernie finished his sentence for him. "No one will." This gave Bernie the opening she'd been waiting for. She took out her wallet and put two fifty-dollar bills on the counter.

Dominic raised an eyebrow.

"We're looking for some information," Bernie explained.

"Like my secret to a perfect espresso?" Dominic asked.

"That too," Bernie said. "But we're wondering if you've heard of anyone selling anything these days."

Dominic looked puzzled. "Like what?" Dominic asked. "Lots of people sell lots of things. You're going to have to be more specific than that. Are we talking a humidifier? A car? A Lego set?"

"I'm not sure," Bernie admitted.

Dominic laughed. "If you don't know, then I certainly don't. And what does that have to do with me, anyway?"

"We understand you buy and sell things . . . kinda like eBay, only different," Bernie told him.

This time Dominic chuckled. "Says?"

"My dad," Bernie told him.

"Your dad is wrong," Dominic said. "I know that's the rumor, but it isn't true. At least not anymore. I got out a while ago. Too much aggravation."

"Okay," Bernie said. "But if you hear . . ."

"I won't," Dominic replied firmly.

Bernie pushed the two fifty-dollar bills toward him with the tips of her fingers. "But just in case you do. Think of this as a retainer. Please. As a favor."

Dominic shrugged. "Fine. If you insist. Just don't get upset if you don't hear from me . . ."

"I won't," Bernie said. She watched Dominic take the money, fold it, and put it in his money clip. Then he took two biscotti out of the domed glass dish on the counter and handed them to Bernie and Libby.

"Enjoy," he said as a guy carrying a toolbox walked into the store. He ordered a latte.

"Talk about a waste of money," Libby said, skirting a pothole as she and her sister walked back to the van.

"First of all, it's not our money, and second of all, I prefer to think of it as using community resources," Bernie told her sister. According to her dad, Dominic dabbled in a variety of criminal activities, which included but were not limited to fencing stolen objects and money laundering. "The problem is we don't know what we're looking for," Bernie continued.

"Duh," Libby said.

Bernie ignored her and went on with what she'd been saying. "Hopefully, Dominic will hear something through the grapevine. I mean, you never know, right?"

"I suppose," Libby said as she got into Mathilda and shut the van door. It closed with a solid thunk. She frowned as a thought crossed her mind. "I hope Dominic doesn't get himself arrested," she said.

"Because you'd missed the coffee?" Bernie asked her.

"And I like him."

"But mostly, you'd miss the coffee."

Libby smiled. "Is that wrong?"

Bernie laughed. "I guess it depends on whom you're talking to," she said while she rested her coffee cup on the dashboard so she could fasten her seat belt. "You know, we could serve these." She indicated her cappuccino with a nod of her head.

"We don't have the space or the people to do that," Libby told her sister as she licked a spot of foam off her top lip.

"We could move the coffee station over to the side," Bernie suggested after a moment's reflection. "That would free up some space."

"I suppose we could," Libby said, "but that isn't the issue."

"Then what is?"

Libby snorted. "Seriously? Think about the morning and evening rushes. We have enough trouble getting people out the door as it is. Add the couple of minutes it takes to make one of these"—she raised her paper cup—"and we're going to be in the weeds."

"You're always so negative."

"No. I'm realistic," Libby told her sister. "Plus, those machines are not cheap."

"We can rent to own," Bernie countered. "That way we can try it out for three or four months. If it doesn't work out, we can give it back."

"True," Libby said, "but we'd have to hire someone else if we did. Amber and Googie don't have the bandwidth to deal with something like this. They're stretched as it is, and so are we, for that matter. I don't think either of us can spare the time."

Which was true. Bernie couldn't deny that. She was

silent for a moment while she savored the taste of foamed milk, cinnamon, and coffee on her tongue. Then she said, "What if we just serve these during our off-hours? Like from ten to twelve and two to four?"

"That's not a bad idea," Libby conceded. "But what about the people who want a latte at eight in the morning?"

"We tell them no," Bernie said. "We tell them to read the sign."

"Which will create ill will and drama," Libby pointed out. She could see it now. "How do you think Robert or Mike Jay or Millie S. will respond if we say, 'No, we can't make you a latte now'?"

Bernie sighed. "You're right." It wouldn't be pretty, that was for sure. She took a bite of the chocolate biscotto Dominic had given her. The texture was good—not over-baked and hard—but the flavor could use some help. Maybe a dash of black pepper or a pinch of cumin or a touch of orange zest. She was wondering where Dominic had bought the biscotti from and how much he had paid per piece—they had a high return—when she realized that Libby was talking to her.

"Okay," Libby was saying, "the coffee is a no go, but there's no reason we can't go back to baking these." She pointed at the biscotto Bernie was eating. "They were a good seller."

Bernie nodded. They had been. Plus, the ingredients were cheap, and they were easy to make. Their only drawback was that they had to be baked twice.

"So, remind me," Libby said. "Why did we stop making them?"

Bernie frowned. "I know there was a reason, but I'm damned if I can remember what it was."

"I can't remember, either," Libby confessed. She took another sip of her cappuccino, leaned back in her seat, and listened to the honking of two Canada geese as they flew by. Then she sat up and asked her sister why the name of Judy Fine's ex sounded so familiar to her.

"It does, doesn't it?" Bernie answered as she started Mathilda up, backed out of her parking place, and drove out of the parking lot. At the intersection of Clarke and Westcott, she paused for a woman pushing a stroller with a cat inside to cross the street before proceeding. "What do you think Cindy would think of that?" Bernie asked, indicating the stroller and the cat with a nod of her head.

"I think she'd die of embarrassment," Libby replied. "And I think that Dad would be mortified."

Bernie laughed. "I'd pay money to see him pushing Cindy in a stroller."

"Me too," Libby said. "And speaking of Dad, I'm going to call him and see what he has to say about Richard Dunne. Maybe he knows something Google doesn't."

"The name sounds familiar," Sean said after he'd heard Libby's question. "I can't place it, though."

"Neither can we," Libby told him. She'd put the call on speaker so Bernie could hear it, as well. "I swear I've heard the name in relation to something. I just can't remember what that something is." She heard her dad chuckle.

"You're getting old, kid," Sean said.

"Yeah, Libby," Bernie chimed in. "It's all downhill from here." Then she asked her dad to dig around and see what he could come up with about Richard Dunne.

"I guess the Internet doesn't know everything, after all, Bernie," Sean replied.

"I never said it did, Dad."

"You didn't need to. It's evident in your tone," Sean retorted, at which point Libby stepped in before her dad and sister could get into an argument.

"Please, Dad," she said. "In fact, could you do that for all the major players involved in this thing?"

"Fine. If you insist," Sean replied, trying to sound miffed and failing.

"I think you made Dad's day," Bernie said to Libby after Sean had hung up.

"I think you're right," Libby told her.

Chapter 24

Libby and Bernie arrived at their destination five minutes later. Wendell's Hardware Store was located in a small strip mall on the older side of town. The shop took up two storefronts and sat between a tanning salon and a dry cleaner. The sidewalk outside the shop was piled high with bags of mulch and topsoil, wheelbarrows, and mowers, a fact that reminded Bernie that it was almost time for her and her sister to fill A Taste of Heaven's window boxes with flowers.

"Guess this is their slow time of the day," Bernie commented as she pulled into one of the six empty parking spaces in front of the shop.

"Better for us," Libby said, thinking it would be hard to have the kind of chat she and Bernie were contemplating if Richard Dunne was busy waiting on customers. "So how do you want to play this? Good cop, bad cop? Appeal to this guy's better nature? Surprise him?"

"I'm thinking, Libby," Bernie said as she turned Mathilda off and opened the door.

"So, you have no idea."

"Absolutely none," Bernie cheerfully admitted as she

got out of the van. "Well, here goes nothing," she said to her sister as they walked over to the door.

"Let's hope that's not the case," Libby said.

"It's a figure of speech, Libby."

"Yes, I know what it is, Bernie," Libby said as she pushed the door open. A bell tinkled as she and Bernie stepped inside.

The place looked empty. There were no customers and no one manning the register. Then someone called out from the back, "I'm over here." When Bernie and Libby looked, they could see a man standing behind the counter at the rear of the store.

They did a double take.

"Do you think that's Richard Dunne?" Libby asked out of the side of her mouth.

"Not who I was expecting, if it is," Bernie replied.

She'd been thinking thin and professorial, with thinning hair and frameless glasses, but this guy was big—Bernie estimated him at six feet, three inches tall and 230 pounds—and he looked as if he'd just stepped off his Harley. He had the whole biker thing going on, with tats up and down his arms, a beer belly pushing out his black T-shirt, a bushy beard that covered his neck, and long dark brown hair tied up in a ponytail.

"I'll tell you one thing," Bernie continued sotto voce, "this is definitely not the person we glimpsed getting into the Escalade."

"For sure," Libby agreed as she and her sister made their way to the rear of the shop. "But maybe he knows who was."

"Maybe," Bernie agreed, but she wasn't feeling optimistic.

When they reached the counter, they halted.

"Yes?" the man said, stopping rescreening the porch door he was working on and looking up. "What can I help you ladies with?"

"Hi. Are you Richard Dunne?" Bernie asked.

Richard cocked his head. "Last time I looked, I was. Why?"

"Good. We have a problem we hope you can solve for us," Bernie continued.

"Plumbing? Electric? Windows? I'm booked out for the next two weeks, but if you can't wait, I can give you the name of one of my friends," Richard Dunne told them. "Otherwise let me look at my calendar, and we can set up a date."

"That's not exactly the kind of problem we're talking about," Libby said as Richard Dunne started reaching for his phone.

"Then what?" Richard Dunne asked, stopping in midgesture.

Bernie decided to get straight to the point. "Recently, the police found an Escalade in a ditch over by Winton Street."

Richard Dunne wrinkled his brow. "Okay. And?"

Good question, Bernie thought. For a moment her mind went blank; then it came to her. She motioned to herself and Libby. "We're following up on the story for the local paper."

Richard Dunne looked suspiciously from one woman to the other. "I don't understand. What does that have to do with me?"

This time it was Libby who replied. "Your ex, Judy Fine, told us you stole it. We were wondering if you would you care to comment on her accusation."

Richard Dunne's face clouded over. "Are you kidding me?"

"No, that's what she said," Bernie told him while she adjusted the collar of the pink-checkered shirtdress, which she'd picked up at a vintage clothing store in Longely last year.

"That's good," Richard Dunne told Bernie. "You do know that my ex is a pathological liar, right? You can't believe a thing she says."

"She said the same thing about you," Bernie lied. "She also said that you had a really bad temper."

"Seriously?" The sisters watched while Richard Dunne took several deep breaths before speaking again. "That's funny coming from her. You want violent?" He pointed to a scar on his upper arm. "This is where she stabbed me with a pinking shears. It took eight stitches to close it up. Ask her about that."

"We will," Libby promised.

"And now if that's all you've come for, I think it's time both of you left." Richard Dunne motioned to the porch door he was working on. "I have to finish this before my customer comes back to get it." And he started stapling again.

Bernie leaned against the counter. "So, I can assume that you and your ex don't have an amiable relationship?"

Richard Dunne slammed the stapler down on the counter. "And what does that have to do with the article you're writing?" he demanded.

"About that . . . ," Bernie said, her voice trailing off.

"Look," he said, "I don't know who you are or what you want, but either level with me or get out."

"Okay," Bernie said. "You got me. We're not reporters."

"No kidding," Richard Dunne said. "I never would have guessed."

Libby continued the narrative. "Actually, we're investigating Ellen Fisher's death, and we'd appreciate any help you can give us."

Richard Dunne's expression changed. He furrowed his brow. "For real?"

Bernie and Libby nodded.

"For real," Libby said. She raised her hand. "I swear."

Richard Dunne scratched the side of his neck. "I don't get it. What's to investigate?" he asked. "Ellen Fisher killed herself."

"Maybe not," Libby told him.

"That's what I read in the paper," Richard Dunne insisted.

"Things may turn out to be a little more complicated than that." And Libby gave him a brief summary of what she and her sister believed had happened.

"Wow. Sounds like something you would see on *Law & Order*," Richard Dunne observed.

"Yeah, it kinda does," Libby allowed.

Richard Dunne took a penny off the counter and began weaving it over and under his fingers while he studied the sisters. "I don't see you as detectives."

"We're not licensed," Libby replied.

"So, then what are you?" Richard Dunne demanded.

"Existentially speaking?" Bernie replied.

"Ha. Ha," Richard Dunne told them. "Remember what I said before about being straight with me or getting out."

"Fair enough," Libby said.

Bernie and Libby both were silent while they thought about how to explain what they did. After a minute, Bernie said, "We're the people you turn to when you can't go through official channels for one reason or another. So, if you know something about Ellen Fisher, I'd appreciate it if you would tell us."

"Like what?" Richard Dunne asked.

Bernie shrugged. "Like anything. We're just trying to build up a picture of her."

Richard Dunne put the penny in the "Take one if you need it" jar. "And if you do find out that Ellen's death isn't kosher, then what?"

"Then we go to the police," Bernie told him.

"Fair enough," Richard Dunne replied. He rubbed the tip of his nose with his knuckle while he thought. Then he said, "I did think something odd was going on. I'm still not sure what it was, though."

"How so?" Libby asked.

"Well, about a month before she died, Ellen told me she thought her house was being bugged, and then she thought someone was following her."

Libby raised an eyebrow. "And were they?"

"I don't know." Richard Dunne hesitated. Then he said, "Let me put it this way. She didn't seem like the kind of person things like that happened to. You know what I mean? On the other hand, she didn't seem like the type of person to imagine things, either."

Libby and Bernie nodded.

"How well did you know her?" Bernie asked.

"I knew her in a casual way," Richard Dunne answered. "Ellen was over at my house a few times when I was still married to my ex. And I helped her move a couple of looms. She wanted to hire me to help her move some more stuff. She was supposed to call me and set something up, but she never did." He sighed. "She was a nice lady. A little nutty but nice."

"And the Caddy?" Libby asked.

"What does that have to do with anything?" Richard Dunne asked.

"Maybe nothing," Bernie allowed. "But whoever was driving it was going through Ellen Fisher's house after she died. We'd like to know why."

Richard Dunne shook his head. "Sorry. I can't help you

with that, but you should talk to my ex again. I bet she's not telling you everything she knows."

"No one ever does," Bernie observed. Then she thanked Richard Dunne for his time, gave him her card, and she and Libby turned and started for the door. Her last comment must have hit home, Bernie reflected later, because Richard Dunne called out to them a minute later. They stopped and turned around.

"Hey," he said. "You want to talk to someone about Ellen Fisher, talk to Selene White. They were tight."

"Anything else?" Bernie asked.

"Well . . ." Richard Dunne paused.

"Please," Libby said. "Anything would help."

Richard Dunne scratched his cheek. "This is just an impression, mind you, but I got the feeling that Ellen was thinking of going somewhere."

"Like a vacation?" Bernie asked him, remembering what they'd found in Ellen's house.

Richard Dunne shook his head. "No. Someplace more permanent. Like she was getting ready to get out of town."

Libby nodded. That jibed with what she and her sister had seen and heard. "Do you know why she was planning on moving?" Libby inquired.

Richard Dunne shook his head again. "Nope." He scratched his cheek. "I didn't ask, and Ellen didn't volunteer. She just seemed more nervous than usual. Or maybe I just imagined it. My ex said I always see things that aren't there."

"And do you?" Bernie asked.

Richard Dunne grinned. "I prefer to think of myself as insightful, someone who sees through the bullshit."

Bernie laughed. Then she and Libby thanked him and exited the hardware store.

Chapter 25

Bernie turned to Libby after they got in the van. "So, what do you think?" she inquired as she started Mathilda up.

"I don't think Richard Dunne took the Caddy, if that's what you're asking," Libby replied.

"Neither do I," Bernie responded. "Which means as the night follows the day . . ."

"That Judy Fine was lying about Richard Dunne stealing the Escalade," Libby said as she watched the sun try to peek out from behind the clouds and fail. "Which leaves two possibilities."

Bernie corrected her. "Three."

"Why three?" Libby asked.

Bernie ticked off the possibilities on her fingers. "The first and least likely. Judy Fine's vehicle was stolen, and she pointed the finger at Richard Dunne because she wants to cause him grief."

"But if that were the case, she would have reported the Caddy stolen to the police," Libby objected.

Bernie nodded. "Exactly. Which makes it the least likely.

That brings us to possibility number two. Judy Fine drove to Ellen Fisher's house in the Caddy, then ditched it."

"And three?" Libby asked as she fastened her seat belt.

"Judy Fine has a partner."

"Or none of the above," Libby said.

"Well, there is that, too," Bernie allowed.

Libby clicked her tongue against her teeth. "We definitely need to talk to her again."

Bernie nodded her head in agreement. "Indeed, we do, Libby."

"And then, more importantly, we come to what Richard Dunne said about Ellen Fisher," Libby went on.

"Yeah." Bernie checked her rearview mirror and started backing out of her parking space. "Maybe Ellen Fisher wasn't imagining things, after all," Bernie mused as she thought about the conversation she, her sister, and Richard Dunne had just had. "Maybe someone was spying on her."

"And bugging her house," Libby added. "Heaven knows that equipment is easy enough to come by these days."

"Which would explain why Ellen Fisher was getting out of town," Bernie observed. She paused for a moment, then said, "What would you do if you were in a similar situation, Libby?"

"I suppose I'd go to the authorities," Libby said after a moment of reflection. "Maybe buy a guard dog and beef up my security system."

"Exactly," Bernie replied. "But Ellen didn't do any of those things."

"She could have been about to," Libby objected. "For that matter, maybe she did go to the police," Libby countered. "Maybe they didn't believe her. Maybe they thought that she was making things up."

"There would be a record if she had gone to the cops," Bernie objected.

"True," Libby said. Then she thought of something else. "If you were in Ellen Fisher's position, if someone was stalking you, you'd go to the police."

"I just said I would," Bernie replied.

"So, what would make you *not* go?"

"That's easy," Bernie replied. "I wouldn't go to the authorities if I was involved in something illegal. Or maybe not even illegal. Maybe something embarrassing."

"Like appearing in a sex video," Libby suggested, thinking of a story she'd read in the local paper a couple of months ago about someone's sex tape turning up in the school library.

Bernie laughed. "That would qualify. I guess that's not something you want to have happen if you're a kindergarten teacher."

"Or a lawyer or a doctor or pretty much anyone," Libby replied.

"Unless you're a sex worker. Then it's called free advertising," Bernie noted as she drove out of the parking lot and started down the street. A school bus pulled out in front of the van, and Bernie slowed down.

"I don't think we're talking about Ellen Fisher here," Libby responded.

"I don't think so, either, but you never know," Bernie replied. The bus stopped. So did Bernie. She watched two kids get off and run into their houses, swinging their bookbags at each other. "She could have had a secret life."

Libby snorted. "Ellen Fisher? Hardly."

"Hey, you never know," Bernie admonished.

"She's Miss Goody Two-shoes, to borrow our mother's expression," Libby rejoined.

"Hey, remember what Dad used to say to us when we were dating? If someone looks too good to be true . . ."

"Then he is too good to be true," Libby said, finishing her sister's sentence for her. "And just to clarify, he said that to you, not to me."

"How can you say that with a straight face?" Bernie demanded. "He said it to both of us."

Libby was just about to tell her sister why he hadn't when she got a text from Amber, asking her to pick up some garbage bags. Evidently, they were down to a quarter of a box at the shop.

"How is that possible? I could have sworn we had another full box," Bernie said to her sister when Libby told her they would have to stop and pick up some. "I mean, I know we go through them quickly, but this is ridiculous."

Libby shrugged as her sister made a U-turn and headed back to Wendell's. It was the closest place. "Well . . . er . . ."

Bernie gave her sister a sharp look. "Well . . . er . . . what?"

"I gave the box to Googie," Libby confessed. "He said he needed the garbage bags to lay under the mulch he was having delivered so he could kill the weeds in the garden he was planting. I forgot to put garbage bags on the shopping list. Sorry."

"Just don't complain about being late," Bernie admonished as she made a left onto Houston Street.

Five minutes later Bernie pulled into Wendell's parking lot. She was heading for the shop when she spotted a white Dodge Ram driving toward the exit at the same time Libby noticed the CLOSED sign hanging on the hardware store's door.

"Now, that's odd," Libby commented, alluding to the sign. "Why would the store be closed?"

"Simple. Because Richard Dunne isn't there," Bernie said, pointing to the Dodge Ram, which was now idling at a stoplight. A moment later, the light changed color, and

Richard Dunne gunned the engine of his truck and sped down Christopher Street.

"He looks as if he's in a hurry," Libby observed. "A family emergency?" she posited. "Whatever it is must be pretty important not to wait for someone to come in the shop and take over."

"I'd say," Bernie agreed. "Although the timing seems a tad . . ."

"Coincidental," Libby said, finishing her sentence for her. "More than a little," Libby added. "I wonder where he's going."

"Let's find out, shall we?" Bernie said as she made another U-turn and headed after him.

When she turned at the corner, she could see Richard Dunne was already midway down the block.

"Slow down," Libby directed. "Otherwise he'll spot you."

"I know that," Bernie said as she applied the brakes.

When Richard Dunne got to the next corner, he made a left-hand turn, and Bernie followed.

"I wonder what we said that spooked him," Bernie mused as she hung back. There wasn't much traffic on Wayfair Street, and Mathilda was easy to spot. The expression *stuck out like a sore thumb* crossed her mind. "Maybe something about the Caddy?"

"Possibly," Libby said. "But why leave the shop if that's the case? Why not call?"

"Maybe this isn't about talking to someone, Libby. Maybe this is about needing to get something, or rather get rid of something."

"Like what, Bernie?"

Bernie shook her head. "I wish I knew."

"So do I," Libby said.

For the next ten minutes, Bernie played a game of cat and mouse with Richard Dunne, and then somewhere around Cobbs Hill, she lost him.

"Damn," she said, looking around. The white Dodge Ram was nowhere in sight.

Cobbs Hill was Longely's only experiment in what the developer had called mixed-use living, which meant that the development contained private houses, town houses, and one small six-story apartment building, all of which were laid out in a tangle of interconnected streets with cutesy names. Bernie stopped on the crest of a hill over-looking the development and surveyed the scene. She saw a postal worker putting the mail in mailboxes, an Amazon truck driver making deliveries, two women walking their dogs, and a school bus dropping off kids, but no Richard Dunne. She tapped her fingers on the steering wheel while she thought.

"I wonder if he lives here," she said to Libby.

"Maybe Judy Fine knows," Libby suggested. She tried calling and texting, but Judy Fine didn't answer.

"So much for that," Bernie muttered as she started driving around the complex again, but she didn't see Richard Dunne's truck parked in any of the driveways, and the three dog walkers she stopped and asked hadn't seen him, either. She had just turned onto Oak Lane and was heading toward the apartment building when she was intercepted by a blue Toyota with the word SECURITY written across both sides in big white letters.

"Can I help you?" the guard asked after he'd exited his vehicle and approached the van. He appeared to be in his fifties, was of medium height, with tired-looking eyes and a slight limp to his walk.

Bernie gave him her most winning smile and explained that they were looking for the residence of a Richard Dunne. "We're delivering an order," she said, rolling down her window partway. "That's Dunne," she added, spelling out the last name.

The guard nodded, went back to the Toyota, and consulted his laptop. He returned a minute later. "Sorry," he said. "We have a Dune and a Donne, but no one living here by the name Dunne."

"Are you sure, Mitch" Bernie persisted, reading his name off the bar pinned to his shirt pocket. "I'd hate to have to take this order back to the store."

"I'm sure," Mitch replied. "Maybe you misspelled the name?"

"I guess that's a possibility," Bernie allowed.

"Are you positive?" Libby asked. "He drives a white Dodge Ram. Big guy. Biker dude."

Mitch snapped his fingers. "Oh him. Yeah. I know who you mean. His mom lives here. He comes by once in a while when her husband needs to go out, to give her, her insulin shot." He shifted his weight. "Now, if there isn't anything else . . ."

Bernie nodded. She was just about to pull away when something else occurred to her. "Just out of curiosity, how did you know we were here?"

"Simple." Mitch pointed to the security cameras. "Big brother is watching."

"When did that happen?" Bernie asked. She'd been so involved in looking for Richard Dunne's truck that she hadn't noticed the overhead cameras. "I don't remember them being here before."

The cop shrugged. "That's because they weren't." He frowned. "It's a sign of the times. Management had them installed last year, after a spate of robberies."

Bernie nodded. "How effective are they?"

"The cameras?" Mitch asked.

Bernie nodded.

The security guard gave her an odd look. "Why are you asking?"

Bernie improvised. "Because we're thinking of installing

a security system in and around our shop, and I'm trying to figure out which company to go with."

"It can get complicated," Mitch allowed.

"It sure can," Bernie agreed. "There are a lot of systems on the market."

"Well, I can tell you one thing right now. Don't use these people," Mitch advised, then named the company responsible for the security system. "These things are always breaking. In fact, the system is down right now."

"But you just said that's how you knew we were here," Bernie reminded him.

"Ah . . ." Mitch looked abashed. He rubbed his chin with his knuckle. "I did, didn't I? Truth is, someone blew you in. Said he was afraid you were casing houses."

Bernie pointed to the van. "Yes, because there's nothing like doing that with your name printed on a van in big black letters."

"The van could have been stolen," Mitch pointed out.

"That's true," Bernie conceded. She rolled down the window all the way. "Can I ask who made the call?"

"You can ask," Mitch said.

"But you can't answer," Bernie guessed.

"You got it," Mitch replied. "I get the call from dispatch and go where I'm told. Probably one of the stay-at-homes made the call," he continued. "They ring up if their neighbor's cat walks across their grass. Talk about too much time on their hands." He sighed and shook his head. "So, A Taste of Heaven is your place?" he asked, changing the subject.

"That it is," Libby said, answering for her sister.

"I heard you guys have pretty good stuff," Mitch told her. "Especially your pies."

"Come by and have one on the house," Bernie offered.

"I just might do that," Mitch replied. Then he jumped

back in his vehicle and escorted them out of the development.

"So much for Richard Dunne," Bernie said to her sister as she headed for the nearest Walgreens to pick up the garbage bags.

"Evidently," Libby replied. She was thinking that she and her sister seemed to be hitting one dead end after the other when Gail Gibson called. She had decided to hold a small informal party to celebrate Ellen's life and wanted to know if the sisters could cater it.

"I realize it's short notice," she said apologetically.

"Don't worry, Not a problem. We'll be more than happy to do it," Libby said. "I mean, you never know," she said to Bernie after she'd hung up. "Maybe we'll come across the clue that cracks the case."

"Now, that would be a pleasant change," Bernie observed.

"Who's being negative now?" Libby asked.

Bernie shook her head instead of answering. She was tired and wanted to go home.

Chapter 26

Three days later, on Saturday afternoon, Gail Gibson greeted Bernie and Libby at the door of her fifties Cape Cod. She was wearing a pioneer dress with a high neck and puffed sleeves, something a settler out West in the early eighteen hundreds might wear. It was not a good look, in Bernie's opinion, not on anyone, but especially not on Gail.

"Sorry about the clutter," Gail told Bernie and Libby as they stepped inside and looked around. "I didn't have a chance to clean up."

"Not a problem," Bernie assured her, because that was the kind of thing you said to a client even when there was a problem.

"Here, let me show you where everything is," Gail said, walking them through the house into the kitchen. "I guess we should invest and do a full reno in here, but I don't really cook, and neither does Dwayne," she said.

One look and Libby wanted to say, "I can tell," but she restrained herself. Over the years, she'd learned that discretion and customer service went hand in hand. Instead, she smiled politely as she studied the small space in front of her, a space that reminded her of the kitchen in her cousin's New York City apartment on the Lower East Side. Galley style, with minimum counter space, the kitchen contained a small scratched white enamel sink, a twenty-year-old refrigerator, and an electric range that Libby was willing to bet had been there since the house was built.

"And I should tell you, the oven doesn't work," Gail continued. "There's something wrong with the thermostat." She gave an embarrassed laugh. "I keep on meaning to get it fixed, but I keep forgetting. I hope that's not going to be a problem."

"Not at all," Libby assured her, thinking as she did that it was lucky they didn't need to use it to heat anything up.

"Good," Gail said as she led Bernie and her sister into the dining and living rooms.

The rooms were small and dark, crowded with a mishmash of too-large furniture. The only bright note was a ninety-gallon fish tank sitting on a cabinet that butted up against the wall connecting the dining and living rooms.

"Nice tank. Salt water?" Bernie said, pointing to it.

Gail nodded.

"I heard they can be tricky to keep going if you don't know what you're doing," Libby noted.

"Yes, they can be," Gail agreed.

"Is that a sea anemone?" Bernie asked, pointing to a small red flower-looking creature waving its tentacles in the air.

"No, it's a jelly," Gail replied. Then she changed the topic to the ad hoc exhibit of Ellen's quilts that she'd created. "Too much?" she asked, indicating them. "Dwayne said it is, but he never likes anything I do, anyway."

"No, not at all. They look great," Libby lied. In her humble opinion, the quilts made the rooms look even more cluttered than they already were. One or two or even three quilts would have jazzed things up, but Libby counted at least twenty quilts in the two rooms. They were tacked to the walls and laid over the sofa, chairs, coffee and end tables, so that wherever Libby looked, she saw clashing colors and patterns. "These are all Ellen's?"

Gail nodded. "She was very prolific." Gail scratched under the neckband of her dress. "I wanted to put the last piece Ellen was working on out here, as well, but it still needs to be finished. It's hard, you know. Whenever I pick it up, I start thinking of Ellen, and I just . . ." Gail swallowed and stopped talking.

Libby patted Gail on the shoulder. "It's okay."

Gail smiled weakly. "It just would be nice to have it on display." She sighed. "I'm thinking of giving it back to Cecilia. She said she would repair the quilt if I can't. I mean, I told her I would. That's why she gave it to me, and I am better at this than Cecilia. She tends to rush things."

Libby patted Gail on the shoulder again. "I'm sure you'll do a splendid job when you're ready."

Gail brightened. "Thank you for that."

"My pleasure," Libby said. "Now, where do you want us to serve?"

Gail laughed and pointed to the dining-room table, which was piled high with stacks of papers, workbooks, and coloring books. "Would here work?"

"I don't see why not," Bernie said.

Gail looked at her watch. "Listen, I need to run out in a few minutes to do an errand. It'll take me about an hour. I hate to ask, but do you think—"

Bernie interrupted. "We can clean off the table. Sure. Not a problem. Just tell us what you want us to do with those," she said to Gail, referring to the piles of stuff on the table.

"Just put everything on the table on the shelves in there,"

Gail replied, nodding to a large mahogany china cabinet, "and shut the doors." Gail apologized again. "I'm so sorry. I was going to do it. Unfortunately, I overslept. I know this isn't great," she said, gesturing around her. "Just do what you can."

"No worries," Libby assured her. "We'll be fine. What made you decide to do this, anyway?" Libby asked Gail as Gail grabbed her bag on her way out the door.

Gail stopped and turned. She tucked a strand of hair behind her ear. "I just thought it would be a nice thing to do." She glanced at her watch again. "Oh my God. Gotta go." Then she turned and hurried out the door, slamming it behind her.

"I wonder where she's going," Bernie said as she checked the time on her phone.

The sisters looked at each other.

"An hour isn't a long time," Bernie observed.

"It's not a short time, either," Libby pointed out.

"It would be a shame to let this opportunity pass," Bernie said.

"Yes, it would," Libby agreed. "So, let's get moving."

She and Bernie spent the next half an hour cleaning off surfaces, bringing in supplies from the van, and setting up. Following Gail's instructions, they'd brought coffee, tea, and sparkling water; a large fruit salad tossed with a lemony poppy seed dressing; a chocolate cream pie and a lemon curd pie; a plate of mini eclairs filled with coffee custard; a platter of sandwiches cut into quarters; and a cucumber, tomato, and feta salad flavored with fresh basil leaves.

"This is really a tough time of the year food-wise," Libby observed as she hurriedly arranged the sandwiches on the platter. "It's still too early for spring produce and too late for the winter stuff."

Bernie nodded as she stole a roast beef on ciabatta with horseradish sauce sandwich from the pile. "Not bad, not bad at all," she remarked after she'd taken a bite. The bread had a nice chewy crumb, the roast beef was freshly cooked—they'd done it in the sous vide, a new addition to their cooking tools—and the horseradish sauce had just the right amount of kick to it.

"March is always tough," Bernie agreed as she chewed. Local strawberries, rhubarb, fiddlehead ferns, and asparagus hadn't come in yet, while the apples, pears, and oranges were past their prime, and people were tired of soups and stews. They wanted bright colors and lively flavors.

"Do you think Gail's husband, Dwayne, will be here?" Libby asked as she arranged the turkey with avocado and homemade mayo on a baguette; the mozzarella, tomato, and basil leaves drizzled with olive oil on focaccia; and the corned beef with mustard on rye; along with the aforementioned roast beef all on a platter.

"I don't know," Bernie replied. "I imagine he will. It is Saturday, so he's probably not at work."

"What does he do, anyway?" Libby inquired.

Bernie laughed. "You know, I don't know."

"Another person we don't know much about," Libby commented as she put the wicker basket containing the silverware out on the table. Then she neatened up the row of coffee mugs near the coffee urn and studied the table. The food was out, the table was set, and the beverages were brewed. They were done. "It's time to go exploring."

Bernie nodded. She'd been thinking the same thing. "We should split up for this. It'll go faster that way."

"Works for me," Libby replied. She checked her watch. "If we're lucky, we'll have about twenty minutes before Gail gets back."

"And everyone arrives," Bernie said. "Fingers crossed," she added. She rubbed the spot on her arm where she'd singed herself this morning. "How about I take the second floor and you do the downstairs?"

Libby nodded as she watched her sister head for the stairs. She took them two at a time. When she got to the head of the stairs, she stopped and looked. The upstairs hallway had a more spacious feel, but maybe that was because there was less clutter and the walls were white, Bernie reflected as she quickly went through the three bedrooms and the bathroom. Evidently, Gail slept in the first bedroom, Dwayne slept in the second bedroom, and Gail used the third bedroom for crafting. Gail's bedroom was full of clothes that needed to be put away, Dwayne's was immaculate, and the crafting room was chaotic.

That room contained shelves stocked with fabric, a fancy sewing machine that had enough buttons for a jet cockpit, a large table that had a half-done quilt laid out on it, and a small sofa, which was piled high with even more fabric. Bernie was thinking that Gail could open a fabric store if she ever decided to stop teaching when Libby called for her to come downstairs.

"I'm in Gail's office," Libby yelled. "I think I might have found something interesting in here. Maybe."

"That's not very confidence inspiring," Bernie called as she hurried down the stairs.

The office, an obvious add-on, was down a narrow hallway and next to the guest bathroom. Next to that was the doorway to the garage.

"Yes?" Bernie said when she got to the office. "So, what's so fascinating?"

"I'm not sure about fascinating, but definitely interesting," her sister replied as she beckoned Bernie inside.

Besides a desk, a file cabinet, and a bookshelf, the office

was crowded with stacks of cartons pushed off to the side, wicker baskets, a couple of garbage bags full of clothes, more fabric samples, and two smallish quilts in various stages of construction.

"What am I looking at?" Bernie asked Libby.

"These." Libby gestured to the small newspaper article and the old snapshot of a lake pinned to the quilt on the left.

"So?" Bernie asked. She didn't get why Libby had called her downstairs.

"Do you think these quilts are Ellen's? Do you think the article and the photo mean anything?" she asked Bernie.

"They don't," Gail said.

Libby and Bernie turned around. Gail was standing in the office doorway, and she did not look happy. "I'll take those, if you don't mind," she said, extending her hand.

Bernie handed her the picture and the article.

Chapter 27

Bernie put on her most ingratiating smile. "We have to stop meeting this way, Gail."

Gail's expression remained frosty.

"I didn't hear you come in," Bernie continued.

"No kidding," Gail replied. She scowled. "What are you doing in here, going through my stuff?"

"What do you think we're doing?" Libby asked.

Two dots of color appeared on Gail's cheeks. "Are you investigating me? Do you think I had anything to do with Ellen's death?"

"Do you?" Bernie inquired.

"Why would we think that?" Libby asked.

"I haven't the faintest idea," Gail replied.

"But if there's anything you want to tell us," Libby said, her voice trailing off.

"Now, that's funny coming from you," Gail replied. "How about you telling me why you were going through my office?"

"We could, but then we'd have to kill you," Libby said. "Not funny?" she asked, looking at the expression on Gail's face.

"Not even a little," Gail told her.

"I thought it was," Libby answered.

"Then you'd better stick to catering," Gail shot back, "because I don't think you'll make it as a comedian."

"Actually," Bernie said, stepping into the conversation, "we were looking for some paper napkins."

Gail blinked. "Why would they be in my office?"

Bernie shrugged. "There weren't any in the kitchen, so I figured you might be storing them in here, and that's when I saw the quilts and the pictures." She turned her gaze to the quilts. "Are these Ellen's quilts?" she asked, pointing.

"As a matter of fact, they are," Gail said, her voice softening. "I tasked myself with finishing them, but so far I haven't managed."

Libby nodded. "Was Ellen thinking of sewing this article and the picture into the quilt?" she asked Gail.

"She was talking about it," Gail allowed.

Bernie widened her eyes a fraction. "Really? How come?"

"It was going to be an experiment," Gail said. She was about to explain when she heard the front door open. A minute later, the sound of people talking floated into the office.

"They're here," Gail announced, imitating Heather O'Rourke's voice in *Poltergeist*. "We'll finish this up later."

"Finish what up later?" Selene asked as she popped into the hallway. Then she looked from Bernie to Libby to Gail and frowned. "What's going on? I'm feeling a certain amount of tension in the room," she observed as she unbuttoned her coat and started taking it off.

"We're good," Gail replied. "It's not a big deal."

"What's not a big deal?" Judy Fine asked Gail. She was right behind Selene.

"What's going on?" Cecilia inquired as she walked in.

"Nothing," Gail replied. "I was just about to explain to Bernie and Libby what Ellen was going to do with the paper and the photo."

"That was so sweet," Judy said.

Cecilia explained. "Ellen was thinking of making quilt squares and having her kindergarteners make drawings, put the drawings in the squares, and take them home, but she wanted to see what the pitfalls would be before she had the class do them."

"In the old days," Cecilia continued, "women used to use paper as an insulation in quilts, as well as other materials, but over time the paper degraded, while things like cotton batting didn't. That's why you don't find paper in antique quilts."

"But sometimes quilters put pictures of loved ones in their quilt," Selene added.

"Sometimes they hid things in there, as well," Judy Fine said. "For example, the slaves used to hide instructions to the underground railroad in them."

"Would Ellen have hidden anything in one of her quilts?" Bernie asked.

All four women shook their heads.

"Whenever we talked about it, she said that she wanted her quilts to speak for themselves," Selene replied.

"Besides," Judy said, "she didn't have any family pictures. She said they'd all been destroyed in a fire years ago."

"Along with everything else that she had," Cecilia replied, taking up the narrative. "Ellen told me it was very traumatic. In the blink of an eye, everything was gone. Frankly, I don't think she ever got over it."

Bernie raised an eyebrow. "Where was this?"

Cecilia shrugged. "I think it was somewhere in Oregon."

Bernie pointed to the picture Gail was holding. "Is that where this picture is from?"

Judy laughed. "No. I think that's Round Lake. She was there for a conference a couple of years ago."

"And the article?" Bernie inquired.

Judy answered. "Oh, she saved it because she wanted the name of the gallery that was holding a quilting exhibition." She sighed. "She wanted to contact them and see if they were interested in some of her work."

"Were they?" Libby asked.

"Yes," Judy replied. "She was so happy." Judy sighed. "Then the place burned down. Faulty electrical wiring. Poor Ellen. She was a poster child for the saying *If she didn't have bad luck, she'd have no luck at all.*"

"The whole kindergarten thing really was a sweet idea," Cecilia observed. "Too bad she never got around to doing it."

"Isn't it, though?" Selene agreed.

The six women looked at the quilts.

"We really need to finish these," Gail said.

"Yes, we do," Cecilia agreed.

"I know I said I would do it," Gail continued, sounding defensive.

"Why don't we do these and Ellen's last one at our next meeting?" Judy proposed.

The three quilters nodded.

"Good idea," Cecilia said. "I believe the meeting is at my house."

"It is," Selene said. "I'll bring the bourbon."

"I have wine," Cecilia told her.

"I was thinking we might need something stronger, given the circumstances," Selene replied.

"Works for me," Gail observed.

"It'll be like going to the funeral all over again," Selene noted grimly.

Bernie looked at the four quilters "I know I asked this before, but I'm asking it again on the chance that someone has remembered something new. Do any of you have anything you can tell me that would help uncover who killed Ellen?"

Selene shook her head. "Sorry."

"I don't have anything, either," Cecilia replied.

"Don't you think we would have told you already if we did?" Judy demanded.

"Yes, I do," Bernie told her. "But sometimes one forgets things, and then something jogs your memory, and you remember."

Gail didn't say anything.

"What about you?" Bernie asked her.

"Well, it's probably nothing," Gail said.

"We'd like to hear it, anyway," Libby told her.

"It really has nothing to do with Ellen," Gail told her.

"Why don't you let us be the judge," Libby said.

"All right," Gail said, and she began. "Okay, a couple of days after Ellen's funeral, someone broke into my house . . . well, maybe not broke in, exactly."

"How so?" Bernie asked, cocking her head.

Gail grimaced. "It was my fault."

"Tell us," Libby urged.

Gail sighed. "I had an early departmental faculty meeting, and I was in a hurry, so I forgot to close the garage door." She indicated the door to the garage with a nod of her head. "I never lock it. The door to the house was open when I came back. I guess someone just wandered in off the street."

"And you didn't think it was worth letting my sister and me know about that?" Bernie asked.

"Not really," Gail replied. "I didn't see the relevance."

Libby leaned forward. "So, what did the police say when you called?"

Gail looked confused. "About what?"

"About the break-in. When you reported it."

Gail frowned. "The person who answered the phone when I called nine-one-one wasn't very nice. She said it was my fault since I'd left the door open and created an attractive nuisance—"

Selene interrupted. "What the hell is an attractive nuisance?"

Libby explained. "That's when someone does something that tempts someone else to commit an illegal act. For example, let's say you stop and get gas and you leave the car running when you go inside to pay, and someone hops in and takes it for a ride. That's called an attractive nuisance, and if the police catch the person who stole the car, he or she is going to be facing a lower charge. Like a misdemeanor, instead of a felony."

"That happened to my cousin in Newark last year," Judy Fine volunteered. "The cops found his car two days later in Trenton."

Gail nodded and finished her story. "And since nothing was taken, the lady I spoke to said if I wanted to report the incident"—she bracketed the words *the incident* with finger quotes—"I should use their online system. They were too short staffed to come out and take the report in person." Gail shrugged. "I never bothered. I mean, what was the point? It's not like they were going to do anything, anyway."

"I wonder if whoever was in here was looking for Ellen's quilt," Libby mused.

"I don't know," Gail told her. "They took my old gym bag, but that was about it. Evidently, they didn't think my TV or computer was worth taking."

"That's the advantage of having old stuff," Selene told her. "No one wants it."

Gail laughed. "Talk about damning with faint praise."

Judy turned to Libby. "On another subject, I know we've been over this before, but you really think that Ellen was killed because she had something that someone else wanted?"

"That's the hypothesis we're still going on," Libby answered.

"Or thinks that she had," Bernie added.

Selene frowned, "I'm sorry, but I still don't see it. I can't imagine what it would be. Aside from everything else, Ellen was very frugal."

"Cheap," Judy said. "The word you want is *cheap*."

Selene nodded. "She definitely had issues. She never wanted to spend money on anything. And then there's the fact that Ellen was so . . . quiet, so risk averse, so deliberate in her actions. I can't imagine her getting mixed up in anything illegal."

"That's what everyone keeps saying," Libby observed as she brushed a strand of hair away from her face.

"Maybe there were compelling circumstances," Bernie suggested.

"I guess anything is possible," Judy Fine said, not sounding convinced. She shook her head. "You think you know someone. But you never really do, do you? Not really. Not deep down inside."

"If I've learned anything over the years, it's that people are complicated," Selene said.

For a moment everyone was quiet as they contemplated the human condition. Then they heard someone in the dining room ask someone else if they knew if there was any oat milk around.

Bernie snapped her fingers. "Damn," she said. "I knew I forgot to put something out."

"Don't worry," Gail said to Bernie. "My husband will be fine without it. He's a bit of a hypochondriac. You know, always worrying about his health."

"Aren't we all these days?" Libby said as she watched Bernie go over to the fridge, take out the container of oat milk she'd purchased earlier, and fill up a small pitcher with it. "What do you think, Bernie?"

Bernie startled. "Oh, definitely," she said.

"Definitely what?" Libby asked.

"What you said," Bernie answered.

Her sister's comment had caught her unaware. She'd been thinking about the quilting squares Ellen Fisher was going to make with her kindergarten class and about how sad it was that she'd never had the chance to do it.

Chapter 28

When Bernie, Libby, and the rest of the Sip and Sew crew walked into the dining room, Bernie counted ten people hovering around the table, helping themselves to the food she and Libby had set out earlier, while an eleventh person, a woman, was standing apart, studying Gail's saltwater fish tank.

"Lovely, isn't it?" Bernie said to her as she set the small pitcher of oat milk down on the table next to the regular milk.

The woman nodded. Looking at her, Bernie decided she was Cecilia's mirror opposite. She was wearing a beige dress that looked like a repurposed tent, bright pink sneakers, and thick support hose. While Cecilia was dressed like a nineteen-year-old, this woman was dressed like someone's eighty-year-old grandmother. "Who would think something this pretty could kill someone?" she remarked to Bernie.

"It was an accident, Alice," Gail snapped. "We've already gone through this."

"I never said it wasn't," Alice responded, turning to look at Gail. "I was just making an observation."

"Well, your tone says different," Gail told her.

"That's not true," Alice protested. "I was just admiring the corals. I didn't think that was a crime."

Gail swallowed. "How can you say something like that?" she cried, at which point Dwayne put his plate down on the far side of the table and walked over to his wife.

"Calm down," he said. "I think you're being a little oversensitive. Alice didn't mean anything. She was just admiring the fish tank."

"Who the hell do you think you are, telling me what to do?" Gail snapped. Then she turned and stalked out of the room.

A spot of color appeared on each of Dwayne's cheeks. Everyone watched as he followed his wife out the door.

Alice sighed. "Oh my. I didn't mean to start anything between those two."

"You haven't started anything that wasn't already happening," Selene assured her.

Libby's eyes widened. "Whoa. What was that all about?" she asked Selene.

Selene shook her head. "Sometimes being married is hard work," she replied. "Communication between people can be . . . difficult."

"Absolutely, Selene," Bernie agreed, "but I believe in this case my sister was talking about the fish tank."

"Oh that," Selene said. She made a clucking noise with her tongue. "So sad."

"But also kind of funny in an awful kind of way," Judy Fine added before Bernie could ask what was so sad.

"If you have a sick sense of humor," Alice said.

"Which I have to admit I do," Judy said.

"Well, I don't think it's funny," Cecilia declared. "For all practical purposes, Gail's brother's life is ruined. I mean, anyone could have made that mistake."

"What mistake?" Libby asked.

No one answered her question. Instead, they went on with what they'd been saying.

"He did know," Judy said.

"You don't know that," Selene objected.

"Yes, I do," Judy Fine answered. "Dwayne told me the owner of Fins and Tails warned Ed, so he knew what could happen, but Ed didn't tell Carl. In fact, he gave him the opposite advice. He told him to keep moving the corals."

Selene wrinkled her forehead. "Dwayne said that?"

"More or less," Judy Fine said.

"You know Dwayne has hated Ed ever since Ed sold him that Acura that caught on fire, don't you?" Selene asked Judy Fine.

"No, I didn't," Judy Fine admitted, "but that doesn't mean Dwayne isn't telling the truth."

Selene shook her head. "I gotta admit I'm lost here," she said.

"You're not the only one," Bernie observed as she straightened the basket the silverware was in and moved the bowl of fruit salad away from the edge of the table.

"That's not what Gail told me," Alice objected, ignoring Bernie's and Selene's comments.

Cecilia snorted. "Of course she's going to say that. Ed's her brother, for God's sake," Cecilia pointed out.

"Obviously, that's not what the DA believed," Judy told her. "Otherwise he wouldn't have charged him."

Libby held up her hand. "Stop." She looked from one woman to the other and back again. "I don't understand. What are you guys talking about? Explain."

A short woman with a headful of curly black hair spoke up. "It was in the newspaper. I'm surprised you didn't see it."

Bernie looked up. "I guess my sister and I must have missed it."

"It was about Gail's brother, Ed," the woman with the curly hair answered.

"That much I got," Bernie told her.

"He just was released from jail," Judy Fine told her.

Libby wrinkled her forehead. She hadn't seen the article, either. "What was he in for?"

"Manslaughter," another woman answered. She was tall and blond, with narrow shoulders and a wide bottom, which the outfit she was wearing—leggings and a short sweater—accentuated. "But that's because his lawyer plea-bargained it down from murder two."

Alice frowned. "Marcy, you make it sound as if Ed should have been convicted on the murder two charge. The prosecution agreed to manslaughter because the case was circumstantial. It was weak, and they knew it."

"How do you know that?" Marcy challenged.

"I have a friend in the DA's office," Alice replied.

"Okay, so maybe he's not guilty in this case, but there's all the other stuff he's done and gotten away with," Marcy asserted as she put a roast beef sandwich on her plate and added a ladleful of fruit salad.

"You don't know that," Diane said.

"Hey, I went to school with him," Marcy countered. "If there's ever been anyone who epitomized the term *bad seed*, he's it. He started dealing in the tenth grade, for heaven's sake. And he beat up Kenny T bad. The only reason he didn't go to juvie was because Kenny wouldn't testify."

Libby held up her hand. "Could someone explain what you're talking about?" she asked, raising her voice.

"It's simple," Cecilia said. She pointed to the saltwater tank. "You see the corals in there?"

Libby and Bernie both nodded.

Cecilia continued. "Some of them are toxic."

Bernie nodded. "I know." Her diving instructor had warned her about that when she'd been scuba diving off the reefs in Australia. "You can get a nasty infection if you get cut. That's why you need to be careful around them."

"Well, it's true you can get an infection," Cecilia informed her. "But"—here she raised a finger to emphasize the point—"I bet what you don't know is that certain kinds of coral can weaponize their venom."

Bernie blinked. "Excuse me?"

Cecilia laughed. "You heard me."

"I heard you," Bernie replied, "but I'm not quite sure what you meant."

"Simple," Cecilia said. "It means that if you piss the corals off, they can spray their toxin into the air and kill you."

"Seriously?" Libby asked.

"Yes, seriously," Cecilia replied. "They're called Zoantharia."

"I thought you were kidding," Bernie told her.

Cecilia shook her head. "I know. I thought that the first time one of the guys at the fish store told me."

"How do you piss them off?" asked a well-dressed Asian woman who had been hovering at the end of the dining-room table.

By now everyone in the room had stopped talking and eating and was following the conversation taking place.

"That's simple. You keep moving them around," Cecilia answered. "Evidently, some corals don't like being moved. Or touched, for that matter. If they get really annoyed, they can spray their toxins into the air and poison you. I know it's hard to believe, but it's true."

"So," Bernie said, "the moral of the story is be kind to your corals?"

"Exactly," Cecilia said.

"Definitely words to live by," Libby observed. "But I'm still not understanding why Gail got so upset."

Selene nodded. "It's complicated."

"It always is," Libby noted.

"According to Gail, her brother has always been difficult," Selene began.

Marcy rolled her eyes. "That's one way of putting it."

"Agreed he has issues," Selene replied.

Marcy snorted. "Issues? Is that what we're calling it these days? Enough with the PC stuff. He was suspended from school for punching a teacher in the face."

"People change," Selene told her.

"He didn't," Marcy retorted. "Like I said, he's bad news," she added. "Really bad news. Gail used to be afraid of him."

"She told you that?" Judy Fine demanded.

"Not in so many words, but she didn't have to," Marcy declared before taking a bite of her sandwich. "I could tell," she said after she'd swallowed.

"So, you were a mind reader back then?" Judy asked her.

"Ha. Ha, Judy. Very funny."

"Or gifted with infinite wisdom?"

"No, Judy, but I have two eyes. I could see what was happening when I used to go over there."

Selene coughed. The two women turned to her. "Are you guys telling the story, or am I?" Selene demanded.

"You are," Judy Fine said sheepishly.

"Then let me do it," Selene told her.

"Sorry," Marcy murmured.

Judy Fine lifted her hands up in a gesture of surrender. "That goes for me, too."

Selene looked from one woman to the other and back again. "Anybody have anything else to say before I continue?"

The two women shook their heads.

"Are you sure?"

The women nodded.

"Okay then," Selene replied, taking up where she'd left off. "The long and short of it is that three or four years ago, Gail's brother, Ed, gave this guy Carl some corals as a present. More to the point, he told Carl how to take care of them. Evidently, the information he gave Carl was wrong." Selene took a sip of water. "And now we come to the crux of the issue. The question is whether he knew what he was telling Carl was wrong or not, because his information led to Carl's death.

"According to Carl's sister, he and Gail's brother had had a bad fight over money Ed owed Carl. After the fight, Ed gave Carl the corals as a way of apologizing. At least that's what Ed told Carl, but Carl's sister maintains Ed killed her brother to get out of repaying him." Selene took another sip of water. "In any case, she called up the DA and lodged a complaint—or whatever you call what she did. Evidently, the DA found some merit in her claim, because he decided to prosecute Gail's brother on murder two, which is why he had him arrested."

Marcy couldn't help herself. "That's because the DA couldn't get him on all the other stuff he's done," she said.

Selene glared at her.

"Don't look at me like that," Marcy told her. "You know I'm right."

"Is she?" Bernie asked Selene when she didn't reply.

Selene sighed. She took another sip of water and carefully put the glass back on the table.

"Well?" Libby inquired.

"I know what the rumors say, but that doesn't mean it's true. People are only too happy to spread gossip and hearsay," Selene replied. "Or throw shade, as they like to say these days."

"What's the difference between gossip and hearsay?" Marcy asked.

"They're pretty much the same," Bernie said. "You can use one as a synonym for the other, except that *hearsay* has a legal meaning, as well."

"Yeah. Like bad person and psychopath," Marcy said.

Selene opened her mouth to reply, but Bernie beat her to it. "Moving along, when did Ed get out of jail?" she asked.

"About a week before Ellen Fisher died," Marcy answered. Her eyes widened slightly as she made the connection. "Why? Do you think he had anything to do with Ellen's death?"

"No," Bernie said as she and her sister exchanged looks.

"I don't see why he should have," Libby added, even though Gail's brother sounded like someone they should talk to. After all, their dad was always talking about casting a wide net and getting something surprising in it.

The sisters were still thinking about the conversations they'd heard when Selene White spoke. She'd just gotten a call from a former Sip and Sewer, Diane Englewood. "She told me she has something to tell you about Ellen Fisher," Selene informed Bernie and Libby. "She wants to arrange a meeting with you."

Bernie nodded.

Libby cocked her head. "Have we met the woman?" she asked.

Selene shook her head. "Diane used to be part of our quilting circle, but she hasn't been around for a while. She and Ellen got into an argument, and then she got carpal tunnel, and she stopped coming."

"You know what the argument was about?" Bernie asked.

"Yes," Selene replied. "It was about stitching."

"Stitching?" Bernie repeated. "Seriously?"

"Yes, seriously," Selene told her." I know it's ridiculous, but there it is."

"I'll call and set something up," Bernie said, reaching for her phone.

After a brief conversation, she and Diane agreed to meet at RJ's at eight thirty that evening.

Chapter 29

At eight o'clock Bernie and Libby closed up for the night. They sent Amber and Googie home, turned off the lights in the store, and locked up. Then they told their dad where they were going, got in Mathilda, and pulled out of A Taste of Heaven's parking lot. It had started sprinkling out, and the sisters watched the raindrops bounce off the pavement and create halos around the street-lights. Small wisps of fog were floating in off the Hudson as Bernie stopped at the bank, rolled down the window, and made the night deposit. She sniffed. The air smelled of damp earth and worms. By now, the rain had started coming down in sheets.

"Smells like spring," Bernie declared as she watched a stray cat run for cover under Mr. Porter's porch.

"And not a moment too soon," Libby said. Even though she denied it, this year the dark and the cold had gotten to her. "We should check the basement when we get back," Libby said, changing the subject. "Make sure the waterproofing worked."

Bernie nodded. Spring showers might bring May flowers, but in their case, it also brought a flooded basement.

And this wasn't a shower. This was more like a monsoon. Bernie drove slowly, avoiding the puddles forming in the road. The rain made it difficult to see in front of her. For a moment, she thought about pulling off to the side, but she was afraid someone would plow into her if she did, so she kept going.

After a few minutes the rain started to let up a little, and Bernie and her sister spent the rest of the drive talking business. They discussed raising prices, whether people would eat sautéed chicken with rhubarb sauce, how much they should charge for the new banana cream tarts they were introducing into the dessert rotation, and whether they should plant marigolds, geraniums, or impatiens in the window boxes this year. They'd just decided on New Zealand impatiens when they reached RJ's. Bernie studied the bar's parking lot as she turned into it. Most of the spots were taken, but then Libby pointed out a space three rows back from the door, and Bernie made for it, beating out a dark green Toyota in the process.

"RJ's looks crowded," Bernie remarked.

"Nice that their business is improving," Libby commented.

"Ready to make a run for it?" Bernie asked her.

Libby put up the hood on her windbreaker. "All I can say is I hope that this Diane Englewood has something useful to say," she griped. She wasn't happy. One, she hated getting wet. And two, she'd planned on spending the evening with Marvin.

"Me too," Bernie replied. She could hear a rumble of thunder off in the distance. A bolt of lightning illuminated the sky. "You ready?" she asked her sister again.

"I suppose," Libby said. "I hate getting wet," she groused.

"Me too," Bernie replied. Then she turned off Mathilda's engine, put the ignition key in her bag, opened the van door, stepped out, and ran for the bar door. Libby followed.

Bernie opened the door. A scream of laughter greeted the sisters as they stepped inside the bar. *The place is packed*, Bernie thought as she and Libby threaded their way through the crowd. A minute later she saw Brandon behind the bar, ringing up someone's tab, and made for him. Just before she and Libby reached him, he looked up, spotted them, and waved.

"A little damp out, is it?" Brandon commented as Bernie and Libby slid out of their windbreakers and bellied up to the bar. He had to raise his voice to be heard over the TV and the buzz of the crowd.

"Busy night," Bernie observed.

"It's definitely nutso," Brandon allowed. "Especially since Vince didn't show up. Again." Vince was the barback.

"Is anyone waiting for us?" Bernie asked.

Brandon pointed to the booth in the back where Selene White and Judy Fine were sitting. "They are."

Bernie and Libby exchanged glances. That was a surprise. Neither sister had expected them to be here.

"No one else?" Libby asked.

"Not that I know of," Brandon replied.

Libby was going to say something when there was a roar from the dart tournament going on in the back.

"The usual?" Brandon yelled over the noise.

Bernie and Libby both nodded.

"Right," he said. "One Scotch on the rocks and one Guinness coming up."

"How come it's so busy tonight?" Bernie asked Brandon while he took a bottle of Johnnie Walker off the shelf and began to pour.

"The bowling tournament is in town," Brandon explained.

"I didn't know we had anything like that here," Libby remarked as Brandon handed Bernie her Scotch and got to work on pouring Libby her Guinness. "Is it a thing?"

"It's most definitely a thing," Brandon told her. A moment later, he gave Libby her beer. "So, who are you guys expecting?"

Bernie answered. "Diane Englewood. Do you know her?"

Brandon wiped his hands on the towel he always had slung over his shoulder. "Does anyone ever really know anyone else?" he asked, pontificating.

Bernie laughed. "Fine. Leaving that philosophical question aside, what *do* you know about her?"

Brandon grinned. He thought for a minute as he scanned the crowd, looking to see if he was needed. Then he said, "Not very much. I know she used to come in once in a while and sit with the Sip and Sew crew, but I haven't seen her in, oh, maybe a year, a year and a half."

That fit in with what Selene had said, Bernie thought. "Anything else?" she inquired.

"Aside from the fact that she's cheap and never tips?"

"Yes," Libby said. "Aside from that."

"Well, I know she worked with Ellen Fisher over at the elementary school, that she hasn't been married, that she went to Europe, that she likes her chardonnay, and . . . I guess that's about it. Oh yes. She had this weird taste in clothes—like nothing ever matched. And now if you'll excuse me"—he gestured toward the crowd, which was two deep in some places—"my public awaits."

"Later," Bernie said, then blew Brandon a kiss before she picked up her drink and headed toward the back.

Libby did likewise, and she and her sister worked their way through the crowd to the booth where Selene and Judy were sitting. It was slightly quieter there, the back room having noise-absorbing acoustical tiles covering the ceiling. Selene looked up when Bernie and Libby sat down. She and Judy had been chuckling over a video they'd been watching on Selene's phone.

"I didn't expect to see you two here," Libby said as she slid in next to Judy Fine.

Judy shrugged. "What can I say? Selene and I felt like having a drink."

Bernie raised an eyebrow. "Really?"

"Really," Selene said. "I mean when Diane comes in, we'll leave. Although I must admit Judy and I are curious to hear what Diane has to say." Selene reached for a potato chip sitting in the bowl in front of her. "She sounded very mysterious when she spoke to me."

Judy took a sip of her dirty martini; then she said, "That's just Diane being Diane."

"What do you mean?" Bernie asked.

"She always exaggerates," Judy replied. "Like if she has a head cold, she'll tell you she has pneumonia."

Selene leaned forward. "So, she has a flair for the dramatic? What's wrong with that?"

Judy shrugged. "Nothing. If we were in the theater. I guess I'm getting old. Too much drama gets to me these days." Then she fished her olive out of her martini and popped it in to her mouth.

"You're saying she isn't reliable?" Libby asked.

"I wouldn't go that far," Selene said. "There's always some truth in what she says, right, Judy?"

"*Some* being the operative word," Judy said.

Libby took a sip of her Guinness and put her glass back down. "Anything would be helpful at this point in the game," Libby observed as she wondered why Selene and Judy were here. Maybe Selene was telling the truth. Or maybe not. At this point, it was hard to know.

While Libby tried to decide, Selene ran a finger around

the rim of her glass. She gave a wry chuckle. "I never thought I'd say this, but I kinda miss Diane."

"Me too," Judy added.

Selene took a gulp of her wine. "Diane knows a lot about quilting," Selene went on. "It was fun talking about it with her."

"What else did you guys talk about?" Libby asked.

"Not politics," Judy said.

"Sewing stuff," Selene replied.

"Anything else?" Bernie inquired.

"Quilting," Judy answered.

"Besides quilting?" Bernie asked.

Selene thought for a minute. "Not really," she replied. Then she said, "You look like you don't believe me, Bernie."

"It's not that," Bernie said. "I just have trouble imagining talking about quilting for all that time."

Judy laughed. "There's more to talk about than you think. There's the history of quilting, quilting techniques, fabric, patterns, to name just a few topics."

"This is a big time for quilting," Selene added. "It's having a moment, as the commentators like to say."

"It's turning into an art form," Judy added.

"Not that it wasn't before," Selene objected.

"Not in the same way," Judy said. "Before you had patterns that people followed. Now things are more free form. More creative."

"I'm sorry," Selene said, "but they were creative back then. Sometimes quilts were the only outlet women had."

"But they weren't free form," Judy said. "There is a difference."

"What is the definition of *a quilt*, anyway?" Bernie asked, intervening before things could become heated.

"I guess," Judy said after taking a minute to think about it, "a quilt is basically two pieces of material with something stitched between them."

Selene nodded. "Like we said the other day, people have stitched lots of things between the two layers—paper, fabric, just to name a few. I mean, the ancient Egyptians made quilts. In the Middle Ages, they wore quilted jackets beneath their armor."

Judy leaned forward. "Do you know that it's rumored that Picasso sewed some quilts?"

"I don't believe that for a minute," Selene responded.

"I read it," Judy insisted.

"On the Internet?" Selene responded.

"No," Judy said. And she mentioned a famous art critic.

"If you're referring to the article he wrote last year, I read that, too, and that's not what he said," Selene replied.

"It certainly is," Judy countered.

Then the two women looked at each other and started to laugh.

"You can see we're rather passionate about quilting and anything concerning it," Selene said.

"Most people aren't," Judy said, "so when we get together, that's pretty much all we talk about."

Libby smiled. "I can see that."

"For example," Selene continued, "right now, hand stitching is popular. Especially using a technique called *sashiko*. Visible mending. It's from Japan."

"I don't think I know what that is," Bernie confessed.

"Sure you do," Judy said. "That's what Ellen used on her quilt."

Bernie tried to remember but couldn't.

"It looks like this," Selene said, and she whipped out her phone to show her. "See?" she said, pointing to a line on the quilt she'd made. "Note how thick the thread is. It's matte cotton, with a tight twist. That means the thread can't be separated into separate strands like embroidery floss can be." She stopped. "Sorry. I get carried away."

"No problem," Bernie said. She glanced at her watch. It

was eight thirty. They'd been ten minutes late, and it had been twenty minutes since they'd arrived. "I wonder where Diane is," she mused, changing the subject.

Selene shook her head. "Weird. She's always on time."

Judy corrected her. "Actually, she's always early."

"The driving wasn't great out there when we came in," Bernie observed. "Maybe she got held up."

Judy frowned. "I hope nothing's happened. This isn't like her."

"Me too." Selene reached for her phone. "I'll call and find out."

Diane didn't answer.

"Let me try," Bernie said. But she got the same result. "I guess she's a no-show," Bernie said after half an hour, two phone calls, and three texts. She looked at the clock on the wall. It was nine thirty. Diane was officially an hour late. Time to go home. Especially since Brandon was too busy to hang out with.

Chapter 30

"Iknew this was going to be a waste of time," Libby complained to her sister on the way home.

Bernie didn't reply. She was too busy concentrating on the road. The rain and the wind had tapered off, leaving downed tree branches, rivers of water, and blocked storm drains in their wake. First, Bernie tried Meadowbrook, but there was an oak tree branch lying across the road, and Hurlbut looked flooded, so Bernie decided to take Hudson Avenue instead. Hopefully, it was clear. As it turned out, it wasn't.

She'd gone about two blocks when she saw flashing red lights up ahead. "I should have taken Warren instead," she muttered to herself. She could see two police cars, a fire truck, a tow truck, and an ambulance parked along the side of the road, their flashing red lights beacons in the darkness. A policeman dressed in a bright green neon raincoat was standing in the middle of the road, directing traffic. When Bernie got closer, she recognized him. It was Mike Winton. He was a regular at the shop, coming in at least once a week and sometimes twice, usually on Tuesdays and Thursdays, to buy a cinnamon bun, a toasted corn muffin with peanut butter, and a large coffee, black, with one sugar.

She rolled down her window as she got closer to him. "Hey, Mike. What's going on?"

"It's Officer Winton to you."

"And you can call me Miss Simmons," Bernie replied.

He laughed and shook his head. Then he said, "There was a bad accident. The driver went off the road and into the ditch." He pointed to the drainage ditch on the right-hand side of the road. It was overflowing with water. It took Bernie a moment, but after a second glance, she could see the rear of a vehicle sticking out of water.

"Did whoever was in there make it?" Bernie asked. She had a bad feeling growing in the pit of her stomach.

"Unfortunately, no," Mike Winton said. "She was gone when the EMTs got here. DOA. Nothing anyone could do."

"Do you know her name?" Libby asked. She had the same feeling in the pit of her stomach that Bernie had.

"Yeah. Diane Englewood." He looked from Bernie to Libby. "Why?" he asked after reading the expressions on Bernie's and Libby's faces. "You know her?"

Libby and Bernie nodded together.

"We were supposed to meet her at RJ's, but she never showed," Libby replied.

Mike Winton clicked his tongue against his teeth. "Well, I hope she's going to be having that drink in that big bar in the sky instead."

Bernie felt a chill moving down her spine. "Me too. So, what happened?"

"My best guess?" Mike Winton asked.

Bernie and Libby both nodded again.

"I'd say it looks as if she was going too fast and she slid off the road and went headfirst into the ditch. This is a bad curve," Winton said. "Too sharp. They ought to have caution signs posted here. We've had two accidents at this spot already this month. And with the rain making the roads slick and the poor visibility . . . well . . ." He put his hands, palms up, out in front of him, and his voice trailed off.

"She couldn't get out of the car?" Bernie asked.

"Unfortunately, she wasn't able to. She probably hit her head on the steering wheel and blacked out. At least that's what the EMTs think," Winton explained after seeing the expressions on Bernie's and Libby's faces. "Plus, the front doors jammed, so she couldn't have gotten out, anyway, even if she had been conscious. The EMTs needed to get the fire engine guys here with their Jaws of Life to get her out." He shook his head. "Really bad luck. From now on, I'm going to have one those escape gadgets in my vehicle, like the ones they advertise on TV. You know, the things that you can use to break the windshield with."

"We should have one, too," Bernie said. Of course, she'd been saying that for the past four years.

"How'd you find her?" Libby asked. There weren't a lot of streetlights on Beechwood plus the road wasn't very well traveled, two facts that made Libby wonder how someone had spotted Diane Englewood's vehicle in the first place. Libby knew she wouldn't have seen it if she had been driving by at this time of night.

"We got an anonymous call," Mike Winton replied. "Then, about five minute later"—Winton pointed to a man standing off to the side, talking to an EMT—"he called it in. Said he saw a car in the ditch. I guess he tried to get the door open, but he couldn't. Like I said, it was jammed."

Libby stifled a sneeze. She hoped she wasn't getting sick.

"What time were you supposed to meet her?" Winton asked.

"At eight thirty," Libby replied.

"The first call came in at eight twenty-five," Mike Winton told them as he and the sisters watched the tow truck back up toward the ditch. When it was as close as it could get, the truck stopped, and two men got out.

Libby, Bernie, and Mike Winton watched one of the men put on high rubber boots, wade into the water, and attach the winch to the bumper of Diane Englewood's vehicle. When he was done, he raised his arm, signaling to the other man, who nodded and started the winch. There was a groan and a creak as it began pulling the car out of the water. A few minutes later, the Kia was on land, water streaming out of the shattered windows.

"Do you think we could take a look inside the vehicle?" Bernie asked.

"Because?" Mike Winton answered.

"Er. Because Diane Englewood was bringing back my raincoat," Bernie lied. "It's my favorite."

Mike Winton raised an eyebrow. "Really?"

"Yes, really," Bernie told him.

"Surely, you can do better than that," Mike Winton told her.

"Not on short notice," Bernie replied. She put on her most charming smile. "So, what do you say?"

Mike Winton checked around him. No one was watching. "You're lucky that I like your cinnamon buns, no double entendre intended. You have two minutes," he told her as he signaled the tow truck driver to stop winching the Kia up.

"I owe you," Bernie said as she put Mathilda into park. She and Libby hopped out, hurried over to Diane Englewood's vehicle, and looked inside.

The inside of the SUV had a layer of mud coating the floor and the seats, and the airbag on the driver's side looked like a large puffball mushroom. A discarded coffee cup lay on the passenger side seat, along with a water bottle and a bag of gingersnap cookies, while the back had a bag of potting soil, a trowel, and a box of tulip bulbs lying on the floor.

"Anything of interest?" Mike Winton asked, popping up behind Libby and Bernie.

Bernie straightened up. "It appears not," she replied.

"And now it's time for you to go," Mike Winton said. He could see his supervisor approaching from the other direction.

Bernie nodded. She and Libby thanked him, got back into Mathilda, and then Bernie put her in gear and drove off. On the way home, Libby called Judy and Selene and filled them in on what had happened to Diane. They both sounded extremely upset.

"Of course, they would," Libby commented afterward, leaning back in her seat and closing her eyes. She'd been tired before, and this had just made her more so. "I mean, who wouldn't be upset given the circumstances?"

"Not that that necessarily means anything," Bernie countered.

"Are you saying what I think you're saying?" Libby asked her.

"That Diane Englewood's death is quite the coincidence?" Bernie replied. "That she might have had help going off the road?"

Libby nodded. "Yes. That."

"On the other hand," Bernie continued, "the roads were bad, and visibility was pretty much at zero, and that curve is hazardous." Bernie had almost gone off the road there herself last year. "Maybe Diane was going fast because she was late to our meeting, and she slid, left the road, and went headfirst into the ditch."

"Is that what you think happened, Bernie? Are you say-ing we were responsible?"

Bernie sighed. "I know that we're not, but it feels as if we are."

"Yes, it does," Libby agreed as Bernie stopped for a light. Then she thought about what her sister had just said and their meeting, and another idea occurred to her. "I wonder what time Selene and Judy got to RJ's."

Bernie nodded. "I've been wondering the same thing. Why don't you call Brandon and ask him if he remembers when those two came in."

Libby did. The answer was three-quarters of an hour before she and Bernie arrived.

"Which would have given them plenty of time to run Diane Englewood off the road and still get to RJ's before we did," Bernie mused.

"True, Bernie, but if they did that, why show up at all?" Libby countered.

"For one thing, it gives them an alibi," Bernie said.

"Well, at the very least, it gives them plausible deniabil-ity," Sean said after his daughters filled him in on what had happened when they arrived home twenty minutes later. He took another bite of the leftover chocolate mocha cake Bernie had brought upstairs with her.

"I suppose it does," Libby said before taking a sip of tea. She needed to warm up. "You really think Judy and Selene could have done something like this?"

"Do you?" Sean challenged before he licked a smidgen of frosting off his fork.

Libby thought for a minute. Then she said, "Honestly, not really. We're talking teachers here. Women whose idea of fun is getting together and sewing."

"Yet two people in their sewing circle have died, and a

third member of the group thinks at least one of those deaths is suspicious," Sean said. "And now we have a second death, of someone who was about to tell you something about the first death."

Libby took a bite of cake. God, she reflected, she needed chocolate in the worst possible way. This whole thing was shaking her up more than she wanted to admit. "I guess I'm just having trouble reconciling what they are with what they could have done."

"Well, you know what they say," Sean intoned as Cindy the cat jumped off the windowsill and onto Bernie's lap. "Looks can be deceiving."

Bernie scratched Cindy under the chin. "Indeed, they can." She'd learned that lesson the hard way with her last boyfriend.

"What's the motive, then?" Libby challenged.

"That's easy," Sean told her. "Three possibilities or variations on them." And he ticked them off on his fingers. "The classics. Money, love, and/or revenge."

Bernie leaned forward slightly. She'd just remembered something she'd overheard this afternoon at Gail Gibson's house. "Maybe whoever did this had some help."

Sean raised an eyebrow. "What kind of help?"

Bernie told him.

"That's a really big stretch," Sean replied.

"I know," Bernie agreed. "But it makes more sense. Gail's brother is certainly a better candidate. Much more physically capable."

"What's his motive?" Sean challenged.

"I don't know," Bernie told him. "That's why we need to check him out."

"Really?" Sean said as he got up to cut himself another sliver of cake. He knew what was coming next.

"Yes, really," Bernie said.

"I suppose you want me to get you his address?" Sean asked when he sat back down.

"Please, Dad," Libby said.

"We could get it ourselves," Bernie told him. "But it'll take more time."

"And considering Diane Englewood's death, the sooner we get a handle on things, the better," Libby pointed out.

Sean sighed. What his daughter had said was true. "Fine," he said.

Bernie hugged him. "Thank you, Dad. I love you."

"That goes double for me," Libby told him.

Sean looked at his daughters and laughed. They definitely had his number.

Chapter 31

The next two days were filled with phone calls and visits from the Sip and Sew crew. At the end of three days, the consensus was that Diane Englewood's death was an accident. The members of the sewing circle believed it, and the police believed it, but Bernie and Libby weren't so sure, even though they had nothing more to go on but a feeling in their gut. In the meantime, Sean had reached out to Clyde and done what his daughters had asked him to do, but now he was sorry that he had. Not that it mattered.

If he hadn't gotten Ed Gibson's address, his daughters would have accused him of being overprotective and not trusting their judgment. Of course, he was overprotective, and he didn't trust their judgment, but that was beside the point. The point was that Ed Gibson was a bad actor. According to Clyde, this guy had done several actionable things, but no charges they'd been able to make stick until now. And even the coral thing was questionable. That was why the DA had pled the case down to manslaughter.

"The guy is like the Teflon Don," Clyde had complained to Sean. "Everything he does slides off him."

"The Teflon Don. Now that's an expression I haven't heard in a while," Sean had remarked.

Clyde chuckled. "You're getting to be an old man. Next, you're going to be talking about how you walked three miles to school every day. Uphill. In a blizzard."

"Actually, it was six blocks. And if I'm old, what are you?" Sean replied.

"Ten years younger," Clyde promptly answered.

Sean smiled, remembering Clyde's comment; then he frowned and rubbed his knee while he thought about the details Clyde had laid out concerning Gail's brother. If what Clyde had said was true, and Sean had no reason to think it wasn't, the brother was definitely bad news, and Sean would be happier if his daughters stayed away from him. Unfortunately, they were no longer little girls, and he couldn't tell them what to do, not that they had listened to him, anyway, even when they were young. The truth was they'd always had him twisted around their little chubby fingers.

"Just be careful," Sean had warned his daughters, thinking about everything that could go wrong.

"Aren't we always?" Bernie had asked him as she glanced through the morning mail. Bills, bills, and more bills. The joys of running a business.

Sean had snorted. "Are you kidding me! If there was a wall with a sign that read KEEP OFF, you'd be on it in two seconds."

"You're exaggerating, Dad," Bernie said.

"Not by much," Libby commented.

"Hey, whose side are you on, anyway?" Bernie demanded.

"His," Libby promptly replied.

Sean smiled as he remembered that. It was a little after ten, and Sean watched the morning sun shining in through the front window of A Taste of Heaven, its beams dancing on the black-and-white linoleum tile floor, while Dolly Parton played in the background. The morning's commuter rush was over, and the lunch rush hadn't yet begun.

The shop was largely empty. Sean noted the three women sitting at the table by the window, nibbling on slices of cinnamon toast, sipping coffee, and quietly chatting, while a twentysomething guy sat at the table near the wall, typing away on his laptop and eating a piece of apple pie. Meanwhile, Amber was counting out the change in the cash register, and Googie was stacking take-out boxes in preparation for the noontime rush.

"Don't worry, Dad. We'll be careful," Libby assured him as she handed him a freshly baked chocolate chip cookie. She'd taken them out of the oven fifteen minutes ago.

Sean thanked her and promptly devoured it. "Nice," he said after he was done and had brushed the crumbs off his hands. "Salted roasted cashews instead of walnuts?"

Libby nodded. "For a change. What do you think?"

"Good choice," Sean told her. "I like it." Then he nodded toward the white bakery box on the counter that Libby was filling up with the same chocolate chip cookies he had just tried. "Are those for Ed Gibson?"

Bernie nodded. They'd packed a small box of the freshly baked cookies to give to Gail's brother. Their mother, Rose, had told them never to underestimate the power of a well-made chocolate chip cookie, and over the years Libby and Bernie had found their mom to be correct in her assessment. It was amazing how a baked treat could loosen people's tongues.

"Your mother would be appalled," Sean commented. Which was true. She'd disapproved of her daughters' interest in anything criminal.

"But she'd be happy we're using her recipe," Bernie told him.

"I suppose she would be," Sean conceded. Then he got back to the subject at hand. "Listen," he said, "don't go anywhere with Ed Gibson."

"We won't, Dad," Bernie assured him.

"I'm serious, Bernie."

"I know, Dad. Where would we go, anyway?"

"Anywhere. Also, don't take anything from him," Sean warned.

"Like what?" Libby asked.

Sean shrugged. "Like something to eat or drink."

"You think he's going to drug us?" Libby asked.

Sean thought back to Tiffany Well's complaint about Gibson putting roofies in her drink, but Tiffany was a well-known grifter, so the story could be true. Or not. Which was why he had decided not to say anything. "Just watch your back."

Libby and Bernie nodded. "We will."

Sean scratched his cheek. He needed to shave. "Maybe you should rethink talking to him."

"We already discussed this," Bernie told him. "Ed Gibson might know something."

"Or not," Sean said. "You're on what we used to call a fishing expedition in the old days," Sean said.

"What's wrong with that? Fishing is good," Bernie told him. "If it wasn't, you wouldn't always be trying to get me and Libby to go with you."

"Ha ha, Bernie. Very funny. I'm not talking about fishing for marlin."

Bernie grinned. "I know. But this guy is the only lead we have so far."

"What is it you always say about casting a wide net?" Libby reminded him.

"I know what I say, Libby," Sean told her. He hated when his daughters used his words against him. "Enough with the fish analogies."

"Seriously, Dad." Bernie pointed to herself. "I have this feeling in my gut about him, and you always say—"

Sean cut her off. Being quoted twice in a row was a little much. "I know, I know," Sean told her. "I always say, 'Go with your gut.' "

Bernie beamed. "Exactly."

Sean sighed. He knew when he'd lost.

"And you'll make the calls," Libby asked as she, Bernie, and her dad walked out of the store and headed to A Taste of Heaven's parking lot.

Sean nodded as he took a deep breath. Another month and the lilacs would be in bloom. He could hardly wait. The older he got, the longer the winters seemed.

"I said I will," Sean told Libby. "But I'm not promising anything. Most of my contacts in the Bureau have retired and moved to Florida or are in the big nursing home in the sky."

"Dad," Bernie exclaimed.

"It's true," Sean told her.

"We're just asking you to try," Libby said, waving to a neighbor walking across the street, then stooping down to pick up a candy wrapper someone had dropped on the sidewalk.

Sean took the wrapper from Libby, walked over, and deposited it in the trash can. Both she and Bernie had asked him to see if he could find out Ellen Fisher's particulars. According to what they'd learned or, more precisely, hadn't learned, Marvin was correct. Ellen Fisher had no living relatives, a sad but not particularly remarkable fact.

What was unusual was that apparently, Ellen Fisher had

had no presence on social media until fifteen years ago. She'd apparently gotten her teaching job at Longely Elementary, bought a house, and started quilting all in one year. None of the people-tracing sites his daughters had searched on their computers had come up with anything about her before then.

Sean figured that could mean nothing—maybe his daughters had gotten Ellen Fisher's name or DOB wrong, although that was unlikely. So, had Ellen Fisher been put in some sort of witness protection program? Had she forged a new identity on her own? If so, whom was she hiding from? What had she done? Was that the reason she'd been killed? Sean guessed it was time to see if his remaining contacts—contact—was up to digging to find out who Ellen Fisher really was. Of course, there could be other explanations, as well.

For example—and Sean knew this was a stretch—Ellen Fisher could have been born into a missionary family in someplace like Zambia or Nepal and been homeschooled, could have worked over there, and could have only recently arrived in this country—but Sean doubted it. The odds for that scenario were unlikely. Not impossible, but highly unlikely.

No. Ellen Fisher had been hiding something. He was convinced of that. But what? On the other hand, his wife had always told him that one of the results of his days in law enforcement was a tendency always to believe the worst about people. And maybe that was true. He was thinking about that when Libby and Bernie kissed him on either cheek and said good-bye.

Sean gave his daughters his standard "Be careful out there" send-off as they hopped in the van.

"We will," Libby assured him as they pulled out of A Taste of Heaven's parking lot.

A moment later, Sean turned and went back into the shop to get a slice of coffee cake and a copy of the local paper to bring upstairs. If he'd stayed outside a little longer, he would have seen a silver SUV pulling out from the curb after A Taste of Heaven's van had gone by it.

Chapter 32

Bernie spotted the silver SUV a couple of minutes after she and Libby had revisited the site of Diane Englewood's accident. She'd decided to stop there since it was on the way to where they were going. No harm in taking a second gander at the scene, she'd reasoned. Maybe they'd missed something. But it turned out they hadn't. Or if there was something there, they hadn't found it.

"What are we looking for, anyway?" Libby had asked.

Bernie had shaken her head as she studied the skid marks indicating the trajectory of Diane Englewood's vehicle when it left the road.

"I don't know," Bernie had admitted as she studied the tire tracks around the ditch. They crisscrossed each other, most of them made, Bernie had guessed, by the tow truck and the emergency vehicles. The water in the ditch had receded by now, but it was still deep. She'd stared into the murky depths, willing an answer to appear, but nothing had.

After a couple of minutes, she'd conceded defeat, returned to the van, and headed out. Five minutes after she'd turned onto Delton Avenue, she caught sight of the silver SUV; then she saw it again after she made a right on Ferris.

"I think someone may be following us," she remarked.

"Why would anyone do that?" Libby asked.

"Because they can't resist my red hair and exuberant personality, obviously," Bernie wisecracked.

"Obviously. Never mind that you don't have, either," Libby informed her.

Bernie took one of her hands off Mathilda's steering wheel and laid it over her heart. "I'm hurt. How can you say that?"

"Easy. Because it's true."

"My hair was red."

"Notice the tense. And, if we're being technical, it was bright orange, and now it's brown."

Bernie corrected her. "Auburn, with expensive blond streaks."

Libby allowed as how this was true. "Fine. But you still haven't answered my question."

"About the car?"

"No, about the bear. Yes, about the car."

"You're a little grumpy today," Bernie observed as she reached up and adjusted the rearview mirror to give her a better look at the SUV behind them.

"So are you," Libby pointed out.

"No, I'm not grumpy. I'm just trying to tell you what I'm seeing. No need to bite my head off." She indicated the rearview mirror with a nod of her head. "See the silver SUV? The Toyota?"

"Yes," Libby told her. At this point, it was three cars down from Mathilda.

"Well," Bernie continued, "it's been with us since we left the accident scene. In fact, I think the driver was parked across the street in front of Mrs. Taylor's place and pulled out right after we did."

Libby shrugged. "It could be a coincidence."

"According to Dad, there's no such thing."

"I wouldn't go that far," Libby told her.

"I'm not so sure," Bernie replied. "At least not in this case."

Libby took a sip of coffee and made a face.

"Don't like it?" Bernie asked her. They were trying out a new blend.

"It's a little acidic for my taste," Libby replied. "Not that I'm not going to drink it, anyway." She changed the subject back to what they'd been talking about. "You know," she continued, "the guy in the SUV could be heading to the mall or to the grocery store, for all we know."

"He could be," Bernie agreed, "but the way he's driving—hanging back, then speeding up to get the light at the last minute, then speeding up to keep us within sight—says . . ."

"He's a lousy driver?" Libby asked.

"No. It says he doesn't want us to notice him."

"Well, if that's the case, he's certainly not doing a very good job," Libby replied as she turned around to get a better look at the SUV and its driver.

"Don't do that," Bernie told her. "Use the mirror instead."

"Why not?" Libby asked as she turned back around.

"Why do you think? Because I don't want him to know that we've spotted him."

Libby rolled her eyes. "What difference will it make?"

"I'd rather have the element of surprise on my side."

"Why do you need it? What are you planning to do?"

"I haven't decided yet," Bernie told her.

"You know what I think, Bernie? I think what happened to Diane Englewood spooked you."

"Hardly, Libby," Bernie said, even though it had. She couldn't stop thinking about how it was a lousy way to die.

Libby studied the Toyota from the side-view mirror. "I don't know. The SUV looks as if it's driving normally to me."

"Well, it doesn't to me," Bernie said as she abruptly changed lanes to see what the silver SUV would do. It stayed where it was. Then, two minutes later, it switched lanes, as well.

Libby shook her head. "I gotta say I think you're getting like Dad—paranoid in your old age."

Bernie smiled. "He's usually correct in his assessments."

"Not all the time."

"But most of it. Wanna bet I'm right?"

"Sure, Bernie. A dollar?"

"Okay."

"How about two?" Libby suggested.

"Living dangerously, I see," Bernie observed.

Libby laughed and took another sip of coffee. "Wouldn't have it any other way."

"You're on," Bernie told her. She and her sister shook hands. "Let's see what we can see, shall we?" Bernie said.

"Yes, let's," Libby said.

Five minutes later, Bernie turned off Harrington and made a left onto Clarington. She checked her rearview mirror. The SUV was still with them. Bernie continued along Clarington. For a moment, she thought she'd lost the SUV at the corner of Fremont, where the house had burned down last month, but then she saw the SUV making the same turn she had.

"He's still on our tail," she observed. "Are you convinced now?"

"A little more so," Libby reluctantly allowed.

"A little more so?" Bernie repeated.

"Fine," Libby grumped. "A lot more so."

"Say it, Libby," Bernie instructed.

"Say what?" Libby asked.

"You know," Bernie told her.

Libby scowled. She hated being wrong. Especially when it came to her sister. "Fine. You're right. Satisfied?"

Bernie grinned. "Yes, I am. Oh, and by the way, don't try to pay me in pennies," Bernie told Libby.

"Who said I was going to pay you in pennies?" Libby protested.

"That's what you tried to do the last time," Bernie reminded her before she checked on the SUV again. Still there, unfortunately.

She squinted as she tried to read the license plate on the SUV. But all she could tell was that the license plate was from New York State. The SUV was too far back now to read, and to make matters worse, the front plate was streaked with dirt. Coincidence? Again, Bernie didn't think so. At least, not unless the driver had been driving through a swamp. No, Bernie was pretty sure the driver had wiped mud on the license on purpose. *Not good*, she thought as she slowed down, trying to get a better look. But she couldn't, because the SUV dropped back another car length.

"Can you read the plate?" she asked Libby.

"I think I see a *B*," Libby replied after she'd studied it for a minute. "Although it could be a *P*. Or maybe even an eight."

"Which is it?" Bernie demanded.

"Sorry," Libby said after another minute of looking, "but I can't tell."

"Thanks anyway," Bernie said. When she reached Longely High School, she sped up. Three minutes later, she took a sharp left into Buckland Park, throwing Libby against Mathilda's door in the process.

"Hey, watch it," Libby cried as some of the coffee she'd

been drinking sloshed out of her cup and onto her jeans. She grabbed a paper towel and blotted up the liquid on her left thigh as well as she was able to.

"Sorry," Bernie said, going as fast as possible down the narrow road, which led past the old farmhouse the park had been named for.

"This isn't good for Mathilda's shocks," Bernie noted as the van jounced along.

"It isn't good for me, either," Libby replied after she hit her head on Mathilda's ceiling.

"Yeah, I'd be worried about killing off my brain cells, too, if I were you," Bernie told her.

"At least I have some," Libby retorted as Bernie went another couple of feet.

Then she pulled off the road, drove across the grass to a grove of pine trees, and maneuvered between the trees. As she killed the engine and peered out the window, she smiled as the aroma of the pine trees washed over her. She didn't see anything except two squirrels chasing each other around a fallen branch, while a cardinal sang in the tree overhead.

Chapter 33

"I think I lost him," Bernie said after a couple of minutes had gone by and no car had appeared. She held out her hand. "I'll take my money now, if you don't mind."

"And if I do mind?" Libby asked just because she could.

"I was being rhetorical, Libby."

"I know you were, Bernie."

"Then why did you say that?" Bernie asked.

Libby shrugged. "Why not say it?"

"I think we've gone about as far as we can go with this conversation," Bernie told her.

"Fine," Libby replied, because she couldn't think of anything else to say. She was reaching for her wallet when she had another idea. "What do you say to double or nothing?"

"Double or nothing on what?" Bernie asked.

Libby told her. "Well, you think we lost this guy, right?"

"Correct," Bernie said.

"And I don't think we did."

"Talk about flip-flopping."

"Ready to put your money where your mouth is, Bernie?"

"Absolutely." Bernie checked the time on her phone.

"According to this, we've been sitting here for six minutes now. We would have seen him drive by if he was still looking for us. My guess is that he's given up and gone home."

Libby finished the rest of her coffee and threw the cup in the trash bag on the floor. "Maybe yes. Maybe no. Whoever is driving could have slowed down, stopped to get gas."

Bernie snorted. "Maybe he stopped to get a latte while he was at it."

"No need for sarcasm," Libby told her sister.

"I just hate to see you waste your money, is all," Bernie replied.

"That's so considerate."

"I like to think so," Bernie said. "So how long do you want to give him?" she asked.

"To show up?"

Bernie nodded.

Libby thought for a moment. Then she said, "Fifteen minutes. After that . . ."

"I win," Bernie said.

"So, we have ourselves a deal?" Libby asked.

"We have ourselves a deal," Bernie agreed, and they shook hands on it.

"I can hardly wait to see who this person is," Libby said as the sisters sat back and waited.

Bernie decided it was pleasant in the grove as she smelled the air and listened to the soothing sounds of the mourning doves cooing and the wind rustling the branches of the pine trees. She leaned back and rested her head against the seat. Her eyes had begun to close—she hadn't realized how tired she was—when Libby poked her in the ribs with her elbow.

"Hey," Bernie yelped, rubbing her side as she sat up. "That hurt."

Libby apologized. "But do you hear that?" she asked Bernie.

Bernie shook her head. "Hear what?"

"That. Listen," Libby instructed.

At first, Bernie didn't hear anything, and then she did. It was the sound of tires on dirt and gravel as a vehicle approached.

"See, I told you," Libby said to her sister.

"It could be a different car," Bernie replied, but a moment later the SUV that had been following them came into sight. The driver was driving very slowly while he looked from one side of the road to the other, trying to spot Mathilda.

"And she's right, folks," Libby crowed as she watched the silver SUV drive by them. She beamed. "Give the girl a pat on the back," she said, referring to herself. Then she turned to Bernie. "I'll take my four dollars, if you don't mind."

Bernie corrected her. "Two dollars."

Libby shrugged. "Can't blame a girl for trying." She watched Bernie take out her wallet. "Now what?" she asked after Bernie had slapped two one-dollar bills into her waiting hand.

"Now we find out who this guy is and what he wants," Bernie responded.

"I have an idea," Libby said.

Bernie put her hands on her chest. "Be still, my heart."

"Do you, by any chance, happen to have that package of AirTags you purchased?" Libby asked, ignoring her sister's sarcasm.

"As a matter of fact, I do." Bernie had bought a couple several weeks ago, thinking that she'd attach one to their cat's collar, but as usual, she hadn't gotten around to doing it yet. "The box is still in my bag."

"Sometimes procrastination is a good thing," Libby said.

A grin spread over Bernie's face. "Are you thinking what I think you're thinking?" she asked her sister.

Libby nodded. "I'm pretty sure I am." She started nibbling on one of her fingernails, realized what she was doing, and stopped. "I just hope this bozo hasn't left the park yet."

"Me too," Bernie replied, although that was certainly a possibility.

The road that went through this part of the park was only four miles long and hilly, Bernie remembered. At the pace the driver had been going, she reckoned there was a good chance they would catch up with the SUV before it left Buckland. On the other hand, if he'd sped up, he would be gone. The other entrance to the park, the one he was heading toward, had three roads adjoining it, each of which would take him in a different direction. At that point, all bets were off as to where he was going.

"Let's find out, shall we?" Libby said.

Bernie took a deep breath and let it out. "Okay, then. Here goes nothing," she said as she started Mathilda up and very carefully and slowly guided her back down the hill. The van was top-heavy, and the last thing Bernie wanted was for Mathilda to roll over.

A few minutes later, both Bernie and Libby spotted the SUV. It was parked twenty feet away from one of the park's exit signs, butted up against the far wall of the amphitheater, where they put on Shakespeare productions in the summer. The SUV was empty, the engine turned off, but after a moment both Libby and Bernie saw the driver leaning up against the trunk of a large oak tree, talking on the phone and smoking a cigarette.

Libby pointed. "Remember the cigarette butts we found in back of Ellen Fisher's house?"

Bernie nodded. "I think we may have found our guy," she said as she studied him.

He was medium height, medium build, slightly balding, with brown eyes, brown hair, and a slight receding chin. He had on a heavy windbreaker, a dark green sweater, a pair of gray slacks, and a black Buffalo Bills' baseball cap. Looking at him, Bernie reflected that there was nothing about him that would make him stand out in the crowd. He was the kind of person who was instantly forgettable, someone whose face didn't register, a definite advantage in certain professions, she decided.

"How do you want to play this?" Libby asked Bernie. The way she figured it, there were two options: confront this guy or surprise him. The problem with the second option was that there wasn't a good place to put the van so they could sneak up on him. This area of the park consisted of grassy lawn with an occasional flower bed. The only place to put Mathilda was behind an old outbuilding whose roof looked to be caving in.

Bernie was heading toward the outbuilding when she ran over a small branch on the ground. There was a loud crack, and the man turned around. When he saw Mathilda, his eyes widened.

Bernie cursed. "So much for options," she said as the man dropped his cigarette and ground the butt out with the heel of his boot. Bernie heard him say, "Gotta go. Something's come up," to whomever he was talking to. She watched him slip his phone into his jacket pocket as she drove over to where he was standing. Then she put Mathilda in park, and she and her sister jumped out of the van.

"Fancy meeting you here," Libby said as they got closer.

The man frowned. He wrinkled his forehead, pretending to be puzzled, but his eyes stayed focused on Bernie's and Libby's faces. "Hey, do I know you?"

Bernie laughed. "Funny thing. That's what we were about to ask you," she said. "My sister and I just want to know if there's anything we can help you with."

The man blinked. "Why would there be anything you need to help me with? I don't know what you mean."

"Well, you were following us. I figured you must want to ask us something," Libby said.

Bernie took over. "Or maybe you want to order something from the shop. We're having a special on pies right now." She cocked her head. "You look like a chocolate cream pie kinda guy to me."

The man shook his head. "I think you're mistaken."

"About the pie?" Libby asked.

"No, about my following you," the man said.

"I don't think so," Bernie replied.

"I don't know what you're talking about," the driver repeated as he started moving toward the SUV.

Bernie stepped in front of him.

"Don't you?" Libby asked. "You've been following us since . . ."

"Delton Avenue," Bernie said, finishing Libby's sentence for her.

The man laughed. "You've made a mistake," he insisted.

"So you said," Bernie told him. She pointed to the SUV. "Been off-roading?"

"As a matter of fact, I have," the man said.

"Funny how only the license plate on your SUV is dirty," Bernie said.

The man shrugged. "I hadn't noticed."

"Did you know that's illegal?" Libby asked.

"Yeah. You can get a ticket for that," Bernie said.

"You can also get a ticket for riding a bicycle without a bell and displaying a dead body in a window," the man replied.

"Well, we're just telling you in case you didn't know, but you obviously do," Libby informed him. "We wouldn't want you to get a ticket or anything."

"Nice to know you're looking out for my best interests," the man said.

"Just trying to be good neighbors," Bernie told him. "In fact, let me help you get that dirt off your license plate. We have some cleaning stuff in the van."

The man feigned a smile. "That's very thoughtful of you, but I believe I can do that myself."

"I won't hear of it," Bernie said as she watched Libby move toward the SUV. "I insist."

"My sister is very persistent," Libby explained as she clutched the AirTag she'd hidden in the palm of her hand.

"It's the least we can do after my sister and I accused you of following us around," Bernie responded. She took a step closer to him, hoping to distract him. "I feel really bad about this misunderstanding."

The man frowned and looked at his watch. "It's fine," he said impatiently. "Don't worry about it. Listen, I really need to go."

Bernie pretended she hadn't heard the man's last comment, seen his foot jiggling, or noticed his obvious desire to get out of there. "Hey, you wouldn't smoke Camels by any chance?" she asked him.

The man shook his head. "Sorry."

"Are you sure?" Bernie asked, and she took a step closer and grabbed his arm, digging her nails into it.

"I'm positive," the man said.

As he took a step back to get away from Bernie, Libby pretended to trip and fall against the front of the SUV. She

let out a small shriek, grabbing the bumper with both hands
to steady herself as she fell. It took her a second to slap the
AirTag under the bumper with her left hand.

"I don't know what's wrong with me today. I hope I'm
not coming down with the flu or something," she chirped
as she levered herself up and dusted the dirt off her knees.
"I hear it's really bad this year." Then she looked down at
the bumper. "Oh dear." She frowned. "I think I might
have scratched your bumper with my ring." And she lifted
her hand to show him the gold topaz ring her mom had
left her.

"I'm sure it's fine," the man said. He rubbed his arm.
"I'm not sure I can say that about my arm, though."

Libby sighed. "Sorry about that. Sometimes my sister
gets a little too . . . excited. We should exchange information," Libby told him. "You know, in case you have to
contact your insurance agent to get something fixed."

"That won't be necessary," the man told Libby.

"Are you sure?" Bernie asked.

"I'm positive," the man said.

Bernie pointed to the bumper. "See? There is a scratch
there."

"Don't worry," the man told Bernie, taking a step back
toward his vehicle.

"But I do," Bernie told him. She turned to Libby. "I
mean, what if he decides to sue us or something?"

"He won't, will you?" Libby asked the man.

"Absolutely not," the man said, taking another step
back toward his SUV.

"See?" Libby said as she patted Bernie on the back. "It's
all good."

"Is it?" Bernie said to Libby, her voice rising.

"Yes, it is," Libby assured her.

"Not a problem. Really," the man said, taking another

step back. Then he turned, hurried toward his SUV, hopped in, and locked the doors.

Bernie smiled and waved to him. The man didn't wave back. "I think we spooked him," she said to her sister as she and Libby got into Mathilda.

"You spooked him," Libby replied.

Bernie grinned. "I believe you're right."

"That was fun," Libby noted.

"It was, wasn't it?" Bernie agreed as she snapped a quick picture of the man before he drove away. "For identification purposes," she explained to her sister.

"Figured," Libby replied. She fastened her seat belt. Bernie did the same.

The beauty of the AirTag, Bernie decided, was that they could do two things back-to-back. When they were done talking to Ed Gibson, they'd go have a chat with the driver of the silver SUV.

Chapter 34

As Bernie drove out of the park, she handed her phone to Libby. Once they got to the park's exit, she made a left and began driving toward 966 Montclaire Avenue, the address of the halfway house Gail Gibson's brother was living in. Located on the outskirts of Longely, Montclaire Avenue and the five square blocks around it comprised the last remaining semi-run-down section of town. Ten years ago, people from New York City had started snapping up properties in town when they came on the market. Now you'd be lucky if you could find a house for less than three-quarters of a mil, Bernie reflected.

"I figure we'll go talk to the SUV guy after we talk to Gail's brother," Bernie said to her sister as she fiddled with the radio.

Libby nodded while she studied the screen on Bernie's phone. "He's heading toward Wide Waters Plaza," she told her sister. The plaza was an office park that was home to a variety of small- and medium-sized businesses.

Bernie grunted to indicate she'd heard.

"This kind of creeps me out," Libby continued, nodding toward Bernie's phone, which was resting on her lap.

"You mean the AirTag thing?" Bernie asked.

Libby nodded.

"Me too," Bernie agreed as she made a left onto Washington and another right onto Montclaire. "It's way too nineteen eighty-fourish for my taste."

"Mine too," Libby agreed. "And yet here we are using it, even though we disapprove."

"That's the problem with technology," Bernie said as she waited for a mother pushing a stroller with a toddler in it to cross the street. "It makes things too easy."

"I think the word you want is *convenient*," Libby said.

"That too," Bernie agreed. "In the end," she observed, "expedience usually wins out over morality." Then she started looking for the address of the house Gail Gibson's brother was residing in. "Here it is," she said a couple of minutes later, pointing to a dilapidated old building.

Located in the middle of the block, flanked by two smaller colonials, the large Victorian had seen better days, Bernie decided. While traces of the original, intricate paint job were still visible on the gingerbread and the turret, time and weather had taken their toll, turning the original colors—dark greens, blues, and yellows—to mere suggestions of their former selves. Bernie noted that the large maple tree in the middle of the lawn looked as if it was barely hanging on, while the house's foundation plantings were growing over and into the porch railings.

"I bet this place used to be really nice," Bernie commented as she parked the van in front of 966. She noted that there was no sign in front of the house indicating who lived there.

"I bet it used to be gorgeous. It's really a shame," Libby said, picturing what the place must have looked like back in the day. "I can't imagine what it would cost to restore it."

"A lot," Bernie guessed. "That's probably why no one's bought it yet."

"Probably," Libby agreed. "*Yet* being the operative word. Although, given the way real estate is going, I wouldn't be surprised if someone bought it and turned it into condos in the not too distant future."

"I wouldn't be, either," Bernie allowed. She sighed. She'd liked Longely better before the Pilates studios, big-box stores, and Starbucks had invaded the town and the independent bookstores, clothing stores, and corner mini-marts had moved out. It was a good thing they owned the building A Taste of Heaven was in, she reflected. Otherwise, they'd probably be out on their ass, like Michael's Deli. He'd had his rent doubled . . . no . . . tripled a couple of years ago.

"What's up?" Libby asked. "You look distracted."

Bernie shook her head to clear it. "Just thinking about Michael and how lucky we are that Mom and Dad bought the building the shop is in."

"God, yes," Libby said. "Everything around here is definitely changing."

"And not for the better," Bernie observed.

"You sound like Dad," Libby told her, giving Bernie's phone back to her.

Bernie chuckled ruefully. "I suppose I do." And with that, she got out of the van and walked to the house.

Libby followed.

"Watch it," Bernie warned her sister, pointing out the cracks in the sidewalk where the pavement had heaved up. "Don't trip."

The steps creaked as Bernie and Libby went up them. Libby rang the bell. While she and Bernie waited for someone to come, they studied the dents and scratch marks on the old oak door. After a minute, a woman wearing pajama bottoms, a sweatshirt, and a serious case of bed head answered. She looked as if she'd just woken up.

"Yes?" she said.

Libby explained who they were there to see.

"Come back another time," the woman told them. "He's at the doctor's." Then she closed the door in Bernie's and Libby's faces before they had a chance to ask when he would be back.

"So much for that," Bernie said as she turned to go. "I guess we'll have to come back later." She took out her phone and looked at it. Libby was right. Their guy had been heading toward Wide Waters Plaza. "But in the meantime, let's see what our stalker is up to."

"I don't know if I'd call him a stalker," Libby objected as they walked back down the steps.

"Then what would you call him?" Bernie asked.

"Bad news," Libby said as she tripped on one of the cracks in the sidewalk Bernie had pointed out earlier.

Bernie chuckled.

"Don't laugh," Libby told her, regaining her balance.

"I wasn't going to," Bernie insisted.

"Right. Then what were you doing?" Libby protested.

"Thinking about this guy's expression when he answers the door," Bernie lied.

"It'll be interesting," Libby replied, even though she was sure that was not what her sister had been thinking about at all.

Ten minutes later, Bernie and Libby arrived at Wide Waters Plaza. Before it had been bought by Witherspoon & Casey LLC, a multinational commercial real estate firm, the area had been a large green space housing a variety of wildlife. Over the years, Bernie and Libby had gone there with their mother to forage for dandelion greens and fiddlehead ferns in the late spring and early summer, but now the plants were gone, along with the deer, wild turkeys, and foxes. The only remnants left of its former incarnation were the geese and the snapping turtles that loitered by the small pond near the complex's entrance.

"I think I liked it the other way better," Libby reflected as she studied the modern brick and glass buildings set on the rolling grass lawns.

"I know I liked it better the other way," Bernie agreed as she looked at the buildings, which ranged from doctor's offices and health-care facilities to tech companies, a small publisher, and an accounting firm. "How long has it been since we used to hunt for frogs here?"

"Years," Libby replied. "We had fun," she added, recalling the past.

"Yes, we did," Bernie agreed, thinking about the time she, her sister, and her mother had seen a mama goose leading her gosling down to the pond. "I miss Mom."

"Me too," Libby agreed as Bernie consulted her phone.

The pin on the map showed the SUV they were tracking was parked in the lot right off Serenity Lane. Bernie made a sharp left and then a right. At the next intersection, she made another sharp left into the parking lot for a building that had a large 278 painted on it. The lot was half full, and Bernie found a spot in the second row, third space from the end.

"So, what's the plan?" Libby asked Bernie.

Bernie turned off the ignition. "We lie our asses off."

"I'm not that good with that," Libby protested.

"You're good enough," Bernie reassured her.

Then she and Libby got out and walked over to the building. Libby opened the heavy glass door, and the sisters entered the black marble and glass lobby. To the left was a list of the businesses housed there. Libby counted six. Two were lawyers, one was an accountant, another one was an insurance agent, while the fifth and the sixth were, respectively, a CPA and an importer/exporter.

"So, which office do you think our guy is in?" Bernie asked Libby.

Libby shook her head. "Your guess is as good as mine."

"Which isn't saying much," Bernie couldn't keep herself from saying.

After staring at the list, they decided to start on the first floor and work their way up, knocking on doors as they went. It wasn't until they got to the last floor that they hit pay dirt.

They were in the middle of showing the picture of the man they were looking for to the receptionist at the Blue River Trading Company when a letter carrier walked into the office to deliver the mail.

"Hey, is that Jack?" the carrier asked Libby and Bernie as he dropped a stack of mail held together with rubber bands on the receptionist's desk.

Bernie and Libby looked at each other. It was the first break they'd had all day.

"It certainly is," Libby said, answering the letter carrier's question.

"Thank heavens." Bernie put on her best smile. "Wow, what a relief. I was so worried we wouldn't be able to find him." And she proceeded to spin a long, complicated story about why they needed to.

"Not a problem," the carrier said when Bernie was done. "He's around back."

Bernie gave him a blank look.

"There's another entrance around the back," the carrier explained. "Jack has a small office there." Then he turned and walked out the door.

Bernie and Libby followed. When they got to the lobby, the carrier pointed to the front door. "You need to go out through there and walk around to the left. The office is on the side of the building facing the holding pond." He made a minute adjustment to the strap of the bag with the letters he was carrying on his shoulder. "Tell him Wendell hopes he found what he was looking for."

"What was that?" Libby asked.

Wendell shrugged. "Something for some client. He was just worried he wouldn't be able to find it. I guess he was going to get some sort of finder's fee if he located it."

"We'll give Jack the message," Bernie assured Wendell as they all went out the front door.

The mail carrier turned right, while Libby and Bernie turned left. They walked around the left side of the building and turned the corner. They could see the holding pond the mail carrier had mentioned from where they were standing. There was a flock of geese waddling around, while a bunch of seagulls squawked overhead. A thin concrete path led around to the back, and Libby and Bernie followed it. In contrast to the front of the building, the back was constructed of brick, and the grounds around it were pockmarked with old soda cans and discarded fast-food wrappers.

Two minutes later, after Libby had sidestepped a small snapping turtle, the sisters came to a door. The door was recessed, making it difficult to see unless you were right there. Constructed of opaque glass, the door had a sign on it that said JACK BRUNO, PRIVATE SECURITY.

Bernie knocked on the door. It swung open. "So maybe not so secure," she noted, referring to the writing on the door.

"He could have stepped out to get a cup of coffee," Libby hypothesized.

Bernie lifted her right eyebrow. "And forgot to lock the door? What if we were clients? "Doesn't look too good," Bernie observed, stepping inside. Libby followed.

The reception area was sparsely furnished—just a worn mud-brown sofa, a rickety coffee table that looked as if it had come from the Salvation Army, and a couple of folding chairs. There were no pictures on the wall or magazines on the coffee table. This was strictly a one-man operation, Bernie thought, looking around.

"Hello," Bernie called out, as she heard faint music coming from the next room. "Anyone home?"

No one answered. She and her sister exchanged another glance. This didn't feel good.

"Jack," Bernie continued. "It's the people you've been following. We'd like to have a word with you."

No response.

"Okay. We're coming in," Bernie warned after another moment of silence.

"Definitely not good," Libby observed.

"Did I ever tell you, you have a genius for stating the obvious?" Bernie said to her sister.

"I prefer to think of it as a God-given talent," Libby replied. She nodded toward the door. "My turn?" she asked.

Bernie nodded. She watched as her sister opened the door to the inner office. She took a step inside, stopped, then took a step back.

Chapter 35

"What is it?" Bernie asked.

Libby turned to her sister. "Well, let's just say I don't think Jack Bruno is going to be answering our questions anytime soon."

"Is he dead?" Bernie asked.

"Well, he sure looks that way from here," Libby told her.

Bernie cursed under her breath.

"I don't get it," Libby said after she and Bernie had stepped inside the inner office. The room was stuffy and smelled vaguely of fried food, cheap air freshener, and dirty clothes.

"Well, he sure did," Bernie noted as she walked over and gently laid two fingers on the inside of Jack Bruno's wrist. No pulse. Not that she'd expected any, given the condition of his forehead. But she had to make sure. Because that was what one did in these sorts of circumstances. "He's still warm," she announced.

"We shouldn't have stopped for coffee at the drive-thru," Libby observed as she did the timeline in her head.

"It's amazing what a difference a minute can make," Bernie commented as she studied Jack Bruno's body. He was sitting behind his desk in an office chair that had seen better days. If you didn't see the single bullet hole in his forehead, you would have thought he was reading the newspaper while sitting at his desk.

Libby took a step back. "Maybe this is a coincidence. Maybe this has nothing to do with the matter we're dealing with."

Bernie snorted. "Yeah, and maybe the tooth fairy is real."

"You mean he's not?" Libby exclaimed.

Bernie laughed. "You know what two coincidences make?" she asked her sister.

"No. What?" Libby said.

"A pattern," Bernie replied as she studied the scene in front of her.

"True. Except in this case, the victims were all killed in different ways," Libby noted. "One was hung, one was run off the road, and one was shot at point-blank range."

Bernie nodded. "Not to mention the fact that the first death was carefully planned, while the second and third weren't," she said as she took note of the expression on Jack Bruno's face. He seemed surprised, she decided. As if this was the last thing he'd expected. And, as it turned out, it was.

"So maybe we're looking for a pair of killers?" Libby hypothesized.

"Possibly," Bernie said. Or had Jack Bruno been shot by a dissatisfied client? A quilter? A friend? A lover? Obviously, he had been shot by someone he knew. Did it have to do with Diane Englewood's or Ellen Fisher's deaths? Was Jack Bruno collateral damage? Was Diane Englewood, for that matter?

Bernie sighed as she unbuttoned the top two buttons of her spring coat. It was still too cold for it, but she couldn't resist the pop of pink. A dash of color this time of year, before the trees leafed out, was always welcomed. She curled a strand of hair around one of her fingers while she thought. Perhaps the most important question was, why had Jack Bruno been following them in the first place? Bernie sighed again. Lots of questions. Questions that would be much harder to answer now that Jack Bruno was dead.

One thing was for certain, though. Indisputable, really. Jack Bruno hadn't seen death coming. No Grim Reaper waltzing into the office, scythe in hand, for him. Judging from Bruno's wound, the position of his body, and the neatness of his office, Bernie figured his killer had walked in, walked up to the desk, taken out their weapon, and fired.

Did Jack Bruno have an appointment with him or her? Unlikely, given that he'd been trying to follow her and Libby a half an hour before. He'd returned to the office only after they'd ambushed him—metaphorically speaking. But Bruno couldn't have predicted that would happen.

Hence, he wouldn't have scheduled a meeting with a client in those circumstances. The last thing you'd want to do was leave your client waiting for you, especially because, given the location and look of the office, Bruno needed all the clients he could get. Bernie closed her eyes and tried to picture what had occurred. She was guessing that while Bruno was following them, someone was following Bruno. They could have been behind the hill, on the other side of the road in Buckland Park.

Bernie leaned over and opened the desk drawer. A Glock 17 was sitting over to the side, within easy reach, next to a box of paper clips, a bunch of rubber bands, a tangle of computer cables, and a box of cartridges. "Look, Libby," she said, motioning for her sister to see what she'd found, as she checked to see if the Glock was loaded. It was.

This was proof, if any was needed, that Jack Bruno knew whoever had walked through his office door and that he wasn't worried about him or her. Otherwise, he would have reached for his weapon. But he hadn't.

Libby nodded as Bernie put the weapon back where she'd found it. She saw what her sister was getting at. Then she thought of something else. Something that set her heart racing. "We just missed meeting whoever did this."

"Ya think, Libby?" Bernie said, looking up. She'd closed the desk drawer and started leafing through the papers on Jack Bruno's desk.

"No need for sarcasm," Libby told her.

"I wasn't being sarcastic," Bernie said.

"You were," Libby countered.

"Okay, I was," Bernie admitted. "Satisfied?"

"Marginally," Libby replied before continuing with what she'd been saying. "If we hadn't been busy looking for this place, if we'd known where it was, if we'd been ten minutes earlier, if—"

Bernie cut her sister off. "I know. I'm aware. We could have ended up like this guy." She nodded toward Jack Bruno. "But we didn't."

"Exactly. But we could have . . ."

"Been killed," Bernie said, again finishing Libby's sentence for her. "But we weren't," Bernie told her impatiently. "We're fine."

"For the moment." Then a new thought popped into Libby's head. "What if whoever did this comes back?" she demanded.

"Why would they?" Bernie replied as she returned to wondering what the link between Ellen Fisher's and Jack Bruno's deaths was. Had Ellen Fisher hired him? Had someone else? Who? And again, why had he been following them? Bernie didn't have a clue. Not even a suggestion of a clue.

Libby coughed, and Bernie turned to her. "What?" Bernie asked, perhaps a little more sharply than she'd intended.

"You don't know they won't come back," Libby said.

"And you don't know that they will," Bernie shot back. She gestured around the office. "Look at this place."

Libby looked.

"Whoever killed Bruno obviously wasn't searching this office for anything. Otherwise, it wouldn't look this neat. It would be torn apart." Bernie clicked her tongue against her teeth. "No. If this person wanted anything, they knew where it was, and they took it."

"Or not," Libby said. "Maybe whoever it was got interrupted, and they're going to come back and finish the job later. For that matter, maybe they hadn't even started yet. Maybe we interrupted them."

Bernie shook her head. "No."

"They could have heard us."

"True, but there was no way for them to leave without our seeing them. This office isn't connected to anything." Bernie pointed to the door. "That offers the only way out. As I said, we would have seen them."

Libby thought for a moment. Even though she hated to admit it, she couldn't think of anything that refuted Bernie's logic.

"No," Bernie reiterated. "I think whoever did this came to do what they did—kill Jack Bruno. I think they accomplished their goal, and they left. End of story. At least for Bruno."

Libby took a deep breath and told herself to calm down. The trick was to concentrate on something else. "How do you think this is connected to Ellen Fisher's murder?"

Bernie shook her head. She had no idea. "Hopefully, there's something in here that will tell us."

"We should call the police," Libby said.

"And we will," Bernie said. "After we take a quick look-see through here and his house." She held up her hand to forestall any protest on her sister's part. "I don't think an hour will make any difference to Bruno at this stage of the game, do you?"

"No, I don't suppose it will," Libby replied as she watched her sister go through Bruno's pockets. She found his wallet, phone, and car keys. The wallet contained a twenty-dollar bill, his driver's license, his PI license, a credit card, and a folded-up sales receipt from a sewing store called Crazy Bee. Bernie unfolded it. There was a list of two other sewing stores scrawled on the receipt's blank side.

"Somehow, I don't think Bruno was shopping for material to make a jacket," Libby said when Bernie showed it to her.

"Or a quilt. We should check these out," Bernie said, referring to the shops, as she put the list in her pocket. Next, she tried to open Bruno's phone. But she couldn't. It was password protected. Not that she was surprised. She gave it two more tries, after which she put the phone back in Bruno's pocket and turned to his desk. "See something missing?" she asked her sister.

"Such as?" Libby replied.

"I'll give you a hint," Bernie told her. "It's rectangular. Portable. Something you're always cursing at."

"A laptop," Libby said. "Of course, it could be at his house," she hypothesized.

Bernie nodded. That was also true.

"Or maybe he doesn't have one," Libby added.

"Everyone has one," Bernie told her.

Libby thought of Mrs. Hurman. "Almost everyone,"

she replied while she started on the pile of papers on Jack Bruno's desk.

She and her sister spent the next fifteen minutes going through it.

The pile consisted of junk mail, old bills, and a few small checks that needed to be cashed. Six of the checks were from an insurance company and two law firms that specialized in divorces, while the seventh check was a paycheck from Costco, where Bruno moonlighted as a security guard.

Libby also found a letter on departmental stationery from the Longely PD, answering a question Bruno had asked about his benefits. She scanned the letter. "Evidently, he worked for them for seven years before quitting," Libby said as she put the letter back in the pile and went on to the rest of mail. Those proved to be bills that needed to be paid. Evidently, Jack Bruno was behind on the rent on his office and was being threatened with eviction. The fact that he couldn't afford to pay five hundred fifty dollars a month said a lot.

"We should ask Dad if he knows him," Bernie said while she opened the top file cabinet drawer. It was filled with client folders. The sisters went through them methodically, taking each one out, reading, and replacing it. Halfway through, Bernie recognized a name. Judy Fine.

"What do we have here?" she asked as she opened the folder. She took out a letter and some notes scribbled on torn-out pieces of notebook paper and read them. "Now, this is interesting," she told her sister. "Two years ago Judy Fine hired Jack Bruno to follow her husband. She suspected him of stepping out with another woman."

"Was he?" Libby asked.

"No. He was going to ballroom dance classes." And Bernie showed Libby the pictures Jack Bruno had taken.

"Maybe Judy's husband wanted to surprise her," Libby

postulated as she handed the pictures back to Bernie. "Wasn't there a movie like that?"

Bernie nodded. "It was Japanese," she said as she set the folder with Judy Fine's name on it aside, closed the top drawer, opened the second one, and studied the contents. It was full of odds and ends. A glass paperweight. A bag of hard candy. Scotch tape. Two packages of pencils. In short, nothing of interest.

The third drawer proved more informative. There was a bunch of letters from a variety of casinos, offering to comp Jack Bruno.

"He must have liked to gamble," Libby observed, waving a couple of the letters in the air.

"So it would seem," Bernie agreed as she began rummaging through the wastebasket by the desk. "Casinos don't send those out to people who don't drop a fair chunk of change on the floor."

A moment later, Libby held up another file. It contained Jack Bruno's divorce papers. "Maybe that's why his wife divorced him."

"It wouldn't surprise me," Bernie said as she continued to go through Jack Bruno's trash. Most of it turned out to be your standard junk mail, but then she came upon a couple of ripped-up letters. One fragment bore the imprint of the IRS, while another fragment was from the New York State Family Court. "Interesting," she said as she dumped the contents of the wastepaper basket onto Bruno's desk and started looking for the other pieces of the torn-up letters.

Libby stopped what she was doing and watched Bernie put the pieces of the letters together. Literally.

"Interesting," Bernie repeated when she was done.

"How so?" Libby asked as she closed the file cabinet drawer and went over to look at what her sister had found.

Bernie pointed. "Well, the IRS was going to audit him,

and the New York State Family Court was about to put a lien on his bank account because he was behind on his child support payments."

"Poor guy," Libby observed. "Things were not going well for him."

"No, they weren't," Bernie remarked as she swept the contents of the wastepaper basket back into it with the side of her hand. "I wonder how much Bruno owed."

"To the IRS?" Libby asked.

"That too," Bernie replied. "But I was thinking more along the lines of a loan shark."

"You don't know that," Libby objected.

"No, I don't," Bernie replied. "But it's a reasonable supposition."

"So, you think Bruno was a compulsive gambler? You think that maybe he was in way over his head and couldn't pay it back, and that's why he was shot?" Libby asked as she looked around the office to make sure she and Bernie hadn't missed anything, not that there was much there to miss. Just a wobbly floor lamp that was tilting to the left, a client chair with a sunken-in cushion, and a grimy area rug that looked as if Jack Bruno had picked it up off the street.

"Well, it might have been the impetus to find whatever the mailman was looking for," Bernie allowed as she checked under the cushion and examined the base of the lamp, while Libby checked the air vents for a camera. Just in case Bruno had been recording client meetings. Because you never knew. Which was what their dad would have told them. They could have saved themselves the trouble. There was nothing there.

"Time to leave," Bernie said, pivoting toward the door.

Libby followed. On the way out, the sisters checked for security cameras, but there weren't any of those, either.

244 *Isis Crawford*

"Of course not," Bernie said as they walked toward the front of the building "That would have made things too easy."

"Maybe that's why he took this place," Libby suggested.

"Or maybe he couldn't afford anything else," Bernie replied as they turned the corner to the parking lot and headed toward their van. On the way, Libby stopped and took off the AirTag she'd put on Jack Bruno's silver SUV and slipped it in her pocket.

"Glad you remembered," Bernie told her.

"Yeah," Libby said. "The last thing we need is the police finding it and hauling us in for questioning." She straightened up. "Do you think we'll find something at Bruno's house, Bernie?"

"One can always hope," Bernie said as she got in Mathilda. Libby followed. A moment later, Bernie pulled onto the main road. "We are due to have our luck change," she noted.

On the way over to Bruno's house, Libby called Brandon and asked him what he knew about him. Not much, as it turned out. There was a rumor floating around that Jack Bruno owed big to a loan shark named Tony Cavelli.

"Told ya, Libby," Bernie mouthed when she heard this. "Anything else?" Bernie asked Brandon. They were on speakerphone.

They could hear Brandon yawn.

"Anything?" Bernie repeated.

"Give me a minute," Brandon said. "I'm thinking."

Bernie restrained herself from making the obvious comment.

"He hasn't been in RJ's for a long time," Brandon said.

"But when he was, who did he hang out with?" asked Libby.

Another moment of silence. Then Brandon said, "Gail Gibson's brother, Ed."

"Anyone else?" Libby wanted to know.

"Not that I remember," Brandon said. "He wasn't a chatty kinda guy. Mostly, he'd come in, have a couple of beers, and stare at the TV."

"Any idea what he and Ed Gibson used to talk about?" Bernie asked.

"If I remember correctly, they used to talk about the college they went to," Brandon replied.

"They went to college together?" Libby asked. She was surprised, although she wasn't sure why she should be.

"Same college, different years. They were both chem majors at St. Andrews."

"Wow," Bernie said. "Who would have thought?"

Brandon laughed. "That's what Ed Gibson said when he found out."

"I wonder if he graduated," Libby mused.

"You'll have to ask him," Brandon said.

"We will," Bernie said.

Then Brandon hung up, and Bernie headed to Jolly John's.

Chapter 36

Twenty minutes later, Bernie and Libby pulled up in front of Jack Bruno's house. It was an unremarkable small Cape Cod built in the sixties and located on an average-looking street one block inside of Longely's northernmost border.

"It looks as if it could use a good paint job," Libby noted.

Bernie nodded in agreement as she parked by the curb and turned off the van. "Not to mention that the lawn looks as if it needs to be reseeded, and the Japanese maple in the middle of it needs to be pruned," she observed as she took a sip of her coffee and a bite of the muffin she'd bought at Jolly John's.

Except for the sound of a garbage truck in the distance and the squabbling of crows, it was quiet. There was very little movement. The street was deserted. No one was playing basketball in the driveway. No one was mowing the lawn or raking up winter's debris. No one was out walking their dog. No one was unloading groceries out of their car or wrestling a toddler into their car seat. The sisters figured the block's inhabitants were either at work, at school, or at day care. Which was more than fine with them. Given what they were about to do, the fewer witnesses, the better.

"No alarm system," Bernie said, noting the lack of signage on the lawn. "So that's a positive."

"He could have one of those video doorbell thingies," Libby pointed out.

"We will see what we can see," Bernie intoned as she and Libby watched an Amazon truck make a delivery to a house down the block and drive off again.

"Or what the cameras see," Libby clarified. Then she said, "What does that phrase even mean?"

"We will see what we can see?"

"Yes."

"It doesn't mean anything. Not really," Bernie replied.

"Then why say it?" Libby asked.

Bernie shrugged. "I just like the way it sounds."

Libby laughed and took a bite of the other corn muffin Bernie had bought. She chewed for a minute, then said, "I think John changed the recipe. What do you think?"

"The same as you, and not for the better." Bernie took another bite of the muffin. "He cut back on the cheddar cheese and added more black pepper to compensate for the flavor loss. And maybe added a touch of what? Sage?"

Libby shook her head. "Thyme. He made the muffins bigger, too."

"A little. But ours are better."

"But theirs are cheaper."

"By five cents."

"These days five cents can make a difference," Libby replied. What with the price of gas these days, lots of people were trying to economize. Fortunately, A Taste of Heaven's customers hadn't cut back on their purchases, but that didn't mean they wouldn't in the future.

Bernie continued. "And the tops of their corn muffins look better than ours. Rounder. A little goldener," she observed.

Libby raised an eyebrow. "Goldener?"

Bernie laughed. "Okay. But you can say browner. Why not goldener?"

"Because English is a strange language." Then Libby took a sip of her coffee while she thought about the muffins. "We could brush the tops with butter midway through baking," she suggested after a moment. "That might do the trick."

Bernie nodded. "We could do a test batch and see if people notice the difference."

"They probably won't."

"Agreed," Bernie said. "But as Mom used to say, there's always room for improvement."

"And appearances do count," Libby added. Something could taste great, but if it didn't look appealing, it wouldn't sell. They'd learned that the hard way. "Should we put in a little more cheddar?" Libby mused. "And maybe another quarter or half a cup of corn kernels. It would give the muffin a little more texture."

"We can try it and see," Bernie said. "What do you think of the coffee?" she asked, changing the subject.

Libby made a so-so gesture with her hand. "It's okay. Nothing great. A little over-roasted. I don't think we have to worry about competition in that department."

"Neither do I," Bernie agreed.

Libby grinned. "Good." She finished her coffee and threw the cup into the trash bag on the floor.

Jolly John's had opened a year ago. So far, they hadn't syphoned off any of A Taste of Heaven's customers, and Bernie and Libby wanted to keep it that way. One of the reasons they'd managed to stay in business for as long as they had was that they always kept tabs on the competition. Just because A Taste of Heaven had been open for the past twenty years didn't mean that they couldn't go under. They were not in the kind of business where you could take anything for granted, especially not your customers.

"Their chocolate lava cake looked good," Bernie noted as she took another sip of her coffee.

Libby finished up her muffin. "I didn't see it."

"That's because you were out the door when John put it in the display case," Bernie told her.

"How is John these days?" Libby asked.

Bernie laughed. "Not jolly."

"He never has been."

"No. He hasn't," Bernie agreed. John Ragnar was a small, skinny guy with a bad complexion and a perpetual scowl on his face.

Libby dusted corn muffin crumbs off her lap. "We should get one of those cakes on the way home. See how it stacks up to ours."

"That's what I was figuring, Libby." Bernie took a last sip of coffee, clamped the lid on the cup, and set it down in Mathilda's cup holder. "Ready to do this?" she asked her sister as she pocketed the van's keys.

Libby nodded and exited the van, with Bernie following. The sisters walked up to Jack Bruno's door. The doorbell was just your standard issue, Bernie noted as she rang it. She and Libby could hear the bell chiming inside. No one answered. Libby rang it again. Just to make sure. And got the same result. Not that she expected anyone to be in there. The sisters looked at each other.

"Guess no one's home," Bernie observed. "Let's head to the back, shall we?"

Libby nodded.

The backyard turned out to be a small plot of scraggly grass with a tired-looking pink flamingo stuck next to a garden shed, a big, neatly stacked pile of wood, and a small greenhouse affixed to the back of the house.

"Now, that's a surprise," Bernie said as she studied the orchids and the ferns. She didn't see Bruno as a greenhouse kinda guy.

"What are those?" Libby asked, pointing at the pots of plants with orange-colored trumpetlike flowers hanging from stalks. They looked like something she'd read about in a magazine article recently. "I can't remember what they're called."

Bernie shook her head. "I don't have the foggiest." Plants were not her strong suit. "But they're pretty. I like their color."

Libby frowned. "I hate having a word or a name on the tip of my tongue and not being able to remember it."

"We should get some of those plants for the shop's window boxes," Bernie suggested as she snapped a picture of them with her phone. "I figure we can show the pics to the guy at Flowers and Things."

"Good idea," Libby commented, still trying to remember the flower's name and failing. There was a reason the name was important. She wished she could remember what it was.

"I guess you never know about people," Bernie continued. She gestured toward the greenhouse. "This would be the last thing I would expect Jack Bruno to have."

"Me too," Libby said, turning her attention away from the greenhouse and toward the shed. The shed had moss growing on the roof and was tilting to the right. It looked as if a strong wind would knock it over. Libby walked over and opened the door. It made a loud groaning noise. The hinges definitely needed to be oiled.

"Nothing of interest here," Libby declared after she'd taken a gander.

Bernie checked the contents of the shed, as well. Just to make sure. Because two sets of eyes were always better than one. Not that she expected to find anything. And she didn't. Just an electric lawn mower, a rake, a snow shovel, a box of snow melt, potting soil, and some seeds. Nothing more. She and Libby checked the walls and the floor for any hidey-holes. Still nothing. She closed the door, and she and Libby walked over to the house.

A BEWARE OF DOG sign was posted on the door. There was no dog and no evidence of a dog's presence. No water bowl. No bones. No poop.

"Must be an old sign," Bernie said to her sister as she dug around in her bag for her lockpicks. "Aha," she said after she found them. She got to work.

Libby watched her. "Having trouble?" she asked her after a couple of minutes had gone by and no progress had been made.

Bernie grunted. "I don't know what the problem is," she muttered. The lock was old, but that shouldn't be an issue. In fact, it should be just the opposite. The new locks were the ones that gave Bernie trouble. She straightened up and rubbed the small of her back. A minute later she tried again. And failed the second time. And the third.

"I guess the third time isn't the charm," Libby remarked.

"No, but evidently, the fourth time is," Bernie said as she felt the lock cylinders move slightly. There was a click. "Yes," she cried. She turned the doorknob. The door swung open. "See, O ye of little faith," she said to Libby. "I told you I could."

"I never said you couldn't," Libby responded.

"You implied it," Bernie said, turning. She stowed her lockpicks in her bag and was about to take a step inside when Libby snapped her fingers.

"Got it," she cried.

"Got what?" Bernie asked.

"The flower's name. It's called Devil's Breath," Libby said. Her eyes lit up. She grinned. "I think I know how Ellen Fisher was killed."

Bernie turned toward her. "Are you saying what I think you're saying?"

"That those flowers are responsible?" her sister replied. "Yes, I am."

"But she was hung, not poisoned," Bernie objected.

"True." Libby closed her eyes as she pictured what she'd read. "The seeds of Devil's Breath, when powdered and treated, contain a chemical, called burandanga, that is similar to scopolamine," she recited. "It's been used in South American spiritual rituals. The compound can lead to hallucinations and loss of will."

"Are we talking zombies here?" Bernie asked.

Libby laughed and opened her eyes. "Not exactly, but close." Then she recited some more of the article she'd read. "Atropine is a classic antagonist that can exert multiple CNS effects. Rohypnol, scopolamine, and burandanga belong to a class of hallucinogens that were cited in a recent UN report on human trafficking as a drug of concern."

"So, you're saying that whoever killed Ellen could have

given one of those drugs to her, waited until it took effect, and strung her up?" Bernie asked.

"That's exactly what I'm saying," Libby was replying when she heard, "Put your hands up over your head and slowly turn around."

When she complied, she saw a policeman standing there with his gun drawn.

"Great," she said to Bernie. "This day just keeps getting better and better."

Chapter 37

"Dad is not going to be happy when he hears about this," Libby predicted when she'd raised her hands in the air.

And she was right. He wasn't.

"What the hell is wrong with you?" he asked Bernie after she'd convinced the officer who'd responded to a neighbor's 911 call about a possible robbery in progress to let her phone her father. "Although I'm not surprised," he added after he'd calmed down. "Bruno was definitely heading in that direction."

"He wasn't fired from the force, though," Bernie said, remembering the letter she'd seen in his office.

"No. He wasn't," Sean told her. "But there were lots of rumors swirling around. He left before he could be brought up on charges. Lucy didn't want the scandal."

"Now, there's a surprise," Bernie said. It was the way Lucy, their esteemed Longely police chief, had conducted business over the years.

"Isn't it, though?" Sean said. Then he hung up and called Clyde, who arrived at Jack Bruno's house twenty minutes later.

Bernie and Libby watched him get out of his car, slam the door shut, and stalk up Jack Bruno's driveway toward them.

"He is not pleased," Libby noted as her dad's best friend approached them.

"No, I am not," Clyde snarled. "You're just lucky Ray is a nice guy," Clyde continued, referring to the patrolman who had answered the neighbor's call.

"Happy to see you, too," Bernie told him.

"This isn't a joke, Bernie. Is it, Ray?" Clyde said.

Startled, Ray looked up from the text he'd been reading and hurriedly slipped his cell into his pocket. "No, sir. No, it's not," he replied, after which he got in his patrol car and started backing down the driveway. Libby, Bernie, and Clyde watched him go.

Once Ray was on the street and had rounded the corner, Clyde turned to the sisters and said, "Lucy told me to tell you that the next time you guys pull a stunt like this, he's going to throw both of you in jail."

"He always says that," Bernie pointed out.

"Yeah, but this time he means it," Clyde replied. "He's serious. So why the hell are you here, anyway?"

"It's a long story," Bernie replied.

"Give me the short version," Clyde ordered.

"We went to talk to Jack Bruno in his office," Libby told him.

"He was following us, and we wanted to find out why," Bernie explained.

"And did you?" Clyde asked.

"Nope," Libby said.

"Like they say," Bernie continued, "dead men don't tell tales."

Clyde frowned. "He's dead?"

"Well, he's not going dancing anytime soon," Libby said.

Clyde frowned. "This is not good."

"Dad implied he was a crooked cop," Bernie told him.

"Maybe *bent* would be a better word," Clyde said. "He liked shortcuts. But you still haven't told me why you guys are here."

Bernie spoke again. "We're here because after looking through his office, we decided to see if there was anything in his house that would explain why he was following us," she responded.

"Any idea why he was?" Clyde asked.

"None," Bernie answered.

Clyde's frown grew. "Were you planning on phoning the crime in?"

"Of course we were," Bernie assured him in her most disarming voice.

"When?" Clyde demanded.

"Right after we went through Jack Bruno's house." No point in lying now, Bernie decided as she watched Clyde shake his head, sigh, and called in the homicide.

"And speaking of Jack Bruno's house, can we go in there now?" Bernie asked Clyde after he'd hung up.

Clyde looked at her and blinked. "I'm amazed."

"At what?" Bernie asked, playing innocent.

"At your chutzpah."

"It's a talent," Bernie told him.

"So, I take it that's a no?" Libby asked Clyde.

Clyde gave her the laser death stare. Then he took a deep breath and let it out. "Are you kidding me? This is now an active crime-scene investigation."

"Twenty minutes," Libby begged. "We'll be in and out in twenty minutes. That's it. No one is going to know."

"That's not the point," Clyde told her.

"Please," Libby pleaded.

"After all," Bernie chimed in, "if it wasn't for us, you wouldn't have found Jack Bruno's body. You owe us."

"In whose universe? And we would have found it, all right," Clyde retorted.

"Yeah," Libby said. "That's true. You would have. But not until people started complaining about the smell."

Clyde sneezed into the crook of his arm. He hoped he wasn't getting a cold.

"We're hoping to find something else in his house that will link him to Ellen Fisher's death," Libby said.

"Something else?" Clyde repeated. "You don't have anything."

"I think we do," Bernie told him.

"Really? Like what?" Clyde demanded.

"Like those," Libby said, indicating the orange flowers in the greenhouse with a nod of her head. "We think someone—maybe Bruno—used them to drug Ellen Fisher and string her up."

Clyde shook his head. "You're wrong. Jack may have been a lot of things, but killing someone like that—no. In the heat of the moment, yes. But what you're saying . . . I don't see it." He frowned. "I thought you were done with the Ellen Fisher thing."

"Hardly," Bernie said.

Clyde glared at her. "We've been through this already. Ellen Fisher hung herself."

"We think she had help." And Libby explained Devil's Breath's properties.

Clyde snorted. "So, the plant has a scary name. Big deal. My next-door neighbor Neal has flowers like that. He bought them from some gardening store in Croton, and they're growing all over the pergola in his backyard. For that matter, I have a weed called deadly nightshade growing around the base of the oak tree in my backyard. So what? That doesn't mean Mike and I are murderers," Clyde continued. "And as for scopolamine, you can get the damned stuff on Amazon. People use it for seasickness."

"Among other things," Libby said.

"At least admit it's a possibility," Bernie said.

Clyde acquiesced. "Okay. It's a possibility. A remote possibility. A very remote possibility. After all, the other plants in there aren't toxic. Maybe Bruno was growing Devil's Breath because he liked the way it looked. Have you thought of that?"

"Yes, I have, but weren't you the one who said that nothing is ever coincidental?" Bernie asked him.

"No. That was your dad," Clyde replied.

"I'm pretty sure you said it, too," Bernie told him.

Clyde shrugged. "Maybe I did. But there's coincidence and then there's coincidence."

"Okay. And which coincidence is this?"

"Don't get smart with me, young lady," Clyde admonished.

Bernie apologized. "Twenty minutes, Clyde. Please. That's all Libby and I are asking for. In case there's a chance that Ellen Fisher's death is linked to Jack Bruno's."

"I'll tell you what," Clyde said to her. "You can read the report. How's that?"

"That's not the same," Libby told him.

"Well, it's as good as you're going to get," Clyde replied.

Bernie glanced at her watch. The crime-scene unit was on the way. They didn't have much time left to get in there.

She made her last pitch. "Okay, let's leave the flower thing aside. But what about the fact that Judy Fine was one of his clients and she was friends with Ellen Fisher? That's one link. And then we come back to the question of why Jack Bruno was following us. I have to assume that he was hired by someone to see what we were doing. It's the only thing that makes sense. Hopefully, something in Bruno's house will tell us who hired him."

"And why," Libby added.

"Because whoever hired him obviously thinks we're involved in this mess in some way," Bernie said, hammering her point home. "They've already gone through our van. How do we know they're not going to do worse?"

"After all," Libby continued, "you always say it's better to be on the safe side."

Then Bernie and Libby stopped talking and gave Clyde a moment to digest what they'd said.

"Trying to guilt me into doing what you want?" he asked after a minute had gone by.

"Is it working?" Bernie inquired.

"Unfortunately, it is." Clyde sighed. "You realize I could get fired for this?"

"You could if anyone knew, but they won't," Bernie reassured him. "We'll be long gone before the forensics team arrives."

"And"—here Libby raised her hand, palm outward, for emphasis—"did I mention that you'd have permanent store credit at A Taste of Heaven?"

Bernie turned toward her sister. "He will?"

"I will?" Clyde echoed.

"Yes, you will," Libby replied firmly, even though the words had just tumbled out of her mouth without her thinking about them.

"So, now you're trying to bribe an officer of the law," Clyde said.

This time Bernie responded. "No," she quickly assured him. "Libby was just trying to show you our appreciation for everything you've done for us and our dad over the years."

Clyde stroked his chin. "Well, when you put it that way."

"There isn't any other way to put it," Bernie said, smiling.

"I guess there's no harm in you guys going in there for a quick look-see," Clyde replied after another moment's thought.

"Thank you, thank you," Bernie cried. She and Libby hugged Clyde.

"You're the best," Libby said.

"Twenty minutes and not a minute more," Clyde said as he untangled himself from the sisters. "And don't touch anything without gloves."

"Of course not," Bernie said. "We know better. This isn't our first time at the rodeo."

"We've got some in the van," Libby added.

"And if I call you and say to leave . . . ," Clyde continued.

"We'll do it instantly," Libby promised Clyde.

"Swear?" Clyde asked.

"Swear," Libby promised.

"Okay, then," Clyde said. "Make it fast." He shook his head at his folly. "I must be crazy," Clyde muttered to himself as he watched his friend's daughters hurry over to Mathilda, take a couple of pairs of latex gloves out of the box on the front seat, and head toward the back door of Jack Bruno's house.

Or maybe I'm not, Clyde thought. The fact that they were being followed was worrying. It certainly lent credence to their hypothesis. In truth, there was a slim possibility that Bernie and Libby were correct in their assessment. Slim, but still there. After all, they had their father's genes, and Sean was the best detective that Clyde had ever had the privilege to work with. He saw things that Clyde missed. So, maybe Libby and Bernie were onto something, after all.

Chapter 38

"How do you want to play this?" Libby asked Bernie as she and her sister hurried back toward Jack Bruno's house. Twenty minutes wasn't very long to accomplish what they wanted to do. In fact, it was totally inadequate, but it was better than nothing.

Bernie thought for a minute. Then she said, "Let's take a quick look through Bruno's medicine cabinet, his bedroom, and his office. We can always sneak back later for a more in-depth look if we need to."

Libby nodded. That was what she'd been thinking, too. She was about to tell her sister that when Clyde spoke.

"Remember," he said to the sisters, who by now were at Jack Bruno's back door. "Twenty minutes and not one minute more."

"How about a few seconds? Can we have a few seconds more?" Bernie asked. "Or how about a microsecond? Or a nanosecond? Or even a picosecond?"

"Don't worry," Libby reassured Clyde as she poked her sister in the ribs with her elbow to get her to shut up. "We'll be out of there when we should. I promise."

Clyde nodded as his phone rang. Bernie rubbed her side while Clyde turned to answer the call.

"Hey, that hurt," she complained to her sister.

"Good. It was supposed to. Why do you always have to cause trouble?" Libby hissed in her sister's ear. "Why can't you ever leave things well enough alone?"

"Because I'm the irresponsible younger sister and you're the responsible older one," Bernie told her.

"Can we switch places?" Libby asked.

"Anytime," Bernie replied as she opened the door and stepped inside. Libby followed.

Bernie started to laugh.

"What's so funny?" Libby asked her.

"I'm just remembering the time you used Mom's thread and strung it across the doorway of your room to see whether or not I had gone into it."

"She was pretty pissed," Libby responded, recalling the incident.

"How long did she ground you for?" Bernie asked.

"Three days. Which was completely unfair," Libby said. "You were the one who should have gotten punished."

Bernie snorted. "How do you get that?"

"Because if you hadn't kept going into my room without my permission, I never would have done that in the first place!"

"Ah, the good old days," Bernie said as she stepped into the narrow back hallway.

Three bundles of folded-up packing cartons tied up in twine leaned against one of the white walls.

"It looks as if Jack was planning on moving," Libby noted as she walked by them.

"Too bad he didn't do it sooner," Bernie remarked. "He might be alive if he had."

The hallway led first to a pantry and then to the

kitchen. Except for a couple of cans of chicken broth, three cases of club soda, six yams that were beginning to sprout, and a bottle of Macallan fifteen-year, double-cask single malt, the pantry's open shelves were empty.

"Well, one thing we know about Jack Bruno," Bernie remarked as she checked out the shelves, "he had good taste in Scotch."

"What's good taste?"

"About one hundred fifty, two hundred dollars a bottle."

"That's nuts," Libby said.

"Not if you like the stuff," Bernie replied. Which she did. And she reached over, took the bottle, unscrewed the top, and took a sip. "Ah," she exclaimed, letting the Scotch roll around on her tongue. "Perfect." Then she took two more sips, screwed the cap on, and put the bottle back where she'd found it.

"Bernie," Libby cried.

"What? Calm down. I just wanted to see what a fifteen-year-old Scotch tasted like," Bernie explained.

"And what does it taste like?" Libby asked.

"Smoky. Worth every penny," Bernie told her as she stepped into the kitchen. For some reason, she'd expected to see dirty dishes piled in the sink and counters littered with pots and pans, but everything was pristine. The floor was sparkling, and the counters were bare.

"I bet Bruno didn't eat at home much," Libby guessed.

"I bet you're right," Bernie said.

"Talk about the fifties," Libby observed, taking in the galley kitchen's harvest gold–colored appliances, Formica counters, and linoleum floor. She indicated the room with a sweep of her hand. "I'll wager this is original to the house."

"I'll wager you're right. I like it," Bernie said as she hurried along. She'd grown tired of stainless-steel appliances, white tiled walls, and pocket lights in the past few years. "A little color is nice, and at least the kitchen doesn't look like an operating theatre," she noted as she and Bernie walked into the dining room.

The sisters stopped in their tracks.

"Wow," Libby commented.

"Impressive," Bernie said. "Someone's been busy," she added.

"That's one way to put it," Libby responded as she took in the damage that had been wrought.

The cabinet drawers of the mahogany china cabinet on the right side of the room were open, and the glasses and dishes that had been stored in there were now in pieces on the floor, while the six dining-room chairs surrounding the oak table lay on their sides. The two leaves that had made up the center of the table had been pulled apart, exposing the table's mechanism. And as a final touch, the three landscapes that had hung on the walls were now on the floor, and someone had made two holes in the plaster-board walls with the hammer that was lying next to the pictures. A tape measure sat next to it.

Bernie went over and studied the holes. Now that she was closer, she could see that someone had placed a series of light pencil dots on the walls in the shape of a square and then had used a hammer to open the spaces. "These openings aren't random," she observed, pointing to the tape measure and the hammer. "I'm guessing that whoever did this came prepared. Which means they knew where to look."

"Only whatever they expected to find wasn't there," Libby commented. "Otherwise, they would have taken whatever it is they were looking for and gotten out. They wouldn't have ripped everything apart."

"True," Bernie said.

"I don't think Cavelli had anything to do with Bruno's death," Libby added a moment later. "This isn't his style."

"No, it isn't," Bernie agreed. "He's more of a broken kneecap kinda guy." She scratched her chin. "Which leads us back to the question, what did Bruno have that was so valuable? Given the financial circumstances he was in, I'd think he'd want to sell it. I know I would."

"Unless, he didn't have it," Libby hypothesized.

"Well, they definitely thought he did," Bernie commented as she took her phone out of her bag, clicked on the flashlight, and looked inside the holes in the walls.

"Anything in there?" Libby asked.

Bernie shook her head. "Nothing here that shouldn't be. Just studs and insulation." She clicked off the flashlight and put it back in her bag.

"Judging by the size of the holes, what they were after has to have been on the smaller side," Libby said.

"That's what I'm thinking, too," Bernie replied as she stepped into the living room. It was in even worse shape than the dining room was. The expression *hit by a tornado* went through her mind as she studied the scene in front of her.

"No holes in the walls here," Bernie noted.

"Maybe they didn't have time," Libby posited.

"No," Bernie said. "I think they did. "Like I just said, I think that they were following some information that they had acquired and that that information turned out to be wrong. Otherwise, they would have gone to work on all the walls." She began to nibble on her lower lip. "What the hell were they looking for?" she asked for the second time.

"And how does whatever it is relate to Ellen Fisher's death?" Libby asked.

Bernie sighed. "That is the question, isn't it?" Right now, she couldn't even begin to guess.

Libby grunted as she studied the chaos in front of her. "I'd be really pissed if this was my place," she noted.

"It's not Jack Bruno's problem now," Bernie observed.

The black leather sofa had been turned over and its underside slit open, while the cushions that had been on it had been disemboweled, as well. The two club chairs that had sat next to the sofa were lying on their sides, with their guts leaking out, while the coffee table drawers were lying open. The contents—a legal pad, a couple of flyers from Bed Bath & Beyond, three automotive magazines, and a bag of hard candy—were splayed out on the floor. In addition, the pictures had been taken off the walls, but the walls themselves were intact. No one had cut holes in them or done any measuring, further proof that Bernie's suppositions were correct.

"You think one or two people did this?" Libby asked her sister.

Bernie shook her head. "Difficult to say. I suppose it depends on the amount of time they were here."

"Maybe the neighbors saw or heard something," Libby suggested. "After all, someone heard us."

"I'm sure Clyde is going to have people go door to door," Bernie replied as she started walking again. She would have liked to linger and make a little more sense of the scene in front of her, but time was a-wasting, as her mother used to say. Hopefully, the forensics team would come up with something.

"I'll take the bathroom," Libby volunteered.

"Okay. Then I'll take the office," Bernie said, at which point Libby hurried up the stairs, while Bernie walked down another hallway to what she hoped was Jack Bruno's office. Fortunately, it was.

Unfortunately, the room was in the worst shape of all. All the desk and file cabinet drawers had been opened, and the floor was awash with the papers that had been in them. Bernie sighed again as she looked at the scene in front of her. There was no way she could go through everything.

She wished she could take the papers home, but she'd just have to take pictures of the relevant data and be content with that. She clicked her tongue against her teeth as she got to work. She started with the collection of papers on the desk.

On top was a confirmation page from American Airlines for Bruno's one-way flight to Belize. It was taking off the day after tomorrow. Another page showed a rental agreement for an apartment in Belize City. The agreement was for a year. So, Bruno had been planning on getting out of town and not coming back for a while, Bernie thought as she took pictures of the documents.

Bernie could understand why as she shuffled through more of the mail. Nothing good was going on in Jack Bruno's life. If I were him, Bernie thought, I'd want to get out of town, too. There were utility bills, cell phone bills, bills for Bruno's mortgage, credit card bills, and a variety of letters. They followed a natural progression. There were escalating demands for payment, threats to cut off service if payment wasn't made and, finally, demands to appear in small claims court for said unpaid bills. Bernie couldn't imagine the stress of being in that kind of situation as she continued to rummage through the papers on Bruno's desk.

She found a couple of books about famous robberies and some brochures about cruises. When she moved an old newspaper, she found a spool of black thread underneath it, along with a receipt from the sewing store Crazy

Bee. Bernie picked up the spool and studied the strands of thread. They were thick and soft and tightly woven. They reminded her of something—she'd seen this type of thread before. She just couldn't remember where.

She'd been doing some reading on fabric, quilting, and thread in her spare time, and she'd found there were a lot of different types of thread. There was thread for sewing and thread for embroidery, thread you used for quilting and thread for mending, not to mention gold thread and nylon thread. So, what kind of thread was this, and where had she seen it before? She tried to remember as she unwound a length of the thread from the spool, bit it off, formed it into a little ball, and slipped it into one of the pockets of her spring coat. No one needed to know, Bernie decided. Especially not Clyde or her sister. After all, what difference would a foot or so of the thread make to the investigation? There was plenty left over.

Bernie patted her pocket and started to look through a series of small notebooks scattered across the desk. They turned out to contain phone numbers, shopping lists, and random observations of people and their movements, people whom, Bernie assumed, Bruno had been hired to investigate. She almost expected to find notes about herself and Libby in the pile, but she didn't. She had thumbed through three of the notebooks and was on the last page of the fourth notebook when she came across three things scribbled in the margin that caught her attention.

"Bingo," Bernie said as she took a picture of the page with her phone.

"Find something?" Libby asked. She'd heard Bernie's exclamation when she was walking down the stairs.

"I think I might have," Bernie replied, and she showed Libby what she'd discovered.

Bruno had scribbled Ed Gibson's name, the letters *HP*, and the name of a store that sold sewing materials in pencil in the margin. Then he had drawn a circle around them, and a question mark next to the circle. Libby was about to comment, but Bernie's phone rang. It was Clyde, telling them they had to get out of Jack Bruno's house pronto. The Longely crime-scene unit was almost there.

Chapter 39

"That was fast," Libby observed.

"Wasn't it, though? Clyde called it," Bernie said. They'd been in Jack Bruno's house for a little under twenty minutes. "Too bad he is right. We could use a little more time. I wonder what else we would find. And speaking of that, anything of interest upstairs?" she said to Libby as they headed for the back door.

"Bruno had a suitcase open on his bed, and he'd started packing," Libby answered.

"Which fits in with the plane ticket to Belize City that I found," Bernie said.

"Belize," Libby repeated. "Do you know you can buy citizenship there and that they don't have an extradition treaty with the US?"

"Interesting," Bernie said.

"Isn't it?" Libby responded. "I wonder if that's why he picked Belize."

The sisters were quiet for a moment.

Then Bernie said, "What do you think HP means?"

"Isn't that the name of a steak sauce?" Libby asked. "Or," she went on, "the initials could stand for Hewlett-Packard, the company that makes office machines. Maybe Bruno was looking to get a new printer."

"Maybe," Bernie replied. After all, it was possible. She changed the subject. "Any evidence of anyone having searched upstairs?"

Libby shook her head. "If they did, they were a lot neater about it. Nothing was torn apart."

"Which means," Bernie said, theorizing, "that whoever searched this house either ran out of time or knew that what they were looking for wasn't hidden upstairs."

"Because they thought they knew where what they were looking for was," Libby suggested.

"Exactly," Bernie agreed. "And they got pissed when they couldn't find it," she said, thinking of the condition of the living room and the dining room.

By now the sisters were in the back hallway and were heading for the exit.

"Find anything of interest?" Clyde asked as they stepped out the door.

Bernie and Libby jumped. They hadn't expected to see him standing there.

"Wait," he said before either sister could answer. "You can tell me later. Right now, you two need to get out of here."

"With pleasure," Libby told him, and she and her sister hurried toward Mathilda.

The forensic team drove up Jack Bruno's driveway just as Bernie and Libby pulled away from the curb.

"Guess we got out of there in the nick of time," Libby observed as she watched the driver park the police van. A moment later, two members of the team exited the vehicle and began lugging their equipment to Bruno's house while Clyde talked to the third team member.

"Do you know that that expression has been around since the fifteen hundreds?" Bernie informed her sister as she drove down the block. She made a left at the corner.

"No, I didn't," Libby replied. She was about to ask her sister why she could remember stuff like that and not remember to get more quarters from the bank when she heard honking and looked up. A flock of geese was flying overhead. The sight made her smile. She decided she wasn't going to miss the winter sky. Not one little bit. "I think it's time to see if Gail Gibson's brother has returned from his doctor's appointment," Libby continued as her sister slowed down to avoid hitting a squirrel crossing the road.

"Funny you should say that," Bernie replied, making a sharp right on Hawley Avenue. "That's just where we're going."

"Great minds, and so on," Libby said as she sat back and thought about how the pieces of this puzzle fit together. She knew they had to. She just couldn't figure out how they did. Or what connected them. Yet. *Yet* being the operative word. Libby was thinking about how to accomplish that when their dad called, wanting a full report.

Bernie listened while Libby gave him one.

"So, what do you think?" Libby asked her dad when she was done talking.

"About Bruno?"

"About Bruno and everything else I just told you," Libby replied.

There was a moment of silence on the other end while Sean considered what he'd heard.

"Dad?" Bernie prompted.

"Okay," Sean responded. "Much as I hate to say it, if I were still on the job, I'd want to talk to Ed Gibson."

"Figured. We're heading there right now," Bernie told him.

"Be careful," Sean warned them again.

"Dad," Bernie cried. "You already told us that. Give us a little credit. We're not children anymore."

"You are to me," Sean told her.

"We get it, Dad," Libby soothed. "Any other suggestions?"

"Yes," Sean answered. "I'd visit the sewing store and try to find out what Bruno was doing there. Somehow, if memory serves, I don't think he was the kinda guy who'd be making his own pants."

Bernie chuckled. "I didn't realize you knew him," she observed.

"Just to say hello to," Sean replied. "He was after my time. But we've had a few conversations over the years."

"And the initials?" Libby asked. "Do they ring a bell?"

There was another moment of silence. Then Sean said, "They might. Let me get back to you on that one." And he hung up.

Libby leaned back and closed her eyes. A catnap seemed like a good idea now. Due to a fender bender outside of the Eastgate Mall and the resulting traffic buildup, the drive over to the transitional house Gail Gibson's brother was living in took longer than expected. Bernie parked behind a rusted-out Dodge Ram in the driveway, and she and Libby got out. Libby rang the bell. This time Ed Gibson answered the door. The sisters could tell it was Ed Gibson because even though he was tall and skinny, while his sister was short and wide, both had the same high forehead, upturned nose, prominent chin, and light brown hair.

"Yes?" he said as he stepped out onto the porch and closed the door behind him. He was holding a crumpled-up paper napkin in one hand and a pint of milk in the other.

Libby introduced herself and her sister.

"Had a good doctor's appointment?" Bernie asked.

A look of confusion passed over Ed Gibson's face. "How do you know about that?" he demanded.

"We were here before," Libby explained. "One of your roommates told us."

He scowled. "She shouldn't have done that."

"Well, she did," Bernie replied.

"What do you want?" he demanded. "I'm in the middle of eating."

"So, I see," Bernie said. "This won't take very long."

"Your sister sent us," Libby lied. "She said you might be able to help us."

"Really?" Ed Gibson's eyes widened. "That's news to me. She never told me anything about helping anybody."

"Well, she did," Libby said, hoping that he wouldn't call his sister and check.

"Do you know a PI called Bruno?" Bernie asked.

"No, I don't," Ed Gibson quickly replied, a little too quickly in Bernie's book.

"That's funny, because he has your name written down in one of his notebooks," Bernie revealed

"So?" Ed Gibson demanded. "That doesn't mean anything."

"Our mistake," Libby said. "We thought he might have wanted to talk to you about contributing to your alma mater."

Gibson blinked.

"We know you know each other," Bernie continued. "We know you guys went to St. Andrews."

"And that you both majored in chem," Libby added.

"This is a small town," Bernie observed.

"So why did you ask me the question if you already knew the answer?" Ed Gibson demanded of her.

Bernie shrugged. "I was just curious to hear what you were going to say. Why did you lie?"

"Because who I know is none of your business, but if you're so curious, go ask him," Gibson replied.

"We'd love to, but we can't," Libby replied.

"Too bad for you," Gibson told her.

"He's dead," Libby said.

"Jack Bruno is dead?" Ed Gibson repeated.

"Shot," Bernie replied. She couldn't tell from Gibson's poker face whether he knew or not.

Ed Gibson shifted his weight from one leg to the other as he looked from Bernie to Libby and back again. "Look, I don't know what this is about or why you're here, but what I do know is that I don't have to talk to you if I don't want to, and I don't want to, so get the hell off my porch."

"You're right," Libby said. "You don't have to talk to us."

"But it would be better if you did," Bernie added.

A spot of color appeared on each of Ed Gibson's cheeks. "I don't need your advice. Now, if you'll excuse me, I have a peanut butter and banana sandwich waiting for me in the kitchen."

"Good choice," Libby observed. She'd always had a weakness for them.

"Are you going to attend his funeral?" Bernie asked Ed Gibson.

"You just don't take no for an answer, do you?" he said.

"Not usually," Bernie said. "You might want to reconsider your story," she told him quietly.

"What story?" Ed Gibson told her. "I don't know what the hell you're talking about."

"That's too bad," Libby said. She shook her head in mock dismay. "I thought you were smarter than that."

"You're on parole, aren't you?" Bernie asked him.

"So, what if I am?" Ed Gibson demanded, his eyes narrowing.

"You're not supposed to consort with known felons, right? Well, Jack Bruno had a couple of convictions under his belt," Bernie lied. "What would your parole officer say if they knew that?" she asked.

"You're trying to blackmail me?" Ed Gibson demanded, his voice rising in indignation.

"Yes, we are," Bernie said.

"No. We're not," Libby quickly countered. "We don't want to get you in trouble. Or, I should say, get you in any more trouble than you're already in."

"Thank you," Ed Gibson told her.

"I'm sure you didn't mean what happened to have occurred," she added. She didn't know if that was the case or not, but she had just read a book by a hostage negotiator and was trying out one of his suggested negotiating techniques.

"For God's sake, what happened wasn't my fault," Ed Gibson cried. "I didn't know he was going to move the blasted things. How many times do I have to say that!"

"You're talking about the corals?" Bernie asked.

"Yes. The corals," Ed Gibson replied. "What else? The store I got them from should have said something. How was I to know if you move them around too much, they get pissed and weaponize their toxins? What happened wasn't my fault!"

"Unfortunately, the court thought it was," Libby told him.

"They're wrong," Ed Gibson shot back.

Bernie tapped her phone's screen with her finger. "Maybe the court was right. Maybe it wasn't. But either way, you can see how bringing your name to the attention of the police might bring you some unwanted attention. Especially with a toxin being involved and all."

Ed Gibson stuck out his chin. "No. I don't see that. I don't see that at all. I don't know what the hell you're talking about."

"I'm talking about Ellen Fisher," Bernie clarified.

Ed Gibson's eyes widened slightly. "My sister's friend? The one who hung herself?"

"That's the one," Libby said.

"Only we think she had help," Bernie added.

Ed Gibson looked from Bernie to Libby and back again. "I don't get it. What do you mean?"

"We think someone gave her a roofie-like substance and then helped her"—Bernie bracketed the words *helped her* with her fingers—"hang herself."

"Okay," Ed Gibson said. "And what does this have to do with me?"

"Well, you're familiar with toxins, aren't you?" Bernie asked.

Ed Gibson's eyes had turned to slits. "Do you know how many toxins there are in the world?"

"I'm talking about atropine-like substances," Bernie clarified.

"We know it's a stretch," Libby said, taking up the story, "but you can see where knowing Jack Bruno . . . considering that he was mixed up with the Ellen Fisher thing . . . might cause your parole officer to . . ." Libby's voice drifted off.

"To what?" Ed Gibson demanded.

Libby shrugged. "To take a closer look at you."

"You're nuts," Ed Gibson declared, but his voice lacked conviction. "What you're saying makes no sense. Anyway, the case is closed."

"Maybe it is. Maybe it isn't," Bernie said.

"Whether it is or isn't, you're talking to the wrong person," Ed Gibson declared. "I had nothing to do with what happened to Ellen Fisher. Absolutely nothing. Now, get off my porch."

"Then tell us who we should be talking to," Libby asked. "Give us a name."

"Just one name," Bernie said. "If you do that, we'll go away." She raised a hand. "I promise."

"This is bull," Ed Gibson protested.

"Are you willing to take that chance?" Libby asked.

Ed Gibson didn't say anything. Neither did Bernie and Libby. The three of them stood there quietly while Ed Gibson decided what to do.

"Just one name," Bernie coaxed, breaking the silence after a minute had gone by. "We won't tell anyone."

Another moment went by. Ed Gibson remained quiet.

So much for that, Bernie thought. She was thinking of another approach when Ed Gibson spoke.

"You have questions," he said, "go talk to my delightful sister or her scumbag husband." Then he turned, opened the door, walked inside, and slammed the door behind him.

"Scumbag husband?" Libby said to Bernie as she heard the lock on the door click. "Delightful sister? Methinks I detect a whiff of sarcasm in the air."

"Methinks I do, too." Bernie readjusted her headband. "I'm thinking it might be time to have a chat with Gail and her husband, Dwayne," Bernie said.

"Indeed, it might," Libby agreed.

"But first, there's something we need to check out," Bernie said.

Chapter 40

"Who knew there were so many sewing shops in Longely?" Libby remarked as her sister made a sharp turn onto Clover Avenue.

"Three is not a lot," Bernie objected as she stopped at the light. Up ahead a big crane was trying to turn. The vehicle behind it beeped.

"It is for this size town," Libby said.

"I guess sewing's becoming a thing again." Bernie bracketed the word *thing* with her fingers. Then she checked the time. The store they were heading toward was only two miles away. If they hurried, they would be back at A Little Taste of Heaven in time for the afternoon rush.

"What do you think we'll find at the shop?" Libby asked.

"No idea," Bernie replied. "Hopefully, one of the salespeople will be able to tell us what Jack Bruno was asking about."

"I'm guessing it had to do with Ellen Fisher's quilt," Libby said. "But what? I just can't figure out how the quilt she was working on led to her death. For that matter, what does Ed Gibson have to do with anything?"

"If I knew that, Libby, we wouldn't be canvassing the sewing shops, would we?"

"No, we would not," Libby replied as she sat back in her seat, folded her arms over her chest, and watched the cars go by. For some reason, there was more traffic than usual this time of day.

They pulled up to Crazy Bee five minutes later. The shop was located between a liquor store and a UPS store in a cul-de-sac off the main shopping area.

"For when you need a stiff one after you have to rip everything out," Bernie said, pointing to Bart's Booze.

"Don't remind me," Libby said, thinking of the time in seventh grade when she'd had to sew a skirt in home ec. She could still see the damned thing. The experience had scarred her for life. She'd never sewn anything else after that. She'd kept putting the zipper in, and the sewing instructor had kept ripping it out because the zipper didn't lie flat. It was wavy. After the eighth time, she'd snuck the skirt out of school and given it to her mother to fix. She still remembered the print on the skirt all these years later and not in a good way.

"Here goes nothing," Bernie said as she got out of the van.

"You can say that again," Libby commented, joining her.

"Okay. Here goes nothing."

"Ha. Ha. Very funny," Libby told her sister as she opened the shop door.

The bell tinkled when Bernie and Libby walked in. They were heading for the counter when they spotted Judy Fine. She was fingering a piece of chintz.

"Judy," Libby called.

Judy looked up and did a double take. "Fancy meeting you here," she said. "I didn't know you guys sewed."

"I don't," Libby said.

Bernie corrected her sister. "We don't. We're not crafty."

"Well, we are, but not in that way," Libby said.

Judy Fine looked puzzled. "Then why *are* you guys here?"

Bernie decided to go the indirect route with her answer, so she dug into her pocket and pulled out the piece of thread she'd taken from the spool in Jack Bruno's house. "I'm looking to match this," she said.

The woman who had been standing behind the counter when Libby and Bernie walked in extended her hand. "Let me see that," she said. "Maybe I can help."

Bernie put the thread in the woman's hand. The woman had a badge with her name pinned to the front of her blue button-down shirt. It read SUE.

Sue looked at the thread for a minute. Then she said, "That's *sashiko*—Japanese mending thread." She pointed to an area in the back of the store. "You'll find some in the back. We have twenty different colors."

"Is it common?" Bernie asked.

"It is now," Sue answered. "Although people don't usually use black."

"People are using it instead of embroidery thread," Judy Fine added.

"It gives a different feel to the design," Sue explained. Then she nodded toward a woman who had just walked in the store. "I need to take care of Claire. Be back in a minute," she promised, and then she bustled off to deal with the new customer.

Bernie and Libby turned to Judy Fine.

"So how are things going?" Bernie asked Judy.

Judy shrugged. "The usual. I thought you said you didn't do crafts stuff."

"We don't," Libby said.

"Then what are you doing with that piece of thread?" Judy asked. "I'm puzzled."

"So are we," Libby told her. "We found it in Jack Bruno's house," Libby informed her.

Judy Fine did a double take.

"Name sound familiar?" Libby asked, nudging.

Judy rubbed her right earlobe with her fingertips.

Bernie smiled and took a step closer to Judy. "That's your cue to say, 'So how is Jack these days?'"

Judy stuck out her chin. "And why should I say that?"

"Because you hired him, and I thought you might want to know how he's doing."

Judy blushed. "How . . . ? Did he—"

"Say anything about your hiring him?" Libby asked, interrupting. "No. He didn't." Which was true. "People talk," Libby lied.

Judy looked at the floor, then back up. "It was a mistake. I should have trusted my hubs."

"How'd you find him?" Libby asked.

"Jack Bruno?" Judy asked.

Libby nodded.

"Why are you asking?" Judy wanted to know.

Libby shrugged. "Professional curiosity."

Judy nodded. "Gail gave me his name. She said that she'd used him before and that he was good, and he was cheap. That I could negotiate my price because he needed the work."

"And why did she need him?" Bernie asked.

Judy looked down at the floor again and mumbled something.

"What?" Libby said. "I'm sorry. I didn't catch that."

"I'm not sure it's my place to tell you," Judy said, looking up.

"Let's pretend it is," Bernie said.

Judy shook her head from side to side. "No. You want to know, ask Gail. Or Dwayne."

Libby lifted an eyebrow, remembering what Ed Gibson had said. "Do you know where we can find either one?"

"Gail is at a workshop, and I imagine Dwayne is at work," Judy said.

"And where is that?" Libby asked.

"Down on Jefferson Street. He does IT stuff for Cannon." Cannon was a company that specialized in manufacturing cardboard boxes.

"So how is Jack?" Sue asked brightly, having returned from waiting on her customer.

Bernie and Libby startled. They'd forgotten she was there.

"You know him?" Bernie inquired.

Sue nodded. "He was in here a couple of months ago, asking the same question you're asking now. Said it was part of a case. Actually, he had a spool of *sashiko* with him."

"I don't suppose he happened to say what the case he was working on was?" Bernie asked.

"He said he was looking for something and there was a big finder's fee if he got it, but that he wasn't having too much luck so far."

"Anything else?" Libby inquired.

"That he was hoping his luck would turn. He seemed nice. I liked him." She stifled a sneeze. "Well, if you see him, tell him I said hello. Tell him we still haven't had that drink he promised me. Two drinks, actually."

"Unfortunately, we can't," Bernie said.

"And why is that?" Judy asked.

"Because he's dead," Bernie replied.

Sue let out a small gasp. "Oh my God, that's terrible! What happened?"

"Someone shot him," Libby told her.

"You're kidding," Sue exclaimed.

"I wish I was," Libby replied, noticing as she did that Judy looked stunned. "Is everything okay?" she asked her.

"It's fine," Judy said.

Libby studied her face. "Are you sure?"

Judy took a step back. "I'm sure. It's just that . . . I'm not feeling well."

Sue looked concerned. "Can I get you a glass of water? Do you want me to call someone for you?"

Judy shook her head. "I'll be fine. I have to go home and take my medicine. My stomach acts up occasionally," she explained as she turned and headed for the door.

"Judy, what about your swatches?" Sue called after her, pointing to two squares of plaid flannel sitting on the counter. "Do you want them?"

Judy stopped and turned around. "Save them for me," she told Sue. "I'll be back later." Then she was out the door.

A moment later, they heard the squeal of tires as Judy took off.

"I wonder what that was all about," Sue mused as she folded up the pieces of material Judy had left behind and put them aside.

"That's a good question," Bernie said. "Definitely makes one wonder." She turned back to Sue. "Can you tell me anything else about Bruno?" she asked her.

"Not really," Sue replied. "Sorry."

"Call us if you remember something," Libby said.

Sue promised that she would as Bernie gave her one of their cards.

Chapter 41

After giving Sue their card, Bernie and Libby left Crazy Bee. They were four blocks away from the fabric store when Libby pointed to a Honda Accord in the McDonald's parking lot across the street.

"Look," she said to Bernie.

"At what?" Bernie asked, taking her eyes off the road for a minute. "I don't see anything."

"There. In the light blue Honda Accord."

Bernie squinted. "I still don't see anything."

"The woman in it. The one talking on the phone. Isn't that Judy Fine?"

Bernie slowed down some more to get a better look. The guy behind her honked, but Bernie ignored him. "You're right. It is," she said. "Her stomach seems better," Bernie commented, referring to the fact that Judy Fine was holding a hamburger in one hand and her phone in the other. "I mean, a Big Mac is my go-to when I'm having digestive issues. Isn't it yours?"

"Personally, I find the fries work better for me." Libby scratched a mosquito bite on her leg. "I wonder who she's talking to," Libby mused, changing the subject.

"Let's ask her," Bernie said. Then she made an illegal U-turn, cutting off the vehicle in front of them.

"Bernie," Libby squealed as the driver of the car in front of them slammed on his brakes.

"Sorry," Bernie called out to the man she'd cut off as he cursed her out. "My bad."

"Apologies aren't going to matter if we're dead," Libby noted after the man had given Bernie the finger and sped off.

"But we're not," Bernie pointed out while she drove into the parking lot.

"But we could be," Libby replied.

Bernie snorted. "We could also get hit by a semi crossing the street or fall into the Hudson and drown."

"I'm serious."

"So am I."

"Do you want to take over the driving?" Bernie asked her sister.

Libby allowed as how she really didn't.

"Okay," Bernie said. She parked a row back and two spaces away from the Honda Accord. Then she and Libby exited Mathilda and walked over to the passenger side of Judy Fine's vehicle. She was so involved in her conversation that she didn't notice them.

"This should be fun," Bernie said to Libby as she rapped on the window.

Judy jumped and let go of the Double Big Mac she'd been eating. Bernie watched it fall into her lap. Then Judy picked the hamburger up, put it back in the bag it had come in, and rolled down the window. "Oh my God," she said to Bernie when she realized who it was. "You could have given me a heart attack."

"Sorry," Bernie said as Judy told whomever she was talking to that she had to go and rested her phone on her vehicle's center console.

"What are you doing here?" Judy demanded.

"We were concerned," Libby told her.

Judy looked puzzled. "Concerned about what?"

Bernie answered, "You."

"Me?" Judy squeaked.

"Well, you left the shop so hurriedly, we were worried that something was wrong. I mean, you told us you had to go home, and when we saw you here . . ." Libby shrugged. "We just wanted to make sure that everything was okay."

Judy's laugh was unconvincing. "That's very sweet of you, but I'm fine."

"Good to hear," Libby said.

"You know," Bernie said to Judy as she opened the door to the Accord and slid into the front passenger seat, "you really shouldn't sit in a parking lot and talk on your phone. It's dangerous. It leaves you vulnerable to carjackers."

"At the very least you should lock your doors," Libby advised Judy as she got into the back of the vehicle. "We could be robbers."

Judy didn't answer. She'd just noticed the stain on her skirt the hamburger had made when she'd dropped it. "Damn," she said, grabbing a napkin and dabbing at the stain.

"Sorry about that," Bernie told her, referring to the stain. "I'll pay for the cleaner."

Judy dabbed harder. "I don't think mayo and ketchup come out."

"I guess your stomach is better," Libby observed. She pointed to the Double Big Mac and the French fries Judy had been eating.

Judy stopped dabbing and looked up. "It was probably just my gallstones acting up at the store," she told Libby. "Sometimes I just get these intense pains, and then they go away."

"Ah," Bernie said. "My mother had gallstones," she lied. "Her attacks went on for days."

Judy's lips imitated a smile. "Guess I'm lucky, then."

"Guess you are," Bernie said.

Then Judy's phone rang. Judy reached for it, but Bernie picked it up first and handed it to her. "Ed Gibson," she said, reading the name on the screen. "I didn't know you knew him."

"Not very well," Judy said after she'd told Ed she would call him back. "Not really."

"And yet he has your number," Libby observed.

"Well, he is my friend's brother. We're arranging a surprise birthday party for Gail," Judy volunteered after a minute's hesitation.

"I'm surprised," Libby said, remembering Ed Gibson's last comments to them. "I didn't think he liked his sister very much."

Judy shrugged. "You know how siblings are. Always fighting."

"I do, indeed," Bernie told her. "So how is Gail these days, anyway?"

"She's fine," Judy told her. She glanced at the clock on the dashboard of her vehicle. "Now, if you don't mind, there's somewhere I have to be."

"Don't we all," Bernie said, leaning back in the car seat.

Judy took a deep breath and let it out. "What's that supposed to mean?"

Bernie beamed. "Nothing. Just a statement of fact."

"You know what I think?" Libby said. "I think Ed Gibson was calling you because he wanted to tell you about Jack Bruno's death."

Judy shrugged again. "So, what if he did? He has a right to, doesn't he?"

"I suppose he does," Bernie allowed. She smiled. "You want to tell me about Gail and Dwayne?"

"I already said I didn't want to," Judy replied.

Bernie decided to take a guess. "Marital issues. They were having marital issues. That's why people usually hire PIs. That or industrial espionage."

"Like I said before, you want to know about Gail and Dwayne, go talk to them," Judy told her.

"I'm asking you," Bernie replied.

Judy clamped her lips together. The fact that she didn't say anything told Bernie everything she needed to know.

"So why did you run out of the shop like that when you heard about Bruno getting shot?" Bernie asked her, changing the subject for a moment. "Curious minds want to know."

"I told you why," Judy repeated, and she started dabbing at her skirt again. "I thought I was getting a gallbladder attack."

"You know we already spoke to Ed Gibson," Bernie told her. "He told us everything," she lied.

Judy lifted an eyebrow. "Do tell."

"He did tell," Bernie replied. "He called Gail's husband scum, or words to that effect."

The corners of Judy's mouth moved up briefly. "Really?"

"So why don't you tell us why he said that," Libby urged.

"I don't see it as relevant to anything," Judy said.

"It might be," Bernie said.

"Or it might not be," Judy shot back.

"Do you want me to tell you why I think it is?" Bernie asked.

"Not really," Judy replied.

Bernie studied Judy's face for a moment. Then she said, "Let me tell you a story." And she began before Judy could object. "When I got out of college, I got an apartment down on the Lower East Side with two of my old roommates. Everything was going fine until one of them started fooling around with the other one's boyfriend."

Judy leaned forward. Bernie could tell she was interested.

"And then one day, out of the blue, Rachel never came home."

"Who's Rachel?" Judy asked.

"The one whose boyfriend was cheating on her," Bernie answered. "They found her body three weeks later floating in the East River."

"That's terrible," Judy exclaimed. "Did they ever find out what happened to her?"

"She was killed, but the police never found out who did it," Bernie answered. "And it made me crazy, because I suspected, pretty strongly suspected, that the other roommate was behind it, but I didn't want to say anything, because I really liked Patty."

"The other roommate?" Judy asked.

Bernie nodded and continued talking. "And I suspect you feel the same way. It tore me apart being in that situation, and I think the same might be true of you."

"I don't know what you're talking about," Judy said as she turned her head away.

"I understand why you don't want to say anything," Bernie continued. "I know this is hard, but three people have been killed," Bernie pointed out, appealing to Judy's conscience.

"You don't know that the deaths are related," Judy protested.

"I'm pretty sure they are," Libby said gently.

The three women sat in the Accord for a minute, watching the flow of people in and out of the fast-food place.

"Please," Bernie said.

"Just tell us what you can," Libby urged. "Anything will help."

Another moment went by. Then Judy spoke. "It's simple, really. Gail suspected that Dwayne was having an affair, so she hired Bruno to follow him."

"Was he?" Bernie urged.

"Yes. He was having it with Ellen. Her best friend," Judy said.

"Gail must have been livid," Bernie said. "I know I would be."

Judy nodded. "I've never seen Gail so angry. She made these comments." Judy stopped talking for a moment and took a breath before continuing. "She was talking about her brother and the corals and saying she'd like to buy Ellen a saltwater fish tank for a birthday present just like the one her brother had set up, and then she was talking about how someone could commit the perfect murder. Just feed them this drug. The one that helps with seasickness."

"Scopolamine?" Bernie guessed.

"Yes." Judy blinked. "Something like it. I forget."

"Why would you do that?" Bernie asked.

"Because in a high enough dose, it makes you real suggestible. Kinda like roofies. Only worse. Gail called it the zombie drug. I thought she was venting. You know how you say things when you're angry? At least, that's what I kept telling myself."

Bernie nodded.

"But then, when you came in and I heard that Bruno had died, it made me wonder." Judy's voice trailed off. "I don't know what to think anymore," she said after a moment had gone by. Then she reached over and turned the key in the ignition. As she did, her jacket sleeve went up, exposing a small tattoo on the inside of her lower arm.

"What's that?" Bernie asked, pointing to it.

Judy hastily pulled down her sleeve. "Nothing," she said. "Just an ill-conceived memento of times past."

"I'm thinking of getting a tattoo myself," Bernie told her.

"Make sure it's something you want to keep," Judy advised as Bernie began exiting the Accord.

"So, what was that thing on her arm?" Libby asked her sister as they walked back to their van.

"I think it was a tattoo of a honey pot," Bernie told her.

Libby frowned. "Honey pot?"

"Yes, honey pot."

You mean like the honey pot in *Winnie-the-Pooh*?" Libby asked.

"Yes, like the honey pot in *Winnie-the-Pooh*," Bernie repeated. "At least that's what it looked like to me."

"That's weird. Why would you have something like that tattooed on your arm?" Libby asked Bernie.

Bernie shrugged. "No idea. Maybe Judy is a beekeeper," Bernie said. "Maybe she just likes bees. Or honey. Or both. After all," she said, thinking about Libby's old boyfriend's tattoo, "Orion had a tattoo of a cigarette lighter on his back."

"I have a question," Libby said as she and her sister got into Mathilda.

"Shoot," Bernie said.

"You know that story you told about your roommates. Was that true?"

Bernie laughed as she started the van. "No. I made the whole thing up."

"That's what I thought," Libby said as they exited the parking lot.

Chapter 42

"Wow," Sean said when Bernie told her dad what she'd seen on Judy Fine's arm. "Talk about a blast from the past."

"You know what that tattoo stands for?" Libby asked him.

Sean grinned. "I can make a pretty good guess."

"Are you going to tell us?" Libby asked after a moment had gone by and her dad hadn't said anything else.

"And the magic word is?" Sean inquired.

"Please," Libby said.

Sean nodded. "Better. It's the Honey Pots."

"Was that a rock band?" Libby asked as she cut her dad a thin slice of cheesecake and handed it to him.

Sean laughed. "Not exactly, although it's a great name for one," he replied as he took the slice and sat back down in his chair.

It had been a busy day, and this was the first chance that Bernie and Libby had had to sit down with their dad and tell him about what had happened.

"Delicious," he said after taking a bite as he watched clouds starting to cover the moonless sky. He checked his watch. Nine thirty. Rain was forecast for later in the evening, but it looked as if it was arriving earlier.

"We used egg whites to lighten the batter," Libby explained as she cut a slice for herself and her sister. "You think it works?"

Sean nodded. "Does for me. I like the dense New York–style cheesecake that you make, but I like this one, as well. It feels . . ."

"Springier?" Libby asked, supplying the word.

"I was going to say lighter," Sean replied.

"That's the idea," Libby told him.

"So, what about the tattoo?" Bernie prompted.

"Are you sure it was a honey pot?" Sean asked.

Libby nodded. On the way home, they'd stopped at the library and checked out a copy of *Winnie-the-Pooh*. She got up, took the book out of her bag, opened it to the right page, and showed the illustration to her dad. "It looked just like that."

Sean nodded. "Interesting."

"Why is it interesting?" Bernie asked.

"A bit of background first," Sean went on after he'd cleared his throat. "Back in the late sixties, early seventies, the women's lib movement came to the fore."

"We know, Dad," Libby said, rolling her eyes. "We're not total dummies."

"I realize that. Do you want to hear this or not?"

"Hear it," Libby said, sitting down.

"Fine. Then let me talk."

"Sorry, Dad," Libby muttered.

Sean took a sip of tea, then began. "As I was saying before I was interrupted, women participated in the movement in lots of different ways. Some read books, some formed consciousness-raising groups that met once a week, and others participated in protests. Some of the more radical groups among them participated in what they called guerrilla theater. For example, a couple of the groups disrupted the Miss America pageant in Atlantic City, while another group—they called themselves Marxist feminists— snuck onto the trading floor of the New York Stock Exchange and burned their bras."

"Seriously?" Libby asked.

"Yes, seriously," Sean said. "If I remember correctly, they were protesting the patriarchal structure of capitalism. However, there were also smaller, even more radical groups. One of the groups claimed credit for robbing a Chase Bank in Scarsdale and stealing a quilt fragment from the thirteenth century that was hanging in the Metropolitan Museum of Art."

"I read about that," Bernie exclaimed excitedly, recalling a chapter she'd glanced through in *The History of Quilts.* "But they were never caught. The money and the quilt vanished, and so did they."

Sean nodded. "That is correct. And you know what they called themselves?"

"The Honey Pots?" Bernie guessed.

Sean beamed. "Exactly."

"So, you're saying . . . ," Libby began.

"I'm saying Judy's tattoo is suggestive that she was a member of the group," Sean said. "She is the right age." He popped another bite of cheesecake into his mouth. "Of course," he reflected, "she could just be really fond of Winnie-the-Pooh, too. That's also a possibility."

"But why identify yourself as a group member of a group that's done something illegal?" Bernie mused.

Sean shrugged. "Good question," he said, thinking back to the gang members he'd arrested. He'd asked them that exact question from time to time, but he'd never gotten a satisfactory answer.

Libby took a sip of her ginger tea. "I wonder if the other members of the Sip and Sew group have similar tattoos," she mused when she was through.

"I didn't see any," Bernie said after a moment of thought, "but then, I wasn't looking, either."

"Neither was I," Libby remarked. She stared at her cup of tea for a moment, as if willing it to answer. She turned to her dad. "Do you think Ellen Fisher was a member of the group? Do you think her death had anything to do with the theft of the quilt?"

"It's possible," Sean replied. "Of course, anything is possible."

"We are making a lot of assumptions here," Libby noted.

"True," Bernie said.

"I would agree with you. Except there is the matter of Ellen Fisher's identity or lack of one," Sean told her. "I finally got hold of my friend," he continued. "The one retired from the FBI. He couldn't find anything on an Ellen Fisher."

"Meaning?" Libby asked.

"That she wasn't in WITSEC, which means the FBI hadn't caught up with her." Sean took a sip of his tea and put the mug down. "But she was obviously involved in something, because why else go to all that trouble?"

"Trouble?" Libby echoed.

Sean explained. "You just don't decide to get a new identity for the hell of it. It's expensive, not to mention a hell of a lot of work. At least so I'm told." And with that, Sean finished his slice of cheesecake, thought about asking Libby to cut him another slice, and decided against it. His potbelly didn't need any more encouragement.

"But what we're talking about happened a long time

ago," Libby pointed out. "Why kill Ellen Fisher now? That makes no sense."

"Something must have sparked it," Bernie noted. She tapped her fingers against her mug while she considered the possibilities. "Of course, there's another direction to go down. Maybe Ellen's death didn't have anything to do with what we were talking about. Maybe it has to do with the affair she was having with Gail's husband."

"You really think so?" Libby asked.

Sean raised an eyebrow. "Love. Money. They elicit powerful emotions. Add revenge," he went on, "and you have the perfect trifecta for bad behavior." Then he thought back to the sequence of events that had occurred in the past couple of weeks. "I think we can safely say what we do know for sure is that someone wants something—let's call it object X—and they don't know who has it. Ellen Fisher's house was searched, and so was Jack Bruno's."

"What about Diane Englewood? We don't know why she was killed, either," Libby interjected. "If she was killed," she added.

"No, we don't," Sean agreed. "But I think it's safe to assume it had something to do with what she wanted to tell you. Three deaths in a very short time. Are they all connected? The probability is high that they are. We can also assume that our perp didn't find what they were searching for at Ellen Fisher's house, because if they had, the whole thing would have ended there."

Libby massaged her temples. "This thing is getting way too complicated."

"Yes, it is," Sean agreed. "There are a lot of threads in play here." He took a sip of tea and cleared his throat before continuing. "Too many. Also, the fact that somebody hired Jack Bruno to follow you and Bernie tells me that whoever is behind this thought that either you had the object or you could lead them to it."

"Or that Jack Bruno had taken it from us and kept it for himself," Libby added, thinking of the condition they'd found his house in.

"Also true," Sean agreed.

"Whatever they're looking for must be very valuable," Bernie observed.

"Well, if I recall correctly, the quilt fragment is priceless, and the Honey Pots were rumored to have stolen over a million dollars from the bank, so I would say we're talking about a fair chunk of change," Sean answered.

"Which is worth a lot more today, what with inflation and all," Libby pointed out.

For a moment, Bernie, Libby, and Sean all sat there quietly, listening to the mournful sound of a tugboat making its way down the Hudson River and thinking about the case.

"I have an idea," Bernie said suddenly, a thought having just occurred to her.

Sean and Libby looked at her.

"I think I know where the money and the quilt could be hidden."

"And where is that?" Sean asked.

Bernie told him.

Libby leaned forward. "What makes you say that?" she asked.

"Simple," Bernie answered. "There was a big woodpile in Jack Bruno's backyard, but there were no ashes in the fireplace."

"Maybe Jack Bruno decided not to build any fires this year," Libby said.

"Then why order all that wood?" Bernie challenged.

"How about his chimney needs to be fixed and he didn't have the money to do it?" Libby suggested.

Bernie shook her head. "No. I think he ordered the wood and ended up not using it because he decided to hide something in the chimney flue instead." Then she turned to her dad and asked him what he thought.

Sean smiled and said, "I think I want another piece of cheesecake." The hell with his potbelly. He'd get started on his diet tomorrow.

Chapter 43

It was a little after two o'clock in the morning when Bernie left Mathilda in the parking lot of the all-night corner store near Jack Bruno's house. Max's Place was three blocks away, and Bernie reasoned if one of Bruno's neighbors woke up and looked out the window, they wouldn't see A Taste of Heaven's van parked in Bruno's driveway and call the cops. She wasn't sure she wanted to risk Lucy's wrath again. The last thing she needed was seeing the inside of the Longely jail, because she was pretty sure that this time he would follow through on his threat.

At this hour of the morning, the houses were dark, and the streets were empty. It was misting out, creating halos around the streetlamps. Wisps of fog dancing like ghosts hung in the air, and Bernie and Libby could see a vapor trail from the plane flying overhead as they walked toward Bruno's house.

They'd gone a block and a half when Bernie stopped and asked her sister if she'd heard anything.

"No. Why?" Libby responded.

"Because I thought I did," Bernie told her.

"Like what?"

Bernie frowned. "I'm not sure. Like maybe something creaking?"

Libby listened carefully. The only thing she heard was the sound of a dog barking somewhere in the distance. "Sorry," she said. "I don't."

"I could have sworn I did," Bernie declared.

"It's probably the wind in the trees," Libby told her.

Bernie listened for another minute. Whatever she'd heard was gone. "You're probably right," she said, and she started walking again.

A couple of minutes later, the sisters arrived at their destination. A light shone in an upstairs bedroom, but other than that, Jack Bruno's house was dark. It looked like all the other houses on the block, except for the crime-scene tape wrapped around the house, cordoning it off from the land of the living. Libby and Bernie ducked under the yellow tape and continued to the rear of the house. Someone, probably one of the EMTs, had left a tarp draped over the woodpile, but other than that, everything looked the way it had the last time they were here. Except for the back door. The police had sealed that shut with crime-scene tape.

"Now what?" Libby asked, pointing to it. If they cut the tape on the door, it would become immediately apparent that someone had been in there, and the most obvious someones were them.

"Guess we go in through a window, unless you have a better suggestion," Bernie whispered.

When Libby allowed as how she didn't, the sisters turned to study the rear of the house.

"At least the windows aren't alarmed," Libby noted.

"I don't think they have locks on them, either," Bernie said as she walked over to take a closer look. Nope. They didn't. So that was good. She went to the nearest one and tried the screen. It lifted. Then she tried the window itself. It wouldn't budge. Closer inspection showed the window was painted shut. She sighed.

"We need a knife," Libby said.

"I've got something just as good," Bernie replied.

"Like what?" Libby asked.

"This." And Bernie reached into her back pocket and pulled out a nail file.

"Isn't that a nail file?" Libby asked.

Bernie corrected her. "It's not just an ordinary nail file. It's a diamond nail file."

Libby snorted. "Well, that makes all the difference."

"Hopefully, it will," Bernie replied, pushing the file's point into the painted space between the sill and the window. Then she used a sawing motion to move the file to the left. "See?" she said as a tear appeared in the white paint. "It works."

"Since when do you carry a nail file—excuse me, a diamond nail file—around?" Libby asked.

"Since I forgot to take it out of my pocket when I broke my nail," Bernie told her as she turned her attention back to the window. She slowly worked her way through the paint on the right side of the window, went on to the left side, and then started on the bottom. Ten minutes later she was done. "Give me a hand," she said to Libby after she'd tried to push the window up by herself and failed. "It's sticking."

They both managed to open the window together, but when they let go of it, it came back down with a loud thud, which sounded even louder in the quiet of the night.

Bernie cursed under her breath. She and Libby stood there listening, waiting to see if the thud had woken the neighbors. After a moment, when no one had popped their head out of a window, the Simmons sisters went back to what they'd been doing.

"Let's try this again," Bernie remarked as she motioned for her sister to hold the window open for her. When Libby did, Bernie slipped the file back in her rear pocket and climbed inside Bruno's house. "Your turn," she said to Libby as she held the window open for her sister.

Libby grunted as she pulled herself up and climbed through. Then Bernie quietly closed the window, and the sisters studied the dining room.

"Looks the same to me," Libby observed.

"Me too," Bernie agreed as she headed over to the fireplace in the living room. Libby followed. They stopped in front of the fireplace. It was the one place in the room that hadn't been touched. The logs were still neatly stacked inside the firebox, waiting to be lit. "Help me," she said to Libby as she began moving them out of the way.

"Why do you think there's something stuck up the chimney?" Libby asked Bernie.

"I already told you. Because it's the only place downstairs that no one has looked," Bernie replied. She pointed to the firebox. "It's pristine. It doesn't look as if anyone used it this past winter."

"Maybe Bruno developed an allergy to smoke," Libby said, citing another possibility, as she stacked the logs Bernie was handing her off to one side.

"I guess we're going to find out," Bernie replied while she handed Libby the last piece of wood. Then she took her phone out of her jeans pocket, turned on its flashlight, crouched down, and stepped into the fireplace.

"See anything?" Libby asked as Bernie shone the light up the flue.

"I'm not sure," Bernie said. She thought she saw something blocking the chimney, but it was hard to tell. "Can you hand me something, like a broom or a mop? I think I remember seeing one in the kitchen."

Libby nodded and went to get it. A moment later she was back, mop in hand. "Here you go," she said, handing it to Bernie. Then she watched as Bernie worked the wooden end of the mop up the flue.

"There's definitely something in there," she said as she gave whatever it was a sharp poke. Nothing happened. "And it's definitely wedged in there pretty tightly," she said as she gave it another couple of sharp jabs. Still nothing. She lowered the mop and was thinking about what to do next when she heard a thump. A duffel bag had fallen onto the fireplace grate.

"Wow," Libby said as Bernie scooped it up and headed to the dining-room table.

"See?" Bernie said as she placed the duffel on the table and unzipped it. There was a smallish package wrapped in cloth sitting on top of packs of fifty- and hundred-dollar bills.

"When you're right, you're right," Libby said as she reached over and fingered the material the package was wrapped in. "I recognize this. Ellen used this material in her quilt."

Bernie took another look. "She did, didn't she?"

"Yes, she did," Cecilia Larson said.

Bernie and Libby whirled around. Cecilia was standing there. It took the sisters a moment to see the gun in her hand, the gun pointed at them.

"Good job. I knew you could do it," Cecilia told them.

Chapter 44

"Do what?" Libby said. "Why do you have a gun? I don't understand."

"I think I do," Bernie said as Cecilia motioned for them to step away from the duffel bag.

The two sisters did what they were told. Cecilia threw a zip tie to Bernie and instructed her to tie her sister's hands behind her back. For a moment, Bernie thought about rushing Cecilia, but Cecilia must have read her mind.

"Don't," she told Bernie. "Because you're wrong if you think I won't shoot you and your sister, because I will."

"Yeah," Bernie said. "What's two more people in the scheme of things?"

Cecilia smiled. "Exactly."

"Fair enough," Bernie said, and she did what she'd been told to do, hoping it would buy her more time.

When Bernie was done, Cecilia instructed Bernie to turn around and take a step back toward her. Again, Bernie obeyed. Again, she didn't feel she had much choice.

"How did you know we were here?" Bernie asked Cecilia.

Cecilia laughed. "Simple," she said. "I put a tracker on

your van. I just followed you here. Talk about convenient."

"I knew I heard something when we were walking over here," Bernie exclaimed.

"You should have listened to your gut," Cecilia told Bernie.

"You really hired us to find the quilt and the money, didn't you?" Bernie asked Cecilia. "That story about finding Ellen's killer was bull."

Cecilia laughed. "Well, Selene and I hired you, if you want to be exact," Cecilia answered as she zip-tied Bernie's hands behind her back, too. "Although I have to say, it took you long enough. I was beginning to think you wouldn't be able to."

"But why?" Libby asked her.

"Obviously, because I couldn't find it myself. And Ellen wasn't talking . . ."

"It's hard to talk when you're dead," Libby observed.

Cecilia nodded. "Give the girl a cigar, as they used to say in the old days. I'd clap if I wasn't holding this gun in my hand."

"So, the text Ellen sent?" Libby asked.

"Selene sent it from Ellen's phone," Cecilia told her.

"And the others?" Bernie inquired.

"What do you think?" Cecilia said.

"I think the same thing obtained," Bernie told her. She shook her head. "And to think I thought Gail Gibson was behind the whole thing."

"She makes a good patsy," Cecilia observed as she indicated with a motion of her hand that she wanted Bernie and Libby to move. "Back into the living room, please."

"What now?" Bernie asked her.

"Now I take your cell phones."

Bernie watched Cecilia while she did.

"Can't have you calling anyone in your hour of need," Cecilia chirped.

"One question," Bernie said.

"Sure," Cecilia told her. "Fire away. Whatever you want to know. It's not like you're going to be able to tell anyone."

"Why did you kill Ellen?" Bernie asked, playing for time.

Cecilia laughed for the second time. "That's simple. She stole the money and the quilt, and I wanted them back, and she wouldn't give them to me."

"Then how did Bruno end up with them?" Libby asked.

Cecilia replied, "We hired him to make sure you were doing what you were supposed to do, and he figured out where Ellen had hidden the money and the quilt fragment before you did. Don't ask me how. In any case, he took them. I offered him one hundred thousand, but he wanted it all. Said he had debts to pay, but it wasn't his to keep. As my mom used to say, 'Greedy is as greedy does.'"

Libby corrected her. "I believe the saying is 'Beauty is as beauty does.'"

"Do I look like I care?" Cecilia said as she put Bernie's and Libby's phones in her tote and zipped it up.

"What about Diane?" Bernie asked. "Why did you kill her? How did she fit into all of this?"

"I feel bad about that," Cecilia admitted. "But what else could I do, given the circumstances?"

"What circumstances?" Libby asked.

"She was going to talk to you, tell you what we did all those years ago," Cecilia replied.

"You're saying she suddenly got a conscience?" Libby asked.

"That's what she said, anyway," Cecilia replied. "Evidently, she didn't like what happened with Ellen. Diane said I had gone too far, killing one of our own, but what else was I going to do? All that money and planning, all those years of keeping quiet and going about our day jobs. We had plans. That money was for our old age. We were going to live by the sea in Costa Rica.

"And then Ellen decides to run off with Dwayne and live happily ever after on the money we took. And on top of everything, she was going to give the quilt fragment back to the museum we took it from in the first place." Cecilia's nostrils quivered in indignation. "Because she felt guilty. Because she felt we were too doctrinaire. I told her not to. I told her to give everything back, but she just laughed and said it was too late. And Diane thought that was perfectly okay . . . well, not exactly okay."

"I'm confused," Bernie said when Cecilia paused to take a breath. "Let me get this straight. You hired us to find the money and quilt fragment that Ellen stole, and then you hired Bruno when we didn't turn them up immediately, but he figured out where Ellen had hidden them before we did and stole them himself."

"That's what I said," Cecilia answered. Then she motioned for the sisters to lie down on the floor by the sofa. Once they had, she took a roll of duct tape out of her tote bag and wound it around their legs several times. Bernie tried to move, but she couldn't. Now she knew what a turkey felt like.

"That should keep you in place," Cecilia said when she was through. Then she walked into the kitchen. Bernie and Libby heard a drawer opening and closing and the click of knobs on the stove. Cecilia was back a minute later. Bernie thought she could smell a whiff of gas, but she wasn't sure.

"What did you do?" she asked Cecilia.

"Turned on all the gas burners, put an old yam in the

microwave with a metal bowl, and turned on the microwave," Cecilia responded promptly.

"You don't have to do this," Bernie pleaded.

"Yeah," Cecilia replied, "I'm afraid I do. You know what they say. In for a penny, in for a pound."

"Don't you feel even a little bit guilty?" Libby asked.

Cecilia cocked her head for a moment while she thought. "Well, maybe a little," she told Libby. "You know what they say about collateral damage."

"What?" Bernie asked.

"I don't have the vaguest idea," Cecilia told her. "Bernie, Libby, it's been a pleasure doing business with you. I figure you've got a half an hour before the house goes up. Maybe less. I promise it'll be quick," she added. "I don't like to see people suffer."

"I can't tell you how relieved that makes me feel," Bernie told her.

"I'm glad," Cecilia said. Then she went into the dining room and picked up the duffel. "Enjoy your next life," she said as she headed toward the door.

"Rot in hell," Bernie yelled after her.

"I don't think Cecilia heard you," Libby said as the door slammed. "This is not good, Bernie. This is not good at all."

"It could be worse," Bernie told her.

"How?" Libby asked.

"I could have left my nail file at home."

"That does not make me feel better."

"Never underestimate the usefulness of manicure implements, Libby."

Bernie waited a minute to make sure Cecilia wasn't coming back. Then she told Libby to wiggle toward her.

"I can't believe she did it," Libby said as she sidewinded her way over.

"It?" Bernie said.

Libby clarified. "Killed three people."

Bernie corrected her. "Five if you count us. But that's not going to happen."

Libby paused for a moment to take a breath. Then she spoke. "She's a kindergarten teacher, for heaven's sake."

"What does that have to do with anything?" Bernie asked her as she rocked herself onto her side.

"Kindergarten teachers don't kill people," Libby said.

"Evidently, this one does," Bernie pointed out. By now Libby was almost next to her. She told her to slide over a little more. "That's right," she said. "Now go up a little."

"Till what?"

"Till you can get your hands in my pocket."

Libby did. They were now butt to butt.

"I can feel the file," she said.

"See if you can get it out," Bernie urged.

Libby bit her lip and concentrated. "This would be easier if your pants weren't so tight," she told her.

"Are you saying I'm fat?" Bernie asked.

"No, I'm saying your jeans are skintight, but take it any way you want," Libby said as she tried to get the nail file out of her sister's pocket. "Isn't there some other way to get out of these?" she asked, *these* referring to the zip ties.

"Not that I know of," Bernie said. She moved a little to give Libby a better angle.

"I wonder what Cecilia would have done if Bruno had an electric stove," Libby mused.

"Probably just shot us," Bernie replied.

"Got it," Libby said after another minute had gone by.

"Thank God," Bernie said as Libby started sawing through her plastic tie with the edge of the nail file. The smell of gas was stronger now, and Bernie tried not to breathe it in, but it was hard not to. She wondered how much longer they had until the yam caught on fire and the metal bowl started sparking. Maybe the explosion would stay in the kitchen. Maybe it wouldn't reach the living room.

"You okay?" Libby asked Bernie as she continued to saw.

"As good as can be expected, given the circumstances," Bernie told her. "I'm sorry," she added fifteen minutes later, as Libby continued working on the zip tie.

"For what?" Libby asked. Her fingers were growing numb from the pressure.

"For everything. For getting you into this."

"It's okay," Libby said as she continued working away. By now a half an hour had elapsed.

A couple of minutes later, Bernie pulled on the zip tie binding her wrists. Was it her imagination, or did she feel a little movement? "I think this might be working," Bernie said.

"God, I hope so," Libby said. "I don't know how much longer I can do this." And she started coughing. The smell of gas was growing stronger.

Bernie gritted her teeth and pulled. She could definitely feel movement. "I think it's coming," she said.

Libby sawed faster and harder. Another minute went by, and Bernie pulled again. More movement. She took a deep breath and yanked as hard as she could. The zip tie came apart. Bernie moved her arms. "Thank God," she said as she rubbed her wrists. They had red welts on them. Then she reached over and grabbed the nail file from her sister. She tried to saw through the duct tape, but there was too much of it. Cecilia had done a good job. "This is going to take forever," she observed after a moment.

"Turn off the gas first. Then worry about the duct tape," Libby croaked.

"I was thinking the same thing," Bernie replied. Using

the sofa, she pulled herself up and hopped into the kitchen as quickly as she could. Her eyes started to tear and her throat constricted as she entered the gas-filled room. She felt dizzy. Her head began to spin. She hopped over to the kitchen table and held on to it so she wouldn't pass out.

"How's it going, Bernie?" Libby called from the other room.

"It's going," Bernie said as she hobbled over to the stove and turned off the burners. Then she grabbed a knife out of the kitchen drawer and began to cut through the duct tape wound around her legs. She was halfway through when the room started spinning. She forced herself to concentrate and managed to cut through the rest of the duct tape. Then she staggered into the living room and opened the window they'd come through and propped it open with a book. Next, she opened the back door before returning to Libby and starting to work on freeing her.

"I'll tell you one thing," Libby said as they stood outside, in the backyard, gulping down breaths of fresh air ten minutes later.

"What's that?" Bernie asked when she could talk again.

"I'll never think about quilts or quilters the same way again!"

Bernie was about to reply when there was a loud noise. They turned to see flames coming out of Jack Bruno's house.

"We could have been in there," Libby said.

"We could have been," Bernie agreed. "But we weren't."

Chapter 45

"I love this time of year," Clyde said four weeks later, as he watched the newly green leaves of the aspen tree across the street fluttering in the breeze. He was upstairs in the Simmons' flat, having brought news of Cecilia's indictment.

"I saw ten robins on Mrs. Reilly's lawn yesterday," Libby announced as she cut into the first rhubarb-strawberry pie of the season. She handed a slice to Clyde and cut another one for her dad.

"Delicious," Sean said after he'd taken a taste. "Just the right blend of sweet and tart."

"I second that," Clyde said, and he took another bite. "Not to mention the crust. How much butter do you use in this, anyway?" he asked.

"Trust me," Libby said. "You don't want to know."

"You're probably right," Clyde replied, thinking of what his doctor had told him after his last checkup.

"So, what happened to the quilt fragment?" Bernie asked as she sat down on the sofa with her slice of pie. It had been a week since the FBI had caught Cecilia Larson hiding out in a Motel Six in Dallas. She'd been on her way to Mexico when she'd been nabbed by the authorities.

Clyde replied, "It's been authenticated and returned to the museum from whence it came." He shook his head. "I'm still having trouble believing Cecilia Larson did what she did."

"Ditto," Sean said.

"You can triple that," Bernie said.

"Count me in," Libby added. "I still don't get it." She leaned forward. "Was that whole Sip and Sew group the Honey Pots?"

"Gail wasn't one. All the others were," Sean replied before Clyde could.

"So, they pulled off this bank robbery and museum heist and then went back to being teachers and the like, as if nothing had happened?" Libby asked.

"Pretty much," Clyde replied. "You know the old expression 'Quit while you're ahead'? Well, they pretty much exemplified it."

"And they didn't spend the money, and they kept the quilt," Bernie said. "What was the point?"

Clyde answered again. "According to Judy Fine, they were going to ransom the quilt, but then everyone started arguing about how they should go about it, so they kept postponing doing it. And as for the money . . ." Here Clyde paused for a moment. "They were going to use it to buy a beach house they could retire to. Judy said that after the two heists, they decided it was time to quit. Especially after Ellen's slipup."

"Slipup?" Libby asked, repeating the word, as she put her fork down and leaned forward, curious to hear what Clyde was going to say next.

Clyde nodded. "According to Selene, Ellen had a panic attack right in the middle of stealing the quilt and took her mask off because she couldn't breathe, or at least that's what she thought," he told the sisters.

"I'm guessing the security cameras got a couple of shots of her," Libby said.

"Indeed, they did," Sean told her.

Clyde took over. "Hence the need for a new identity and cosmetic surgery. She settled here because Judy and Cecilia were here." Then he brought out a picture and laid it on the coffee table for everyone to see. "This is what Allison Beech, aka Ellen Fisher, used to look like," he told the sisters.

The two women studied the photograph. Sean kept eating, as he had seen it before.

"It's amazing what a difference a nose job makes," Bernie finally remarked.

"Isn't it, though?" Sean agreed as he took another bite of pie.

Libby cut herself a second sliver. "What sparked all this? Everyone was seemingly happy, and then all hell broke loose."

Clyde sat back in his chair and spoke. "Love and greed. Two of the most powerful emotions there are. None of this would have happened if Ellen hadn't been having an affair with Gail's husband and the two of them hadn't decided to run away together." He shook his head. "One thing led to another." He shook his head again. "It's amazing how events cascade."

"You'd think that Gail would have been the one that killed Ellen," Bernie observed.

"One would think," Clyde said.

Bernie wrinkled her brow. "But Cecilia killing Ellen? I understand the impetus, but it got her the opposite of what she wanted."

"As actions like that so frequently do," Sean observed.

Clyde bent over and scratched his ankle. "The killing was an accident—at least it was according to Cecilia. She thought if she strung Ellen up for a minute or so, she'd come clean. But that's not what happened. Cecilia miscalculated. The scopolamine was supposed to act as a truth serum, but it didn't. Then, when Cecilia strung her up, she cut off circulation to her carotid artery. Death came pretty fast."

"That's what Cecilia told me when I spoke to her before you booked her," Bernie said. "Do you believe that?"

"Well, let me put it this way," Clyde said. "The DA is charging her with three counts of murder two, plus two counts of attempted murder."

Bernie took another bite of her pie, while Clyde took a sip of coffee. "What's going to happen to everyone else?" she asked.

"Selene and Judy have been charged with aiding and abetting Cecilia. Ordinarily, they'd both be charged with murder two, as well, but since they've turned state's evidence, the DA has knocked down the charges. They'll get a long stay in jail, though."

"But Gail is in the clear, right?" Libby clarified.

"Right," Clyde answered.

"And Dwayne?" Bernie inquired.

"Ditto," Clyde said. "He had no idea what was going on." Clyde took another bite of his pie. "The funny thing is that Dwayne and Gail are back together again. Dwayne told me he didn't appreciate what he had to begin with."

"At least something good has come out of this," Libby commented.

"One last question, Clyde," Bernie said. "The Devil's Breath. That's a pretty obscure plant. How did Cecilia know about that? Did she get it from Bruno?"

"Now, that's an interesting story," Clyde replied as he

thought about the sequence of events. "Evidently, Judy Fine had been in Peru several years ago on some sort of spiritual pilgrimage that involved the seeds from Devil's Breath. Anyway, when she hired Bruno, she went to his office, and he had a vaseful full of them on his desk."

"Did he know what they were?" Libby asked.

"His ex said he didn't. He just liked the way they looked. In any case, he and Judy got to talking, and she asked for some cuttings—which he gave her. According to Bruno's ex, Judy Fine wanted a reminder of her trip."

"So, Cecilia got the scopolamine from Judy?" Bernie asked.

"Exactly," Clyde said.

"Did Judy know what Cecilia wanted it for?" Bernie asked.

"At first, Judy said she didn't know, but then she allowed as how she did. In fact, she confessed she was the one who suggested it. She said that she was hoping it would act like a truth serum, that she had no idea Cecilia was going to use it for something else, as well."

"Do you think she was telling the truth?" Bernie asked.

Clyde shrugged. "Your guess is as good as mine."

For the next five minutes, the four sat there quietly, watching Cindy the cat chase a dust mote around the room.

Sean was the first one to break the silence. "I can't believe how lucky you were," he told his daughters.

"I know," Libby said.

"If you hadn't gotten out of there when you did . . ." Sean fell silent, unable to finish the sentence, as he thought of Bruno's house burning down to the ground.

An overwhelming sense of gratitude rushed over him. He got up and retrieved the bottle of cognac he kept for special occasions. Libby went downstairs to get the crystal glasses. When she came back, she set them on the coffee table. Everyone watched Sean uncork the bottle and pour a little of the cognac into each glass. Everyone reached over and took theirs.

"To us," Sean said, raising his glass.

"To us," Clyde, Libby, and Bernie chorused.

"May we live long and prosper," Libby added.

And with that, everyone clinked glasses and drank.

"This was a rough one," Sean observed.

"You can say that again," Libby remarked.

So Bernie did.

RECIPES

The following recipes are from my three daughters-in-law. Not only are they wonderful human beings, but they are excellent cooks, as well. Guess you could say I lucked out.

NIC'S EASY WEEKDAY SAUCE

This recipe feeds a hungry family of six any night of the week.

Ingredients:

For the sauce:
2 tablespoons extra-virgin olive oil
1 large yellow onion, peeled, halved, and thinly sliced
½ teaspoon dried rosemary
½ teaspoon dried oregano
½ teaspoon salt
½ pound fresh mushrooms, rinsed and sliced (white or
    baby bella work fine here)
2 cloves garlic, peeled and minced
1 teaspoon garlic powder
1 teaspoon onion powder
Two 28-ounce cans San Marzano whole peeled tomatoes
¾ cup red table wine, preferably dry
1 can cannellini beans (optional)

For the pasta:
1½ pounds rigatoni or penne pasta
1 teaspoon salt, plus a pinch for the cooked pasta
1 pound fresh spinach (optional)
1 teaspoon extra-virgin olive oil
¼ teaspoon garlic powder
½ cup freshly grated Parmesan or pecorino Romano
    cheese, for serving

Directions:

Heat the olive oil in a medium Dutch oven over medium heat. Add the onion slices and cook, stirring occasionally, until translucent, about 5 minutes. Stir in the rosemary and oregano and ¼ teaspoon of the salt and cook until the onions are soft, about 5 minutes. Add the mushrooms and cook, stirring occasionally, until they soften. Next, stir in the garlic, the remaining ¼ teaspoon salt, the garlic powder, and onion powder.

Pour the tomatoes and their juices from one of the cans into a large bowl and mash well with a potato masher. Add the crushed tomatoes to the mushroom-onion mixture. Repeat with the second can of tomatoes. Fill one empty tomato can halfway with water and pour into the sauce.

Bring the sauce to a slow boil over medium heat and add the wine. Stir the sauce and return it to a boil. Then lower the heat and simmer until the sauce has thickened, about 45 minutes. Taste and adjust the seasoning. If you chose, add the cannellini beans for an extra bit of protein (Beans are a great trick for adding more nutrition to a basic meal.) Cover and set the sauce aside.

Next, fill a large pot with water, add the salt, and bring to a rolling boil over high heat. Add the pasta and cook until it is al dente, about 11 minutes. Drain the pasta and return it to the pot. If you add spinach, place it in the colander before draining the pasta. The hot pasta will wilt the spinach without overcooking it.

Toss the pasta with olive oil, the pinch of salt, and garlic powder to give it flavor ahead of the sauce. Add a few ladles of the reserved sauce to the pasta and stir until coated. The pasta will soak some of it up. Add more sauce as desired. Any remaining sauce can be served on the side for those who prefer extra-saucy pasta.

Divide the pasta among bowls or plates and serve at once with grated cheese for sprinkling on the side.

BETSY'S ORANGE OLIVE OIL CAKE

This cake is light and flavorful, easy to make, and keeps well.

Ingredients:

1⅓ cups extra-virgin olive oil
3 large eggs
1¼ cups whole milk
¼ cup orange juice
2 tablespoons grated orange zest
¼ cup Grand Marnier (or similarly flavored orange liqueur)
1¾ cups granulated sugar
1 cup all-purpose flour
½ teaspoon baking powder
¼ teaspoon cinnamon
Confectioners' sugar, for dusting the finished cake

Directions:

Prepare a 9-inch springform pan by lining the bottom with parchment paper and then spraying the bottom and sides with Pam or a similar cooking spray. Preheat oven to 325°F.

In a large bowl, combine the olive oil and eggs, and whisk vigorously until well blended. Add the milk, orange juice, Grand Marnier and orange zest and whisk to incorporate. Fold in the sugar and mix until blended. Add the sifted flour, baking powder, and cinnamon and mix just to incorporate. Do not overmix, or the cake will be tough. The batter will be on the thin side. Don't worry. It's supposed to be.

Pour the batter into the prepared pan and bake for 70 minutes, or until the cake is golden brown on top and a toothpick inserted in the center comes out clean. Start checking for doneness after 60 minutes.

Remove the cake to a wire rack and allow it to cool for about 1 hour before releasing the clamp on the springform pan and removing the pan's sides.

Dust the cake with confectioners' sugar before serving.

ALFAJORES: DULCE DE LECHE SANDWICH COOKIES

This recipe is from Olivia. It was her dad's favorite cookie.

Ingredients:

2 cups all-purpose flour
2 cups cornstarch
3 teaspoons baking powder
1 teaspoon salt
1 cup unsalted butter
½ cup granulated sugar
4 large eggs
One 13.4-ounce can dulce de leche
1 cup unsweetened shredded coconut, for decorating (optional)

Directions:

Grease 2 baking sheets.

Mix together the flour, cornstarch, baking powder, and salt in a large mixing bowl.

With an electric mixer, cream together the butter and sugar in a large mixing bowl until fluffy. Add the eggs and beat until incorporated. Next, add the flour mixture and mix on low speed until a soft dough forms.

Preheat oven to 350°F. On a lightly floured surface, roll out the dough to one-third-inch thickness. Then cut into circle shapes with a biscuit cutter or a wineglass. You might want to refrigerate first to make it easier to roll.

Transfer the circles to the prepared baking sheets and bake until golden brown, about 10 minutes. Transfer the cookies to wire racks to cool completely.

To assemble the cookies, spread 1 teaspoon dulce de leche on 1 cookie, and then place another cookie on top to form a sandwich. Roll the sides in shredded coconut if desired. Repeat this process with the remaining cookies.

Store the cookies in an airtight container in the refrigerator until serving.